Small Packages

Lambda Literary Award Winner

KG MacGregor

Bella
BOOKS

2009

Bella Books, Inc.
P.O. Box 10543
Tallahassee, FL 32302

Printed in the United States of America on acid-free paper
First Edition

Editor: Cindy Cresap
Cover Designer: Stephanie Solomon-Lopez

ISBN 10: 1-59493-149-6
ISBN 13: 978-1-59493-149-9

To the lesbian families who welcome children into their homes.

Acknowledgments

If you survived the earthquake in *Without Warning* and the angst of *Aftershock*, you're due a heartwarming tale. This one should make the journey worthwhile.

When the California courts ruled that gays and lesbians were allowed to marry, I snatched *Aftershock* back from the typesetters to change the epilogue, from a commitment ceremony to a wedding. Since that book went to press, voters have passed Proposition 8, taking away that right. I've decided to give up on trying to guess where the wind will blow, and quit choosing those ambiguous words that could mean domestic partner or significant other. Anna and Lily are married. End of discussion.

As always, I want to thank Jenny for taking her pencil to my next-to-last draft and reminding me that she has the final word on the technical edit. She always flinches when I report back that Karen or the Bella proofreaders found dropped words, inconsistencies or other stupid stuff. I love working with people who take as much pride in these books as I do.

Small Packages is special, because it's my final book with Cindy Cresap as my editor. When I heard the news that she was dumping me for a better job, it gave me pause to take stock of all the things I had learned from her after seven books together. I'm a far better writer because she never pulled a punch. I wish her much success and laughter…and I hope she misses working with me as much as I'll miss working with her.

About the Author

KG MacGregor was born in 1955 into a military family in Wilmington, North Carolina.

Following her graduation from Appalachian State University, she worked briefly in elementary education, but returned to earn a doctoral degree in journalism and mass communications from the University of North Carolina at Chapel Hill. Her love of both writing and math led to a second career in market research, where she consulted with clients in the publishing, television and travel industries.

The discovery of lesbian fan fiction prompted her to try her own hand at romantic storytelling in 2002 with a story called *Shaken*. In 2005, MacGregor signed with Bella Books, which published Goldie Award finalist *Just This Once*. Her sixth Bella novel, *Out of Love*, won the 2007 Lambda Literary Award for Women's Romance, and the 2008 Goldie Award in Lesbian Romance. In 2008, she proudly announced the return of the *Shaken* Series with its first installment, *Without Warning*.

To KG, there is no better praise for her work than hearing she has created characters her readers want to know and have as friends. Please visit her at www.kgmacgregor.com.

Chapter 1

Lily slid through the warm, churning water, coming to rest on Anna's lap. This was her favorite way to kick off the weekend, a Friday night soak in the hot tub, especially on the cool nights of early autumn. Tonight was a special occasion, the second anniversary of her sobriety. They had celebrated earlier with dinner at Empyre's with Anna's sister Kim, her husband Hal and two-year-old Jonah.

"Your nephew was hilarious tonight."

Anna laughed. "I know. I couldn't believe he told the waiter his daddy's pee-pee was bigger than his."

"Like a giant's," Lily added.

"And did you see Kim? She just shrugged and said, 'Well, it is.'"

"That's so much more than I wanted to know about Hal."

"You wouldn't believe the things Kim used to tell me about their sex life. I went through about a year when I couldn't even make eye contact with him."

Anna's shyness about sexual things when they first met was

one of the things Lily had found endearing. "It's funny to think you used to be so bashful about that stuff."

"I still am, just not with you."

"It's a good thing." She ran her hands through Anna's hair, newly cut to the top of her shoulders. "This is so damn sexy."

"I was worried you wouldn't like it."

"I love it. It feels thicker." She fluffed it around Anna's shoulders, only inches above the water line. "I couldn't imagine what kind of surprise you were bringing home."

"You know how impulsive I am."

Lily laughed and shook her head. "You are many things, Anna Kaklis, but impulsive isn't one of them. How many times has Jonathan cut your hair exactly the same way?"

Anna leaned back and spread her arms along the edge of the hot tub. "God, how old am I? Thirty-five?"

"For a few more weeks."

"And I've worn my hair long since I got back from college. So that means Jonathan's trimmed it at least fifty times."

"I bet he freaked when you told him to cut it off."

"It was his idea. There was another lady in the salon who wore hers this long. I told him I liked it and he said mine would look great like that."

"He was right." As far as Lily was concerned, Anna could shave her head and still be beautiful, but this cut, barely long enough to pull back in a tie, gave her a quality Lily secretly loved. It made her look older, like an elegant woman in her mid-thirties instead of an ingénue. "I think it's gorgeous."

"I think you're gorgeous."

"I bet you say that to all the naked women who sit on your lap."

"Just the really small ones."

Lily took advantage of Anna's position to cup both of her breasts. "Careful with the pygmy jokes. I have hostages."

"Easy, baby." Anna closed her eyes, a sure sign she was concentrating on the sensation. She had complained earlier of PMS, which meant her nipples were hypersensitive, almost to

2

the point of pain.

In their three years as lovers, Lily had mastered a feather-like touch, the only direct contact Anna could bear during the days that preceded her period.

"We need to trim that bougainvillea," Anna said.

Lily resisted the urge to give Anna's nipples a twist. "Excuse me, did you just respond to my loving caress of your breasts with a gardening observation?"

Anna blinked and cocked her head. "Sorry. I just opened my eyes and it was the first thing I saw."

"You're supposed to have a little more control over what comes out of your mouth." Feigning a pout, she scooted backward off Anna's lap.

"Don't go. I liked what you were doing."

"Too bad. My amorous mood is shattered now. Who knows if it will ever come again?" She held the back of her hand to her forehead dramatically as she climbed the steps of the tub. "Besides, I'm getting waterlogged."

Chester, their basset hound, looked up from the chaise lounge and thumped his tail as Anna stretched across the deck and threw the levers that turned off the jets and the heater.

Shivering against the chill, Lily wrapped a towel around her torso and tucked it in front. Then she got a playful urge and picked up Anna's towel as she darted for the house. "I think you should stay out here with your bougainvillea."

"Oh no, you don't!"

She squealed with laughter when she heard Anna's wet feet slapping against the concrete pool deck. "No running!" she yelled, not even looking over her shoulder for fear of losing a step. By the time she reached the French doors of the kitchen, she could practically hear Anna breathing down her neck, but she scooted inside and spun the deadbolt just in time.

Chester ran into the kitchen through his doggie door and began to bark.

"You're going to be so sorry," Anna said menacingly.

Lily whirled and pressed her back to the door. She could

hardly contain her hysteria as she envisioned Anna standing on the other side of the door, naked and dripping wet, her arms folded indignantly. But when she turned to taunt her again, Anna was gone.

Lily cupped her hands around her eyes and peered through the glass. Anna must have gone back to the safety of the pool to wait her out, knowing she would eventually relent and take her towel outside.

"Next time, you might want to check the lock in the family room."

"Aack!" Lily screamed at hearing Anna's voice behind her. She dashed into the dark dining room, but not fast enough to keep Anna from snagging her towel on the way by. Now she was naked and standing in a room with an enormous window that faced the street.

They squared off on opposite sides of the formal dining table, lunging first one way then the other to keep the maximum separation. Anna had cut off her escape route back into the kitchen.

Chester ran from one to the other, barking frantically.

"I can see your little boobies bounce," Lily said.

"You should talk. The neighbors are about to get a look at your little butt." Her fingers hovered over the light switch.

"You wouldn't dare."

No sooner had the words left her lips than Anna wrapped herself in the towel and clicked the switch that lit up the entire room, exposing Lily to anyone who happened to be on the street.

Lily squealed again and bolted across the brightly lit foyer for the dark living room, where she ducked behind the couch and pulled Chester close to keep him quiet. This room also had a large window, but there was no overhead light. She was relieved to see that the street was deserted in front of their house, so no one had caught the peep show.

Anna entered the room from the opposite doorway, the one near the kitchen. "Why do you run from me? I only want to kiss

4

you and tell you how much I love you."

"Bullshit. You want to tickle me."

"Why would I do something so mean? Just because you locked me outside naked?" Her voice was growing closer.

Lily was cornered. Her only hope was to jump out suddenly and skirt the coffee table in a beeline for the doorway. But the instant she sprang up, a strong hand caught her wrist and pulled her down sideways onto the couch. Anna writhed beneath her, already groping for her ribs.

Lily tensed in anticipation of a tickling frenzy, and wrapped her lips around the closest nipple in hopes of forcing a stalemate.

"Oh," Anna said, nearly moaning.

"Oh?"

Anna's hands left her ribs and began stroking her hair. "Oh," she said again as her body went still.

Lily sensed the shift from playful to serious and responded in kind, gently licking the breast as her hands began to wander over Anna's smooth skin, which was still damp from their soak in the hot tub. They were shielded from curious eyes by the back of the couch, but Lily was so intent on her desires that she hardly would have cared had they been on the front lawn.

Her mouth dipped lower across Anna's abdomen, but a squeeze on her shoulder stopped her from going lower.

"Stay up here with me. I need to hold you."

Lily's heart pounded with passion whenever Anna used the word "need." She nestled close to resume the kisses on Anna's tender breasts, and ran her fingertips through the soft curls at the apex of her thighs.

Anna parted her legs and moaned her approval when Lily found her center. Her fingers began to brush Lily's shoulders in a rhythm that matched the slow, teasing strokes.

This was a rare but familiar dance, one Lily had seen on only a handful of occasions. It almost always came at this stage in Anna's cycle, and usually at the end of a demanding work week. The hallmark was an intense physical craving, at least outwardly. Lily was willing to bet that an emotional release would accompany

Anna's climax, and when it did, their connection to one another would be closer than ever.

As if on cue, Anna began to whimper and dig her fingers into Lily's back.

Lily quickened her strokes and left Anna's breast to draw even with her face. "That's it, baby. Let it go," she whispered.

Anna shuddered hard and released a sob before burying her face into Lily's neck. Then her body went limp.

The next few minutes passed quietly as Lily waited for a signal that Anna's emotional wave had passed. She knew from experience that the tears were meaningless, nothing more than a release of pent-up sensitivities.

"I have no idea where that comes from," Anna finally said.

"But it's all okay, right?"

"It's wonderful." She tightened their embrace and sighed. "I love my life with you."

Those were Lily's favorite words. "Nothing you'd change?"

"Not one little thing."

Since their wedding on the beach eighteen months earlier, they both had worked hard to mesh their lives as a couple. Anna gave up her long hours at the dealership, and Lily cut back on her legal caseload, freeing them to make the most of their weekends. Whether on excursions to the desert or California coast, with friends or family, or even just relaxing in their comfortable home, they spent the time together. If it wasn't a perfect life, Lily couldn't imagine what was.

"You know what I like best?"

Lily wanted to say the sex, but she didn't want to break the spell, this pensive mood that impelled Anna to speak her heart. "Tell me."

"I like how the rest of the world falls away, how it's just you and me. We don't let other things take over and come between us. And I know you're always going to be here."

"I will." It was true. From the moment they said their vows, she knew Anna would be the one constant in her life, the anchor she needed. What had thrilled her even more was the recognition that Anna needed her just as much.

"I don't want this to ever change. I know we're supposed to get older and start taking in cats…"

Lily chuckled, not minding at all that Anna had shifted things back to a playful level, especially in the context of them growing old together. "Only a true lesbian would say something like that."

"You really think I'm a lesbian?" That was Anna's running joke.

"What else would you call a woman with a wife?"

"Good point."

Lily extricated her limbs and pushed herself up to a sitting position. "I'll go get our towels and lock up. You just lie there looking beautiful."

"I'll do my best."

She returned minutes later to find Anna gone. "Did you just run upstairs naked?"

Anna called down. "I stole your towel, remember?"

Lily climbed the stairs and entered the master suite, where Anna was sitting on their bed beside a small wrapped package that looked like a CD. "What's this?"

"Something for you, I think."

"You didn't have to get me a present."

"I know, but I'm really proud of you." She held out the package. "I'll save you the trouble. It's a collection of love songs from Broadway. It reminded me of our trip to New York last year."

Lily leaned over to deliver a kiss. "Your sister's right about you. You've turned into a romantic mush ball."

"Kim?" Anna called out as she opened the back door of her sister's house.

"Come on in. I'm back in Jonah's room."

Anna followed the voice down the hallway. "Where's my little—" She stopped when she saw her very pregnant sister squatting awkwardly to pick up Jonah's toys. "Let me get those."

She quickly gathered the brightly colored blocks and shapes, absently running the wheels of a plastic car across the carpet to make them spin.

"My hero," Kim said drolly. "Hal took Jonah over to Mom's. If I go sit on the couch, will you help me up before you leave so I won't be stuck there?"

Anna laughed and steered her toward the living room. "Sure, I'll help you up. Can I get you anything?"

"Did you bring a handgun?"

"No weapons."

"Then smother me or something." Kim slumped onto the couch in a heap.

"I see. So did Hal and Jonah leave to give you a break, or did you run them off with your cranky mood?"

"They ran for their lives, Miss Sunshine. I'm betting you won't last longer than fifteen minutes."

"That's about all I've got anyway. Lily went to a special AA meeting for women. They had a guest speaker or something."

"Hal and I appreciated you guys inviting us along last night. Two years without a drink is a big deal."

Anna loved her family for the way they had stepped up after Lily's fall into alcoholism. Not only did they offer their understanding and support, they also refrained from drinking in her presence, even though Lily insisted it was all right. Kim, being pregnant, had an easy excuse, but she also complained that even smelling it on Hal's breath made her want to throw up. "We were glad to have you. Besides, dinner with Jonah comes with entertainment."

"Can you possibly tell me where that child gets that chatty streak? He'll say anything to anyone."

Anna knew where he got it—from his mother. "I can't possibly guess," she answered, rolling her eyes at her sister's irony.

"Look at my ankles. They're like pumpkins."

Anna pulled Kim's feet into her lap and tugged off her terrycloth slippers. "Don't you dare tell anyone I did this." She began to knead her sister's swollen feet.

8

"Oh, my God. Would you believe me if I told you that feels better than sex?"

"Not in a million years."

Kim laughed. "Yeah, that was sort of a crazy thing to say. But it does make you one of my favorite people in the universe."

"This one's been harder than Jonah, hasn't it?"

"Jonah was a breeze. I only gained twenty-two pounds, and if it hadn't been for that and the fact that Hal treated me like I was made of crystal, I might never have known I was pregnant." She wiggled her toes. "This time I look like a Volkswagen Beetle."

"At least you don't look like a Dodge." Anna thought her sister more beautiful than ever, but Kim had threatened to maim the next person who dared to comment on her "glow."

"Can you imagine how much weight I would have gained if I hadn't thrown up for three straight weeks?"

"You'll forget all of this in about ten days when your baby girl gets here."

"Let's hope she sleeps better than Jonah."

"Maybe that's the trade-off. A tough pregnancy means an easy baby."

"When are you and Lily going to discover this bliss for yourself?"

"You know, it's funny. I always thought I wanted children, but I'm not so sure anymore."

"Because I complain so much? You know what a princess I am."

"No, believe it or not, I make some of my decisions totally independent of you." She smirked and dug deeper with her thumbs into Kim's arches. "You and Hal had eleven years to get ready for Jonah. Lily and I are still on our honeymoon."

"And in eleven years you'll be what? Fifty? And then you'll be seventy-five when he gets out of high school."

"Where did you learn math?"

"Besides, Hal and I had been trying for four years before Jonah came along. If you wait too long, Lily will be buying diapers for both of you."

"Very funny."

"Seriously, Anna. You always wanted children. Remember how we used to talk about our kids playing together?"

Anna shrugged. "And I used to think I'd grow up and marry a man. That didn't happen either." Though technically, it had.

"Is that why you don't want kids? Because we both know you don't need to do the nasty to have babies. I hear a turkey baster will do the trick. You just stand on your head and get Lily to squeeze."

She sighed and shook her head. When it came to sex, there wasn't anything off-limits to Kim. "You are the crudest person I know. They're doing some cool things with fertility treatments these days."

"If anyone knows fertility treatments, it's me. I'm lucky I'm not having quadruplets."

"Right." Kim and Hal had struggled to conceive both of their children. "Anyway, you remember my friend from Seattle?"

"Carolyn?"

"Yeah, she and her partner had a baby together. Vicki carried it, but it was Carolyn's egg."

"That's perfect. You could get Lily to have your babies."

"Except that Lily is even less interested in having babies than I am." She thought about their romp through the house the night before. "Besides, we're happy with things the way they are. Why have our own kids when we can rent them from you?"

"Speaking of that, are you and Lily still up for babysitting?"

"We're excited about it." They had offered to shower Jonah with attention for a couple of days after his sister was born so he wouldn't feel jealous of the new baby. "We're going to spoil him and give him back."

"You can't possibly be worse than your father. Jonah comes home practically bouncing off the walls. Sometimes I think George gives him coffee."

Anna gave Kim's feet one last squeeze and stood. "Do you want me to help you off the couch?"

"No, I want my husband to find me here and to think I've

been trapped all afternoon. Then he'll feel guilty and I'll get him to shave my legs."

"…courage to change the things I can, and the wisdom to know the difference." Lily squeezed the hands she was holding and joined the group in their sign-off ritual. "Keep coming back!"

As she walked out of the meeting with her sponsor, Virginia, she accepted congratulations for her two years of sobriety from several women. "I like these women-only meetings."

"So do I," Virginia said. "It's so much easier to identify with our stories."

"I don't mind all the different stories so much. I just appreciate being able to come to a meeting without worrying about getting hit on."

Virginia nodded. "Right…they call that the Thirteenth Step. Did you have the same problem with the gay and lesbian group?"

"In some ways, it was worse. People just seem so desperate to hook up."

"They want a partner who can keep them from drinking."

"Nobody can do that."

"No, but you're lucky to have Anna."

"I know." Lily hated to think how difficult it might have been to stay sober had she not had support at home every step of the way. Anna had simply wiped alcohol from both of their lives.

"Have you decided anything about your job offer?"

Lily smiled at the mention of the one thing she had been trying to put out of her head this weekend, her meeting with Wes McLean, the retiring executive director of LA County's guardian *ad litem* program. "It wasn't exactly an offer. He just asked me to think about it, and that's what I'm doing."

"What did Anna have to say?"

"She feels the same way I do, that it's the opportunity of a lifetime." The executive director of the county's program coordinated a network of volunteer attorneys to advocate for

11

children, particularly wards of the state or those involved in custody disputes, in order to ensure their ideal placement. It was the sort of job that became a career, and one that paid nearly twice what she made at the Braxton Street Legal Aid Clinic. "But it's also a huge commitment."

"Since when are you afraid of commitment?"

Lily chuckled. Besides being her sponsor, Virginia had become a trusted friend with whom Lily could talk about the insecurities that had led her to drink too much. "Very funny. It's just that Anna and I have finally got things right where we want them. She's hired a couple of managers and cut back on her time at the dealership. It doesn't seem fair for me to turn around and take on a job that could have my phone ringing at all hours of the night."

"But you just said Anna thinks it's a great opportunity."

"She won't stand in my way if it's what I want, but that doesn't mean she wants me to take it. Besides, I can't leave Tony high and dry after the way he took me back when I got out of rehab."

"I know you owe Tony a lot, but you've been out of rehab for almost two years. Besides, he's not going to blame you if you jump ship for an offer like this."

"It's not an offer," she reiterated. "We just talked."

Virginia looked at her dubiously. "They came after you, Lily, so it's obvious they want you. And why wouldn't they? You understand perfectly what kids in the system need."

"I'm sure I could do the job." *Blindfolded.*

"So what's the real reason you're dragging your feet?"

Lily almost laughed. No matter how much she hedged, Virginia usually read her like a book. "You're almost as good as Anna."

"I can usually tell when you're worried about falling. Why does this job scare you so much?" They reached Lily's car, where Virginia leaned against the driver's door, clearly determined to finish the conversation.

"Because it's all about schmoozing lawyers and judges to get them to volunteer their time, and that means cocktail parties and three-martini lunches. Wes McLean drank two double bourbons in the middle of the day and went back to work."

"Maybe you can change the way it's done."

"What if I can't?"

"It won't matter, Lily. You don't drink. That's all you have to say."

Virginia was correct, but that didn't make this any less frustrating for Lily. "It's not that easy and you know it. Most people accept it just fine, but there's always the asshole who says 'just one little drink won't hurt.' I don't think I can face that every day."

"I can see how that would be annoying, just like having someone blow smoke in your face. But do you honestly think you'd be tempted by it?"

Lily sighed. She was lucky not to struggle with temptation the way others did. "I don't know. I've never had to deal with it. We don't do that social thing at the law clinic."

"You were thrilled last week when you told me about this. What's changed?"

"Nothing. I've just been thinking about it."

"Lily, I'm not worried about how you'll handle someone pressuring you to drink. You're a lot stronger than you probably realize." Virginia folded her arms and looked at her seriously.

That wasn't at all the answer Lily had expected. "If I'm standing here telling you that I'm worried about temptation, shouldn't you be advising me to avoid it?"

"No, because your downfall isn't temptation. It's disappointment. What I worry about is that you'll always look back on this opportunity and think about what could have been. And that's when you'll start to struggle."

Lily slumped against the adjacent car, suddenly anxious about the changes such a move would mean. "You really think I should take it?"

"That's totally up to you, but I think you should consider it seriously if it's a job you would enjoy. Don't let your fears decide. Like I said, you're a lot stronger than you think."

It was a dream job if ever there was such a thing. As long as she could remember, she had wanted a career in which she could help children the way she had been helped by her adoptive mother and their attorney friend, Katharine Fortier. This was the chance to do that. Like Virginia said, all she had to do was get past her fears.

Chapter 2

Anna twisted back and forth in her chair, excited to see the note from the community relations coordinator from the LA Dodgers. This was the perfect Friday night date. Without even looking, she hit the speed dial on her phone.

"This is Lilian Kaklis."

No matter how many times Lily answered her phone that way, it never failed to bring a smile to Anna's face. Lily's decision to change her name after their wedding both surprised and honored her. "What color do you bleed?"

"Dodger Blue!"

"I was hoping you'd say that. You up for a game tonight?"

"In the skybox?"

"Better. Front row behind the Cubs dugout."

"Have you been doling out sexual favors again?"

"Writing checks is more like it. They hit me up at last month's Chamber meeting for a donation to their youth charities, and now the PR guy is offering two tickets."

"I'll have to check my social calendar. I'm very popular, you know."

"For someone of your beauty and esteem, I'm not at all surprised."

"Why, it so happens I'm free."

"How did I get so lucky? Can you be ready to go by six thirty?"

"Sure. Have you heard anything from Kim?"

Today was her sister's due date. "Not a word. Hal's driving us all crazy. He's been walking all over the lot checking out his cell phone signal to make sure it's working."

"You ought to send the poor guy home."

"I can't. Kim made me promise to keep him busy all day. I guess he was driving her crazy too."

She was interrupted by a knock from Holly, her sales manager. "Anna, the guys are here with the new TV."

"Great. Have them take it to the media room. I'll be there in just a minute." She reached into the bottom drawer of her desk and retrieved the two DVDs she had ordered from Germany. One was a scenic trip through Bavaria, pointing out interesting sights from inside various BMW models. The cinematography of the film was such that it almost gave the feeling of driving the car on the autobahn, right down to the dashboard features. The second DVD held detailed information—engine specifications, safety features, option packages and performance—on each model in the BMW's North American line. The latter was menu-driven and could be used as a sales tool to educate a potential buyer about a specific model. "My new toy is here," she told Lily.

"I like toys. Are you going to bring it home to share?"

Anna felt herself blush at the innuendo, though she was sure Holly hadn't heard Lily's remark through the phone. "I doubt it. It's the plasma TV."

"The one that won't even fit in our house?"

"That's the one. It's over five feet wide. I'm having it mounted in the customer lounge. We're turning it into a media room."

"Now all you need is one of those old-fashioned popcorn carts."

"What a great idea! You're brilliant."

"And you're either biased or the world's biggest flirt. Or both. I've got to get back to work. Are you finished bothering me?"

"I am. I'm off to play with my toy. But be ready to roll at six thirty." She laughed to herself, because they both knew Lily would be the one kept waiting.

With the DVDs in hand, Anna briskly walked down the stairs to the showroom, where the delivery crew was already busy with the installation. She supervised the placement of the HD screen and studied the operator manual as they finished.

The large room held several black leather couches and captain's chairs, with glass and chrome side tables holding recent issues of *Car & Driver*, *Motor Week*, and of course, brochures on the various BMW models. An air purifier helped preserve the rich aroma of the leather, Anna's idea for mimicking the new car smell.

She had designed this room at Premier BMW to introduce new customers to the joys of driving, especially the joys of driving performance BMWs. She couldn't wait to show it off to her sales staff at their Friday morning meeting.

Chester's excited bark announced the arrival of Anna's car in the driveway.

In predictable fashion, she stormed through the side door and charged through the family room to the hallway. "I know, I know. I'm late."

Lily chuckled from the kitchen doorway. "I already laid out your jeans."

Anna spun back and gave her a quick kiss. "What would I ever do without you?"

"You'd probably wear a business suit to the ballpark. We'll make it if you hurry."

"We can sing the national anthem in the car on the way over," she answered, darting up the stairs.

Lily filled Chester's water bowl and waited by the door with their jackets in hand. Even after a warm day like today, the ballpark would be chilly once the sun went down.

Anna appeared, already sporting a Dodgers sweatshirt along with her jeans and sneakers. She stopped at the mirror in the small bathroom and tucked her hair behind her ears before putting on her Dodgers cap. "It's weird not being able to pull my hair through the back of my cap anymore."

"It's normal though…losing your hair as you get older."

"Very funny." Anna mussed Lily's hair as they rushed outside to the car. "Did you tell Tony about your job offer?"

"No. I decided not to say anything unless I definitely make up my mind that I want it."

Anna shook her head as she backed down the driveway. "Some days I don't understand you at all. I thought you said this job was perfect for you."

Actually, it had been Anna who had said that, but Lily had agreed at the time. "It's a perfect job, but that isn't the part of my life that I need to be perfect."

"What does that mean?"

"I've been thinking about the other night when you terrorized me in the dining room."

"You mean the night you locked me outside naked?"

"I didn't lock you out. The door got stuck, and I was trying to figure out how to get your robe to you through the keyhole."

Anna snorted and accelerated onto the busy 405. "What about it?"

"Just something you say a lot…that you love our life. I love our life too. Why would I take a chance on changing it?"

"Some changes are good, Lily. We both spend too much of our time working not to enjoy what we do. I'm lucky because I have the perfect job. But you don't. You hate it when Tony hands you a criminal case, and that's half of your cases these days. I can tell as soon as you get home when you're working on one. You're drained and your voice is down."

Lily couldn't deny Anna's assessment. A community grant from the public defender's office had doubled their criminal caseload at the clinic, swamping her with jury trials that ate up her work week. Family law—cases involving divorce, child custody and adoption—was Lily's specialty, so she was a natural to lead the court's program on child advocacy, and it would get her out of the day-to-day grind of the courtroom. After her talk with Virginia, she was confident she could handle the social pressures of the job, but she couldn't bring herself to say yes just yet. "I guess I'm worried about making such a big change. I'm supposed to have lunch with two of the board members on Monday. If they like me, we'll see where it goes."

"If they like you? I bet this is more about your liking them."

That was probably true, she realized. When the outgoing executive director had contacted her, she had gotten the distinct impression she was at the top of their list. "They won't make a final decision until the first of November. That gives me six whole weeks to obsess about it."

"I'll support whatever you want to do. I hope you know that."

Lily reached over the console and took Anna's hand. "I do, and I appreciate it."

They rode in comfortable silence to the ballpark, where Anna flashed the VIP parking pass she had received in the packet along with the tickets. The second inning was already underway when they made it to their seats.

"Promise me you didn't sleep with somebody to get these seats," Lily said, low enough that no one else could hear. Their seats were in the first row, right behind the on-deck hitter.

Anna plucked a menu from the pouch in front of her and waved to one of the attendants who watchfully serviced those in the premium box seats. "Feeling decadent?"

"Very." Her mouth watered in anticipation as Anna ordered hotdogs and curly fries. "Do you realize we're sitting close enough that the umpire can actually hear us?"

"Just try not to get arrested." Anna pulled on her jacket. "Every time we come out here I think about our first game."

"Yeah, the one where that advertising creep was fawning all over you."

"Were you jealous even back then?"

"Damn right. I wanted you all to myself."

"I didn't even notice him. I was too busy trying to impress you."

"You were not."

"I was. Seriously." She paid the attendant and they both dug into their piping hot fries. "I didn't realize why at the time, but I distinctly remember feeling very proud of myself for scoring those tickets."

Lily grinned. "And I distinctly remember trying on about thirty different outfits so you'd think I was cute."

"And now it's four years later and you're picking out my clothes too." She polished off her hotdog and began licking her fingers.

"I can hardly trust you to dress yourself. You didn't even own a pair of jeans until—"

"Hold that thought. My hip's vibrating."

"I beg your pardon."

Anna pulled her cell phone from her pocket and checked the display. Her face lit up instantly. "It's Hal."

Lily automatically started gathering up her jacket and their trash.

"How long?" She grabbed Lily's wrist as she stood. "Tell her she has to wait. We're at the ballpark. It'll be forty-five minutes at least…the Dodgers, two to nothing in the top of the third."

Hal had probably earned a smack for asking the score, Lily thought as she followed Anna up the stairs and through the concourse.

"We're going to be aunties again. You ready?"

Anna paced the hallway for what felt like the thirtieth time. Kim and Hal were in the birthing room with Dr. Beth Ostrov, the fertility specialist who had helped them conceive first Jonah, and now their daughter. Jonah was climbing from chair to chair in the waiting room under the watchful eye of Anna's parents. Lily had dashed home to trade Anna's two-seater Z8 for her X3 SUV so they could take Jonah home with them for the weekend.

The doctor emerged and met her eye. "You're Anna, right?"

She nodded.

"Kim said for you to come on in. It's probably going to be another hour or two."

Anna entered and found Kim and Hal running through their relaxation drills. The room was decorated in a homey style, with a braided oval rug, pictures on the walls and comfortable chairs surrounding the hospital bed. It was easy to see the appeal of a low technology, low intervention birthing experience. Equipment was readily available for any type of emergency response, but Kim was healthy and her pregnancy was considered low risk.

"Did you come to watch me suffer?" Kim greeted her with a grin, the first one Anna had seen in a month.

"What are you smiling about? Did you get drugs?"

"No, we were just talking about baby names."

"Have you decided?"

"We have to look at her and make sure it fits. Where's Lily?"

"She went home to switch cars so we could take Jonah tonight."

"Are you sure you want to do that?" Hal asked. "He's out there climbing on the ceiling right now."

"We'll be fine. Besides, he'll probably be asleep before we get out of here." Kim and Hal traded teasing looks, but Anna was confident she and Lily could handle things.

Hal stood and stretched. "I'll go out and check on him. Don't let her have any babies until I get back."

Anna chuckled. "Believe me, if she starts giving birth, I'll come tearing through that door like an M5." Hal had worked at the dealership long enough to recognize her reference to BMW's most powerful car. She walked around and sat on Kim's bed. "You feeling okay?"

Kim's face fell instantly. "God, remind me never to have sex again!"

"That's a first. Is it that bad?"

"Remember how Hal hyperventilated when Jonah was born? He can't stand it when he knows I'm in pain, and right now I feel like I'm about to give birth to a sofa."

Anna took her hand and rubbed it warmly. "I think you married the best guy in the whole world."

"I should have married Lily. She wouldn't have done this to me."

"You're going to have the most beautiful daughter."

Kim grimaced and took several rapid breaths between her teeth. "Beth said she probably wouldn't come until midnight, but I have a feeling this little girl will be here by ten thirty."

The clock behind the bed said ten after. "I hope she'll wait for Lily."

"I hope Lily drives like a bat out of hell." She gripped Anna's hand as a contraction went through her. "I love you, sister."

Anna's eyes misted. "I love you too."

Hal returned quietly and took his place on the other side of the bed. "You want anything?"

Kim seized again, this time stronger than the one before. "Maybe a stopwatch."

"Are you serious?"

She nodded vigorously and Hal pressed the call button by the door.

Moments later, the doctor entered. "Is she getting impatient?" As she helped Kim into the stirrups, Anna moved toward the door.

"I'm going to wait for this miracle in the other room."

"Chicken," Kim said through gritted teeth.

"In a word, yes." She pulled the door closed and turned to find Lily coming down the hall. "You just made it. We're having a baby right now."

"Is everything okay?"

"Fine." She steered Lily into the waiting room and delivered her update. Her father was slumped in a chair, clearly exhausted from chasing Jonah, who was sitting on the floor with an array of books. Hal's father, Harold, Sr., chatted with Martine. Harold was divorced from Hal's mother, who lived in Florida. Hal wasn't particularly close to either of his parents, but his father had come around a few times since Jonah was born.

Anna stood in the doorway, an eye on the door to Kim's room. Ten minutes passed before two nurses entered. "Something's happening," she announced. "The nurses just went in."

One by one, the Kaklis clan gathered behind her to watch the door, except George, who stayed behind to keep Jonah occupied. At ten thirty sharp, one of the nurses emerged, pulling off her rubber gloves and tossing them in a nearby receptacle. She didn't look their way, so there was no discerning the news.

"That had to mean something," Lily whispered.

The next person to exit was Dr. Ostrov. The smile on her face sent them all into a frenzy. "She's gorgeous. Seven pounds, nine ounces."

"And Kim?" Anna asked anxiously.

"She's doing just great. Even Hal made it this time," she said. "The OB nurse is still cleaning up a little, but when she comes out, you'll be able to go in. Just try not to rush the door."

"Thank you, Dr. Ostrov. We appreciate everything," Martine said.

"I love my job." Her smile still in place, she turned and disappeared down the hall.

After an eternity of eight or nine minutes, the OB nurse appeared and waved everyone down to the room. "They're doing great, but you don't want to overwhelm them, okay?"

They tiptoed into the room *en masse* to find Kim sitting up in bed, her auburn hair freshly combed away from her face. In her arms was a dark-eyed, red-faced darling with a shock of her father's jet-black hair. "Everyone, meet Jonah's little sister, Alice Martine Phillips."

Martine was visibly moved at the honor of her namesake and reached out to caress the infant's head.

Lily began snapping photos with her digital camera. "That's a great one. Get over there, George, and try not to scare the little thing." The whole family posed in every conceivable combination, with Harold and Lily trading off to be in the pictures.

Anna was relieved when her earlier prediction came true and Jonah succumbed to his busy day, falling asleep on Hal's shoulder.

Hal walked them to the garage to retrieve the car seat and Jonah's things for the weekend. "Last chance, Anna. He could wake up in the morning and be a pistol."

"We'll handle it, Hal. Even if you have no faith in me, Lily knows all about kids. That's her specialty at work." She shot Lily a wink.

"That's right. If he gives us any trouble, I know how to put him up for adoption."

"He hates me," Anna said, the anguish plain on her face as she turned to back out of her sister's driveway.

"No, he doesn't," Lily replied. "He was probably just anxious about not being in on the action. George said he cried the night he stayed over there too."

Jonah had been upset all day, obviously distressed at being separated from his mother and father. None of the activities he usually enjoyed—a dip in the pool, a Popsicle, toys and games—distracted him from his tears for more than a few minutes. After two straight hours of near hysterics, Anna finally gave in and decided to take him home.

"He's never been like that before. He didn't even want me to hold him."

Lily felt sorry for Anna. It was rare to see her grapple with a loss of confidence about anything, but she was clearly feeling helpless about Jonah's distress. "Put yourself in his shoes. There was a lot of excitement last night, so today was a letdown. And with all the talk about the new baby coming, he was probably feeling insecure that his mom and dad were with her and leaving him out."

Anna sighed. "I hope he doesn't learn to associate us with feeling like that."

"He won't. He loves you." Lily could only imagine how

disappointed Anna was at throwing in the towel, but given Jonah's obvious suffering, it was probably for the best. And despite her assurances to Anna, she too was worried about how he would feel the next time they all were together. "At least Kim and Hal got a little bit of rest."

"I wish it could have been more."

When Anna was intent on beating herself up, there wasn't much Lily could do about it. Her only real consolation would come when she was sure things between her and Jonah were okay. "Look at it this way. It gave us an excuse to see Alice again."

Anna managed a sheepish smile, but Lily could tell she was still upset.

"We'll go back over there in a couple of days. I'll bet you anything Jonah is back to his old self." She reached across the console to pat Anna's thigh. "Besides, there's a silver lining in all this. I have you all to myself for the rest of the weekend."

"Hmm…lying on the couch watching TV has some appeal."

"That's not quite what I had in mind, but it's a start." In fact, relaxing together in the family room was one of their favorite pastimes on the weekend. Often, their evenings on the couch led to making love, but not always. Sometimes it was enough just to be close without the worries of the day.

It was near the end of their second movie before Lily sensed that Anna had fully relaxed. The signal was a soft kiss on the top of her head as they lay entwined in the dark family room. Anna then squirmed for the remote.

"Do you want to watch another movie?" Lily asked.

"I have a better idea. You go fix us a peanut butter and jelly sandwich and I'll take this lazy hound for a W-A-L-K. Then I'll meet you upstairs and we can watch something from bed."

"Sounds like a plan."

Lily made the sandwich and cut it in half. Then she poured a tall glass of milk and carried the snack upstairs. As she changed into a nightshirt, she heard Anna return with Chester.

"Turn on the local news and see if the Dodgers won."

Lily clicked through the channels as Anna changed for bed.

"I saved you some milk."

Anna climbed into bed and eyed Lily's nightshirt, which sported a blob of strawberry jam just above her breast. "Did you save me this too?" She attached her lips to the stain.

"Keep that up and I'll be smearing your half of that sandwich all over me."

"Peanut butter as an aphrodisiac...sounds like a great idea."

"It would only work on someone like you." Lily groped for the remote control and turned up the volume. "The news is on."

"...got two homers in the bottom of the second. Was it enough to beat the Cubs?"

Anna groaned. "I hate TV news. Why can't they just tell you who won?"

"They don't call it commercial television for nothing."

The next teaser showed footage from what was evidently a protest, followed by a mug shot of a young woman. "...*protesting what some are calling the callous actions of the San Francisco police.*"

"Wow, I thought that was you for a second," Anna said.

Lily stared at the photo on the screen before it faded to a commercial. Though very thin and younger by at least ten years, the woman pictured had nearly identical facial features. "I looked a lot like that when I was younger and my hair was long."

"That looked like a mug shot. People all over LA will see that tonight and think it was you." Anna nudged her teasingly. "I wonder how many calls we'll get."

"I can't wait to see what I did."

The news program returned and went straight into the story from San Francisco.

"*Police officials in San Francisco are on the defensive tonight following the killing of a homeless woman who was taken hostage after an attempted bank robbery late Friday afternoon. She's been identified as twenty-two-year-old Kristy Parker, who, according to witnesses who knew her, had lived on the city's streets for several years. The robber, forty-year-old...*"

Lily sat up ramrod straight. "Oh, my God."

"What is it?"

"Didn't you hear? They said her name was Kristy Parker." From Anna's confused look, it was clear she hadn't made the connection. "Anna, my name was Parker. I wonder if...never mind, that's ridiculous."

"You think she might be related?"

"No." She shook her head, refusing to give credence to such a coincidence. "It's hard to tell what people really look like from just their mug shot. Besides, I bet there are thousands of Parkers in the Bay Area."

Chapter 3

Lily couldn't shake her nervousness about having lunch with two directors of the guardian *ad litem* program, despite Anna's assurances that they—and not Lily—were the ones trying harder to impress. She thought of Virginia as she ordered sparkling water, and was pleasantly surprised when the directors followed suit. "Do you mind if I ask a question?"

"Not at all," Kenneth Thompson said. He was a senior partner in one of the largest firms in LA. "That's why we're here, to make sure you have all the information you need to make the decision that's right for you."

She appreciated that he genuinely seemed to want her to weigh their offer carefully. "I can't help but wonder why the board would be interested in someone who's had only seven years experience. There must be hundreds of attorneys who are better suited for this job."

Esther Cohen nodded. "There are, but frankly, we don't want someone who's burned out and needs a change of scenery. People like that tend to cycle through jobs, and we'd end up filling this position again in three or four years." If anyone knew about professional burnout, it was Cohen, who headed up child and family services for the county.

Thompson shifted in his seat and leaned closer. "Lily, I'll be honest with you. Our top priority was to find someone who would see this as both a challenge and an opportunity to make a real difference in the lives of children. We asked around and Rusty Evans told us we should talk to you, and there isn't anyone whose recommendation we hold in higher regard."

Rusty Evans was Lily's favorite judge in family court, and she was deeply honored to hear such high praise coming from him.

Cohen jumped in on the double-team. "We also spoke with the dean of the law school at UCLA, and she said you were highly recruited by a number of firms. The fact that you chose the Braxton Street Legal Aid Clinic tells us a lot about your character."

Lily could feel herself blush at the compliments. She wondered if they knew about her DUI. "Are you considering anyone else?"

"We're looking at a couple of other candidates, but as I said, you came highly recommended, and that means a lot to us."

"Would it...would it make a difference if you knew I got arrested a couple of years ago for driving drunk?"

"And that you completed a rehab program?" Cohen added, her eyebrows arched.

Lily smirked. "You guys are pretty good."

Thompson smiled back. "That came up in our background check, so we followed up on it. We talked to Richard Anston, and he assured us you were a success story. Was he right?"

Judge Anston was the one who had denied her request for driving privileges so she could attend a day treatment program. That had forced her into residential treatment at Redwood Hills. "He was, but I wanted to be sure you knew about it. That's always going to be a part of my record."

"People make mistakes, Lily. What matters most is how they handle them."

Lily breathed a sigh of relief, acknowledging to herself that she was interested in the post. "So if I said I wanted to be considered, what would be the next step?"

Both directors smiled. "We need to talk with the rest of our board and ask them to put together a financial package. You look it over and see if it meets your needs. Then we'll set up another meeting and go from there."

She thought back to her earlier conversation with Wes McLean. "Wes said you probably wouldn't make a decision until November."

"That's when we have our next official board meeting. We can't do anything formally until then, but we'd like to go in with a strong recommendation."

"Then I guess I'll wait to hear from you."

As she returned to her car, she checked her missed calls. One was from her friend, Sandy Henke, who worked in social services and had access to a statewide database. Lily had called her the day before on the off chance she could find out anything about the mysterious Kristy Parker in San Francisco. She punched a button to return the call.

"Hey, Lil. I'm on my way to do a home visit, but I wanted to give you an update on that woman."

"Did you find anything?"

"Yes and no. She's on file, but she aged out of foster care four years ago, so I had to turn in a special request to get into the archive."

"Right, they said she was twenty-two."

"She's also on special status because of the circumstances. They do that so the press can't get into the database and pull out things that are supposed to be confidential."

"You won't get in trouble for this, will you?"

"No, I went through channels...for a change."

Lily chuckled. Sandy had worked for social services for over fifteen years and knew all the shortcuts. "I don't really expect you to find anything. It was just freaky because she looked so much like me and had the same last name."

"Yeah, I saw the picture. Anyway, I just called to tell you it might be a day or two before I get something back."

"It's no big deal." On the short drive back to her office, she laid out the speech to Tony, reminding herself that the new position would give her greater impact on the lives of children at risk. If ever she needed assurance that such a job was worthwhile, she had only to think about her own precarious start, and that of women like Kristy Parker, whose childhood struggles had led to a life on the streets, and to a death that came much too soon.

Anna emptied the plastic bag of its contents, one carton of steamed rice and another of shrimp and vegetables. Cooking was not her forte, but she ranked herself among the very best when it came to take-out, which she picked up a couple of nights a week to give Lily a break in the kitchen.

Chester lumbered into the family room, his low bark announcing Lily's arrival.

A few moments later, Lily appeared in the kitchen doorway with a sly grin. "Come kiss me, Amazon. I have news."

Dinner was forgotten as Anna took Lily in her arms and delivered a loving kiss. "I take it your meeting went well."

"I'm going to do it, Anna. I've decided to take the job if they make me a firm offer."

"That's my girl!" Anna smiled her approval. "I've been hoping you'd say yes. What was it that pushed you over the edge?"

She took out plates and chopsticks as Lily told her the details. She wasn't surprised to hear that support from a couple of judges had given Lily the confidence to take the leap. "One of these days, you're going to realize what I've been telling you since the first day we met. You can do anything you set your mind to. I've never met anyone so capable in my life…except when it comes to reaching things on the top shelf. You're really no good at that."

"Keep it up, and I'm going to start biting your ankles."

"Is that your cell phone?"

Lily followed the chirping sound back into the family room. Moments later she returned, her face nearly white and her voice shaking. "That was Sandy. She said that woman who was killed in San Francisco...Kristy Parker. She was my sister."

Lily was glad Anna was driving. Her simmering rage at Karen Parker—the woman who had abused and neglected her—bubbled over in short bursts that caused her to dig her fingernails into her palms. "You know what kills me, Anna? Some states won't even let gays and lesbians adopt, but people like Karen Parker can have all the children they want."

"There's no rhyme or reason."

"Social services should have taken Kristy away the minute she was born." She pounded her fist against her thigh.

"How long after you left was she born?"

"She was twenty-two. So I was eleven years old and already living with Mom when she came along." She snorted. "I bet if Mom had known about her, she would have tried to get custody."

Anna patted her forearm. "I know your head's filled with what-ifs, but there probably wasn't anything you or Eleanor could have done."

"I know. That's what's so frustrating about this."

They reached Sandy and Suzanne's home in Sherman Oaks and Lily hopped out, barely waiting for Anna to put the car in park. She charged up the front steps toward the ranch-style house and rang the bell. Anna caught up with her just as Suzanne opened the door.

"Sandy's in the dining room."

Lily blew past her to find Sandy arranging folders on the dining table. "God, look at all of this."

"Eighteen reports in all, but most of them are from foster parents. Kristy's first contact with social services happened when she was five." Sandy pointed to the first file. "A hospital worker said Karen brought her in with a dislocated shoulder. Kristy was filthy and malnourished. They put her in a foster home, but returned her after four months." The second file was thicker. "This is the big one. When she was eight, her teacher reported that she was acting out sexually at school, which, as you know, is a pretty sure sign of sexual abuse. They investigated Karen's boyfriend, but never filed charges. Social services argued that Kristy was better off in foster care, and since Karen never showed up for court, the judge agreed."

"What are all these others?"

"Apparently, Kristy was a handful. She stole things and lied… got into fights with the other kids in the home. They moved her fifteen times in six years."

Lily went through the reports one by one, confirming Sandy's summary.

Anna picked up one and read it silently. "I don't know how either of you do what you do."

Sandy sighed. "Some days I wonder myself."

"I do it because it's the only way to save the Kristy Parkers of the world," Lily answered flatly. "Is this all?"

"I think so. My supervisor—Donna, you remember her—was able to get the birth date from the police report, and we worked forward from there. Nothing came in after one o'clock, so I don't think we're going to find any more."

"I appreciate you guys doing this. I know you're not supposed to go fishing through the records without a good reason."

"I told Donna why you wanted to know and she didn't bat an eye. She knows you're one of the good guys."

Lily paged through the reports again, noting various social workers' observations that Karen's parenting—or lack thereof—never resulted in criminal charges. If they had charged Karen with abuse for yanking Kristy's arm out of the socket, they could have petitioned right then to sever parental rights. That would have made Kristy eligible for adoption at five years old. She could have been removed from the home permanently and spared an abysmal upbringing that likely included being sexually molested. "This last report was when Kristy was fourteen years old. Shouldn't there be more? Surely she didn't go back to Karen."

"If you look at the last paragraph of that one, it says she ran away from her foster home. Social services never located her after that."

On the way home, Lily cradled the stack of reports, the only tangible link to a sister she never knew she had.

"I can't even imagine what you're feeling right now," Anna said.

"What do you think about all of this?" Anna had barely said a word as Sandy walked them through her reports.

"It's all pretty incredible. It's amazing to me how you seemed to know it was her, but I have to admit I had the same feeling that first night we saw her on the news."

"It's really ironic. After all these years, I find out that I have a sister. And now she's dead. I wish I'd…"

"You wish what?"

"I wish I'd had the chance to know her. Maybe if we could have connected, even in the last few years, I could have helped her."

"What would you have done?"

"I don't know. But if she'd had some place to go…"

"You know, she might not have wanted that. Some homeless people actually prefer living on the streets."

"Karen Parker is responsible for this, but the state could have done something. If they'd pulled Kristy out of the home when she was little, she might have had a chance with another family." Lily sighed in exasperation. "When Mom died, I felt like I'd lost the only family I'd ever had. Now it's like—"

"That's not true, Lily." Anna reached over and took her hand. "I'm family, and my family is yours too. Not only that, we just grew by one the other night."

"I know. You're right. But it's going to be hard not to think about what it would have been like to have had a little sister."

"Let's go out and grab a bite." Anna was dead on her feet after several days of running back and forth between the two LA dealerships. If she could last one more day until Friday, she could relax. When she saw Lily already collapsed on the couch, she didn't dare ask what was for dinner.

"I'm too tired to get up. Besides, Sandy's coming by around

eight."

"What for?"

"I don't know. She left a message at work that she wanted to stop by. Suzanne's fortieth birthday is next month, so maybe she wants to talk about a surprise party or something."

"Soup?"

"And a grilled cheese sandwich, please."

Anna chuckled at her fate. Lily had ordered the one thing she had mastered in the kitchen. She changed into shorts and a T-shirt and fed Chester before fixing their simple dinner.

"You're awfully handy to have around," Lily said as she finished her sandwich. "Just for that, you get to hold the remote."

Anna quickly tuned in the Dodgers game. "If we win two out of the next three, we'll get the wild card spot in the playoffs."

Lily craned her neck to peer out the window at the sound of a car in the driveway. "There's Sandy."

Anna loved it when their friends or family came over…unless she and Lily were chasing each other through the house naked. She opened the side door and ushered Sandy in, noticing the manila folder she gripped tightly.

Sandy wasted no time getting to the point of her visit. "Lily, remember the other day when I told you how we ran the query on Kristy Parker?"

Lily nodded, her face a mask of confusion.

"I quit checking the queue after that last report, but the query kept running. Our IT guy printed out three more reports for me this afternoon." She nervously opened the folder and pulled out the papers. "Turns out Kristy Parker had a little boy of her own, and he's currently somewhere in the foster care system in San Francisco."

Lily's mouth began to move, but no sound emerged.

Anna took the folder and sat on the couch next to Lily. "What do you know about him?"

"Just what's in there. His name is Andres and he turned four a couple of months ago. The first report says they took custody when he was about a year old because Kristy OD'd and ended up in the hospital. But he went back after about five months and stayed with her another year or so. The second time was after they found him in a park by himself."

"Did they sever parental rights?" Lily said, breaking her silence.

"What difference does that make if Kristy's dead?" Anna asked.

"If they severed rights, he might be up for adoption already."

"That would be a good thing, right? I mean, if he has a new family…" Swallowing the rest of that thought seemed like a good idea, given the incredulous look on Lily's face. It was obvious she had something else in mind, something that sent Anna's stomach into a dive bomb.

Sandy reached over and flipped the file to the end. "They never severed rights. It looks like they left it open for her to get him back if she found work and a place to live."

Lily turned back to Sandy. "Where is he living?"

"I'm not sure. I'd guess he's in a foster home, probably still in San Francisco, but the specific locations are coded so that the information is secure."

"Can we find him?" She glanced uncertainly at Anna. "Just to see if he's okay?"

"Maybe, but you'll have to get in touch with the office up there. His social worker is a guy by the name of John Moss. His number's there." She gestured at the note clipped to the top of the folder. "I got it off the state directory. You can call him tomorrow. He might not tell you anything, though. In fact, he could get in trouble if he did."

Lily nodded absently, staring at the report. "I need to try. That's the least I can do."

The wheels spun in Anna's head to come up with the right words, something supportive but noncommittal. She understood Lily's concern, but she couldn't help but be unsettled about the implications. "Yeah, call him and see what he knows. Maybe this kid is doing okay."

Sighing heavily, Lily slumped against the couch back, clutching the folder to her chest. "Andres. Andres Parker. My nephew."

When Sandy left, Anna sat quietly as Lily committed the scant information in the report to memory. Finally, she said, "I bet you don't sleep a wink tonight."

"Where's your head on all of this?"

"I think it's pretty amazing. I can understand why you want to know all about this little boy."

"I need to find him, Anna," Lily said emphatically.

"I know you do."

"But what?"

"I didn't say anything," Anna replied defensively.

"You didn't have to. I could hear it in your voice. You don't want me to pursue this."

"I never said that. I said you should talk to the social worker and find out how he is."

"And then what?"

Anna was surprised by the sharpness of Lily's voice. Somehow this had turned into a confrontation. "I can't answer that." She pushed up from the couch and started to pace. "I know where you're coming from—"

"You can't possibly know where I'm coming from. You've had the chance to know your family and be part of their lives. I haven't."

"But that's just it, Lily. Kim and I don't share one drop of blood. We're sisters because we shared our lives. You didn't share anything with Kristy Parker except for that miserable excuse for a mother."

"Which means we shared a childhood, even if it wasn't at the same time. You can't say that about Kim."

Anna blew out an exasperated breath. "This isn't a competition. Kim is my sister, and if you say you feel the same way about Kristy Parker, I accept that. But this business about finding this little boy…that just feels like you might be opening a big can of worms."

"Anna, I have to. I don't know how else to explain it."

"You don't have to explain it." In truth, she understood Lily's feelings better than she did her own. "But I have to tell you, the idea of rushing into this scares me half to death."

Lily closed the folder and clasped her hands on top. "Anna, I promise you I'm not going to rush into anything unless both of us are on the same page, okay? I just need to see this boy and make sure he's okay."

"What if he isn't?"

"Then I'll do whatever I can to make sure he ends up in the right place. He needs someone on his side, just like I did when I was little. If I can get him the help he needs, there's a good chance he'll turn out all right."

Anna breathed a quiet sigh of relief. "I think we're on the same page then."

Chapter 4

"I appreciate your help, officers," Anna said as she walked the two uniformed policemen back to their cruiser. "If there's ever anything I can do for you, just let me know."

She pressed two fingers to her brow to ward off a headache. The last thing she needed now was a migraine, but the swirling darts of light she had seen the moment she arrived at work warned her that one was on the way, whether she needed it or not.

Vandals had paid a visit to the BMW dealership overnight, leaving sixty-two flat tires, one for each auto on the front lot. Every car tipped slightly, though the direction varied depending on which tire was punctured.

Their insurance would cover the damage, and already a crew was hard at work replacing the pierced tires. Surveillance cameras had captured the entire episode, and one of the teenagers was well known by the officers on this beat. It was just a matter of time before the police apprehended the boy and his cohorts, but Anna knew from Lily's work with troubled families that it usually took more than arrest and punishment to turn these kids around.

She just hoped they wouldn't make a habit of taking out their frustrations on Premier Motors.

"Anna Kaklis, you have a call on line two. Anna Kaklis on two," the loudspeaker barked.

As she pushed through the glass door into the showroom, a sharp pain pierced her forehead. The moment Holly or Brad arrived on the lot she would hand off this mess and head home to bed. If she waited too long, she wouldn't be able to drive herself.

"This is Anna Kaklis. Can I help you?"

"Hi, honey."

Anna slumped into her office chair and closed her eyes.

"I struck out. Sandy was right about the social worker not telling me anything."

"Not even how he was doing?"

"Nothing. He said he couldn't give out that kind of information."

"Well at least you tried, sweetheart. You knew it was a long shot." Anna held the silent phone for ten full seconds. "Lily, are you still there?"

"Yeah...I made an appointment to see John Moss in person on Monday morning."

Anna felt a surge of panic as she imagined Lily going off to San Francisco and returning with a small child in tow. She took a deep breath and calmed herself with the reminder that Lily had promised not to take any steps on her own.

"Did you hear what I said?"

"Of course." She couldn't help her agitated tone as her headache grew more pronounced by the second.

"Please don't be upset with me, Anna. I didn't know what else to do."

Anna sighed as she ground the heel of her hand into her forehead in order to quell the pain. "Lily, I'm not upset. Well, actually I am, but not with you. You know how annoying a flat tire can be?"

"You had a flat tire?"

"I had sixty-two of them. A couple of kids came through the

40

lot last night and popped one on every single car. And if that's not enough, I'm getting a migraine."

"Anna, you should go home and go to bed."

"That's just what I plan to do. Can we talk about this later?"

Within two minutes of hanging up the phone, Anna was in the ladies' room throwing up. That was a sure sign her headache would get worse, and as soon as Hal arrived at the dealership, she enlisted him to drive her home.

Careful not to jostle the bed, Lily sat on the edge and gently placed the icepack on Anna's forehead. "Does that feel good?"

Anna grunted.

In the four years she and Anna had known each other, she had witnessed a half-dozen such headaches, but it was clear this was one of the worst, already spanning two full days. "Should you take some more medicine?"

"What time is it?"

Lily leaned sideways to see the clock on the bedside table. "Almost nine."

"I guess." Anna shifted the icepack to one side. "Just the painkiller, not the one with caffeine. I need to sleep this off."

She helped Anna sit up long enough to take the pill and then eased her back against the pillow. "I'm going to sleep in the guest room again tonight so I don't bother you."

"Mmm…that's probably best."

That proved to be a good decision, as Lily tossed and turned all night. Her head was filled with thoughts of what she might discover in talking on Monday with the social worker in San Francisco.

She was surprised the next morning when Anna appeared in the kitchen. "I bet you're starving. What can I fix you?"

"Just some toast…maybe hot tea."

Lily jumped up to prepare it as Anna slid onto the bench behind the small table in their breakfast nook. "How's your headache?"

"I think the worst is over, but I'll probably go back to bed.

I'm sorry I'm such rotten company." Anna took a sip of tea. "I know you want to talk about your sister's son, but I don't think I can right now."

"It's okay." Lily sat across from her with a cup of coffee. "I guess there really isn't much to talk about right now anyway. I just need to go check things out first." What she wanted most from Anna was a show of support that she should do whatever was needed for the boy, even if that meant bringing him to LA for a few weeks while she worked on getting him into the best permanent placement. There was no way to know for sure about Andres, but children who had been neglected early in life tended to have an array of problems, both physical and behavioral. Lily suspected it would be difficult to find a suitable home, but she knew how to champion that for him. She hoped Anna would agree that the important thing was the child's well-being, not whether or not they were mildly inconvenienced for a few weeks.

Anna gave her a weak smile. "I can tell you're worried. Don't be. I was a little freaked out the other night, but I know we'll do the right thing."

That was just what Lily needed to hear, and she felt a wave of relief. "I love you, sweetheart. I want you to feel better."

"Me too."

"I was thinking of taking Chester for a long walk today. Is that okay, or would you rather I stayed home in case you need something?"

"You can go." Anna planted a kiss on the top of her head as she walked by toward the door. "I'm going to take another pill and conk out."

Lily tightened her seatbelt as the jet banked right over the ocean on its way up to San Francisco. The flight would take only an hour, but the minutes would drag by as her excitement grew.

Andres Parker. The social worker had called him Andy. Like Lily and her sister, he bore only his mother's name, though his given name suggested Latino heritage. According to Moss, his father had been murdered in a gang-related shooting, and the only known relative was Karen Parker Haney. Moss had hedged when it came to specific information, but he implied that he had ruled her out as a guardian for Andy. Lily shuddered to think that had even been a consideration. He would have been better off homeless at four years old.

She smoothed the wrinkles from her olive-green dress, one of the conservative outfits she usually saved for court appearances. She needed to make a good impression on John Moss in order to gain leverage in securing the best placement and care for the boy.

Other than a name and birthday, Lily knew almost nothing about Andy Parker. Was he healthy? Was he happy? Did he have any special needs? What did he look like? The file Sandy had pulled together showed that in just the last year in foster care, he had already lived in four different homes. From her experience with the foster care system, that was a red flag, usually signaling a child who had difficulty adjusting to his or her environment, or a child with unmanageable needs. Given his home life with his mother, that wouldn't be a surprise.

The bigger question for Lily was what she would do if she found him. If his care was inadequate, how could she help him? If there were legal matters involved, she certainly could advise and assist, but the fact remained that, even as his aunt, she lacked standing. She couldn't insert herself into the decision-making process where this child was concerned unless she assumed the role of guardian. If she eventually decided to do that, she first had to pass muster with Moss.

"Feeling better?" Hal asked from the doorway to Anna's office.

"I lived," she answered. "I appreciate the ride home the other day."

"No problem. Kim was worried about you, but didn't want to call in case you were sleeping."

When he left, she shut her office door and took a seat behind her cluttered desk. Then she placed a call to her sister. "I need some advice. You got a minute?"

"This better be good. I only get about three minutes of adult time every day."

Anna related the news about Lily's nephew and her trip to San Francisco to meet the social worker.

"That's amazing. Lily must be thrilled."

"She's pretty excited."

"No wonder. This is huge. How come you're not jumping up and down?"

From her sister's elated reaction, Anna got a sinking feeling in her gut that her quest for support would go unmet. "Because she has no idea what she's getting herself into. That kid could have all sorts of problems. His mother was into drugs, and he's been bounced around from one place to another."

Kim didn't answer, which caused Anna to panic even more.

"What if she comes home and says she wants that boy to come live with us?"

"That boy has a name," Kim said sharply.

"Andy. What if she wants Andy to come live with us?" She was annoyed to hear herself on the verge of hysteria.

"You need to calm down. You know Lily wouldn't bring him home unless you were all right with it."

"I know that." She also knew she was getting ahead of herself. "What I'm worried about is what's going to happen if she wants to bring him home and I don't. How do I tell her no without sounding like a heartless bitch?"

"Oh, you're not going to like this."

Anna had the same feeling.

"I think you need to try looking at it through Lily's eyes. She lost her mom and then out of the blue, she loses a sister she never knew she had. Try to imagine how important Andy must be to her."

"So in other words…" She wanted Kim to spell it out.

"Don't even think about telling her no."

Anna added guilt to the range of emotions she was experiencing. She wasn't surprised by her sister's admonitions, and grudgingly admitted to herself that Lily's perspective was more important than her own. It didn't quell her anxiety, though, nor her hope that Lily would find the boy—Andy—already placed in a good home with a bright future.

Lily swung her crossed leg nervously in the reception area of the busy government office, growing anxious that this might turn out to be a wasted trip. John Moss was forty-five minutes late for their appointment, apparently called out this morning by police to a domestic disturbance involving children. She understood these types of emergencies—as an attorney working with disadvantaged families, she had been called out plenty of times herself—but she hoped Moss could resolve the matter quickly and still have time to meet with her today.

Everywhere she looked around the office people were on the phone or scrolling through information on their desktop monitors. About half the desks were empty, their owners likely in the field checking on the status of their charges. The waiting area was overflowing.

A middle-aged woman stepped up to the other side of the long counter. "Is there a Lilian Kaklis here?"

"Yes, right here." She hurried up to the counter with her purse and folders.

"I have a message for you from John Moss. He's going to be tied up for another hour or two. He apologizes, but he's dealing with an emergency this morning."

"It's okay. I understand." Though it was frustrating to wait, at least she was sure he remembered their appointment. Maybe he would even feel a bit guilty for having her cool her heels for so long and he would be more cooperative about releasing information on Andy.

When she turned back to the waiting area, she found that her chair had been taken. With an hour to kill—and nowhere to sit—she headed outside in search of a coffee shop. Using her cell phone, she left Moss a message that she would return at eleven thirty. As she moved forward in the line to order her coffee, her phone rang, the caller ID registering an unknown local number.

"Ms. Kaklis, John Moss here. I'm sorry to keep you waiting. I just got your message."

She hoped he wasn't calling to cancel. "I understand how emergencies are. I just hope you'll have time to see me."

"Absolutely. I've been stuck here waiting for a policeman to sign a release form, which he just did, so I'm leaving the scene now. Why don't you meet me downstairs in twenty minutes? We'll grab some coffee and talk about Andy Parker."

"That would be great, Mr. Moss."

"Call me John. Mr. Moss was my dad."

"John. I'm Lily, and I'll be right in front of the building."

True to his word, twenty minutes later a slender man in his late thirties rounded the corner and strode toward where Lily had been pacing nervously. Only a few inches taller than she, he was dressed in khaki chinos and a tweed sports coat, and his striped tie hung loosely from the collar of his denim shirt.

"Lily Kaklis?"

"That's me," she answered, her smile fixed in place as she held out her hand. She couldn't say why, but she liked him at once.

"John Moss. Nice to meet you, and I'm really sorry I kept you waiting."

"I understand. It happens to me in my work all the time."

"What kind of work do you do?" He gestured with his hand in the direction of the coffee shop where she had just been.

"I'm an attorney, a family services attorney at a legal aid clinic in LA. I do a lot of work with social services on getting kids in the right placement." She wanted this man to know that she knew her stuff, and also that she was his comrade.

He stopped abruptly on the sidewalk. "I don't mean to sound rude, but would you mind terribly showing me some ID?"

Lily opened her wallet and pulled out her driver's license. "You want to see my state bar card?"

Moss inspected the driver's license and handed it back. "That won't be necessary, but thanks for the offer. I Googled you on Friday after you called."

"So you already knew what kind of work I did." She wasn't exactly annoyed by the pretense, but it heightened her awareness that this was a serious matter.

He pushed his hands into his pockets and looked at her sheepishly. "Actually, I knew what kind of work Lilian Kaklis did. I just needed to make sure that was you before I started talking about Andy. I'm sure you're aware of all the privacy restrictions in place regarding kids in state custody."

"Yes, but we covered that on the phone last week, so I'm hoping we're past all of that. You must have had a good reason to ask me up here."

He began to stroll toward the coffee shop. "I was… intrigued."

"Intrigued?"

"To tell you the truth, I didn't believe you when you called on Friday. I thought you might have been another reporter. Some guy called last week trying to find Andy so he could do a survivor story, showing everyone how, because of the police actions, some poor child was now orphaned."

"You thought I was a reporter?"

"Yeah, but when I found your bar listing, I did some checking on your maiden name and found your adoption records. They were never sealed, you know, so linking you to Karen Parker Haney was pretty easy. Her paper trail goes back quite a way with us."

Lily scowled at the mention of her birth mother. "So now that you're convinced that I'm related to Andy, will you tell me about him?"

"I am satisfied that you're related to him, but I'm going to want to know more before I give away any confidential information."

"Such as?" Lily realized her heart was starting to race as she got closer to finding out something.

"Mostly, I just want to know what's in this for you." They each ordered coffee, paying separately, and climbed the spiral staircase to the loft, where they sat at a small table overlooking the entrance.

She toyed with her paper cup as she chose her words. "I've lived in foster homes too. If there is anything I want, it's peace of mind that he's all right, that he's in a good home where he's being taken care of."

"And what if he isn't?"

Lily's stomach lurched. "Is there something wrong with him?"

"I didn't say that. I just want to know what you plan to do if you find out…say, that things aren't as good for him as they should be, or even that they could be. What will you do?"

"I…think that I would…" she stammered, suddenly feeling like a dog that had chased a car and caught it. "I suppose I would try to do whatever I could to make it better. Maybe ask for a new placement, or some extra services. It would depend on the circumstances."

"And would you ask as Andy's aunt? Or as a lawyer? Or as your garden-variety critic of the system?"

"I don't know exactly what I'd do. But I'm not a critic of the system any more than you are. In fact, I'm a part of it too. I want what's best for all these kids."

"Let me just ask you point-blank, Lily. If you found Andy's situation to be lacking, would you be willing to take him into your home, as his aunt?"

She sighed heavily, her frustration mounting. "Can't you just tell me how he's doing?"

"I can," he replied calmly. "But I want to know what it means to you. You obviously care about Andy, or you wouldn't be here. I care about him too, and I want what's best for him."

Lily felt her face turning red at the gentle reproach. John Moss had all the traits of a first-rate social worker. If she weren't able to see for herself how Andy was doing, she was at least relieved to know that the boy had this kind of advocate.

"Are you interested in custody?"

"No, it's just not…" *Not what?* Not something she could ask of Anna?

"That's too bad. I would like very much to place Andy with a relative who can give him some stability. His grandmother—your biological mother—has asked for custody."

Lily was stunned to hear this. "Karen Parker? You've got to be kidding!" Her mind raced back to the cocktail waitress she had seen in Oakland last year, hardly the motherly type. "Why would she want Andy?"

"I can't say for sure, but we got an adoption petition from James Lafollette. He's one of those litigation attorneys. It's my guess he approached her about filing a wrongful death suit against the police department. Being Andy's guardian would help her case a lot because it would give her legal standing."

That possibility fit perfectly with her view of Karen Parker. "You're not actually going to place him with her, are you?"

He shrugged. "Not if I can help it. As I told you on the phone, I looked into her situation back when Andy first came to us, and we made the decision then that he was better off in regular foster care. But she wasn't asking for custody then."

"Can't you just make him eligible for a private adoption? Surely, you've got enough ammunition against Karen Parker to keep him from going to her home."

"That's what I'd argue for him, but you know how judges are about wanting to place kids with family members."

"John, his whole life would be ruined. Karen Parker isn't anyone's family. She already had two kids she didn't take care of." Lily was so angry she was ready to cry.

"That's why I'd like another option." Moss wore his poker face, but he had to know he was pushing all of her buttons. "What kind of life do you want for Andy?"

"I just want him to be saved from all of this. I want him to have a happy childhood and be loved. I want him to have a chance to make something of himself." She blinked back tears at the thought of how Eleanor Stewart had rescued her from what would have been a life of despair.

The two sat silently, sipping their coffee for several minutes. Finally, John spoke. "My car's in the garage around the corner. What do you say we take a little ride out toward Candlestick

Park?"

Lily jumped to her feet immediately and pitched her empty cup in a nearby bin. "Thank you."

Lunch was the proverbial rubber chicken, made worse by the cold, sticky fruit sauce on top. The eight diners at Anna's table had practically fought over the bread basket, giving up on the main entrée and the too-cooked mixed vegetables. At least the salad had been edible, and now she was looking forward to the chocolate mousse.

This was the annual Entrepreneur Awards Luncheon for the Greater Los Angeles Chamber of Commerce. As one of last year's winners for her sweeping acquisition of three new dealerships, Anna was seated near the speaker's table with several of the movers and shakers who had made their mark in LA's business community. The subject of conversation at Anna's table was the mayor's promotion of a small business tax break. Anna favored it, as did several others, but some of the more successful businesses felt they were subsidizing their competition.

To Anna, it seemed the Chamber membership was divided into two factions, one that focused solely on the needs of the business community, and another that championed improving the quality of life throughout the county through things like mentoring, youth programs and neighborhood franchising. She was part of the latter group, especially since, through Lily, she had gotten a closer look at the struggles of those on the lower end of the economic spectrum. Bettering their lives would have a positive impact on everyone.

A tapping on her shoulder took her away from an anti-city hall tirade.

"Dave, hi. How are you?" Dave Cahill owned a string of office supply franchises throughout southern California. He was the Chamber's vice president, and would ascend to the top job after the next election, two months away. Like Anna, Dave and his businesses were ardent supporters of several projects that benefited children, either in the schools or in the neighborhoods.

"I'm sorry to interrupt, but I wonder if you'd mind joining a few of us for a short meeting after lunch. I promise it won't take long."

"Sure." She nodded. If Dave was getting behind something, chances were she would too.

"Great. We'll meet in the Palm Room down the hall. Oh, and Geri just ordered a sandwich tray," he added with a nod toward her unfinished lunch.

"Then I'll definitely be there."

Anna walked into the room after the luncheon to find a small group of the Chamber's elite members, including several past officers. Anna knew them all because she had served as the organization's treasurer a few years ago.

"Anna, thanks for joining us," Dave said eagerly.

When she saw the smiles throughout the room at her arrival, she realized with trepidation that this meeting was about her. "Hi, everyone." She glanced about nervously. "What's this about?"

"This is about your campaign for vice president. Everyone in the room wants you to run, and we'll all do our part to help you get elected."

Anna had worked like a dog the last time she had served the Chamber. However, she knew from others who had held various posts that only the job of president was more demanding than treasurer, so the vice presidency wouldn't be a huge burden.

"Why me, Dave?" There were lots of Chamber members with more business experience than she, and Anna was almost certain she wouldn't get much support from the old guard.

"Because you're the kind of leader we need, somebody who has shown that she knows how to operate a sound business and make it grow."

Geri Morgan spoke up. "Somebody who can be a good role model for other women and young people in the business community."

Dave leaned in and added, "And somebody who cares about the whole community, not just her own business interests. I hope to start the ball rolling on some new projects during my term, and I'd like to see someone coming along behind me who will keep them going."

Anna was staggered by their praise. "Well, I…"

"Just say the magic word, and we'll worry about the rest."

Anna sucked in a deep breath. It was a two-year commitment, as the charter called for the vice president to automatically succeed the president. If Lily took the job as executive director of the guardian *ad litem* program, they would both be swamped again, but at least she would have a platform for advocating better business practices and more community involvement. "Okay. I'll do it."

The room erupted in applause, and everyone rushed forward to offer their thanks and congratulations.

Lily squirmed in anticipation as Moss spun his Honda Civic south on 101 toward the infamous stadium on Candlestick Point.

"What kind of work does your husband do?" Moss asked.

Lily chuckled at his assumption. "She sells cars."

Momentarily perplexed, Moss recovered nicely as understanding dawned. "And do you two have any children?"

"No, but we have a basset hound, and my spouse and I seem to take turns acting like children from time to time."

"I know what you mean. My wife says I do that too."

"Do you have children?" She genuinely liked this man, and was glad the wheels of fate had landed Andy's case on his desk.

"Two boys, twelve and nine. I tell you, sometimes after a really tough day, I have to go straight to their rooms when I get home and tell them how much I love them."

She was tempted to tell him she was interviewing to become the director of the guardian *ad litem* program, but decided to save that for even more leverage later. "Believe me, I understand. We see some horrible things in this line of work. Still, I like knowing that I'm doing something about it."

"Me too. Here we are."

Moss parked and led Lily up the steps to the porch of a narrow three-story house. The garage took up the ground level, so the front door entered on the second story. They were expected, as he had called on the way over.

"Nice to see you again, John. Come on in."

"Hi, Mary Beth. Sorry about the short notice."

"Not a problem. We've just had lunch."

Moss and Lily entered the small living room, where he made the introductions. "Lily, this is Mary Beth Shull. She and her husband have been foster parents with us for about eight years."

"Hi, Mrs. Shull. I'm Lily Kaklis," she eagerly offered, barely able to avert her eyes from the three young boys huddled around the TV. If one of them was Andy, he was awfully big for four years old.

"Call me Mary Beth. Even the boys do."

From the abundance of gray hair, Lily surmised Mary Beth was in her mid-fifties. She doubted seriously that any of the children in the room belonged to her and her husband. In fact, besides the actual presence of the boys watching the TV, there wasn't much evidence that children lived here at all. There were no toys, games or books of any kind in the room. Things were neat and orderly, giving the impression Mary Beth ran a tight ship.

"It's nice to meet you. Thanks for letting us come."

"It's all right. I told Andy someone was coming to see him, and he slipped upstairs to the bedroom without finishing his lunch. He's pretty shy."

"Can we go up there?" Lily realized she was shaking.

"Right this way." She fell in behind Mary Beth, and Moss brought up the rear. Straight ahead at the top of the stairs was a small bathroom, the upward toilet seat a sign that its last visitor had been one of the young boys. To the left was a closed door, presumably the Shulls' bedroom. The room on the right was open, with two sets of bunk beds visible from the doorway. Apparently, all four of the boys shared this small room.

"Andy?" the foster mother called.

53

Lily stepped into the room behind her, her eyes drawn immediately to movement in the corner behind the tall chest of drawers. A small boy squatted low, his green eyes wide as he watched them enter the room. Even in his crouched position, Lily could see that he was quite small for his age, probably less than thirty pounds. His complexion was slightly darker than hers, and his curly hair was brown, both evidence of his Latino parentage.

"Andy, do you remember John?"

If he did, he didn't let on.

"Hi, Andy. How are you, buddy?" Moss smiled a friendly greeting to the boy. "I brought someone to see you today. This is Lily. Can you say hi?"

Lily slowly squatted, careful not to crowd the child in the corner. From here, she noticed that his hands tightly clutched a small toy car. "Hello, Andy. What's that you're playing with?"

He didn't answer, but meekly held out the toy for her inspection, as though afraid she would take it from him. He was dressed in oversized red gym shorts, most likely hand-me-downs from children who had stayed with the Shulls over the last eight years, and a faded blue T-shirt with a racecar on the front.

"That's a nice car. Is it fun to play with?"

Andy nodded and pulled it back.

"He really likes to play with cars," Mary Beth interjected. "We have about five or six of those little cars here that he keeps hidden under the bed so the other boys won't get them." She walked to the lower bunk on the left to retrieve his stash.

Andy followed her with his eyes, seemingly anxious about his secret place.

"One of my friends likes cars too, Andy," Lily said.

"Behavior-wise, he's not a whole lot of trouble," she went on. "He doesn't talk much and he plays by himself a lot. But he's a very picky eater, and he doesn't wash himself very well."

Lily had learned some of those same things about herself from the adoption papers her mother had saved.

"How's his asthma been?" Moss asked.

"He has asthma?" Lily was momentarily startled by this piece of information. She still had a few problems with the condition, and knowing its hereditary nature, she wondered if Kristy also had suffered with it.

"From what I can tell from his records, it seems to be a little worse in the summertime. I had to move him down to the couch the other night because his coughing was keeping the other boys awake."

The image of the small boy alone downstairs in the night almost broke Lily's heart. She knew the most effective medication for an asthma attack was a double-edged sword at night. It usually stopped the coughing, but stimulated the senses, making it difficult to fall asleep.

"Mary Beth, why don't we go back downstairs for a while and let Lily visit with Andy?"

Alone with the bashful boy, Lily adjusted her dress and sat cross-legged on the floor. His wide eyes never left her as she reached out to drag the other cars over to the space between them.

"Which one of these is your favorite, Andy?"

Wordlessly, he slowly crawled the few feet to where she sat and pointed to a small convertible.

"This one?"

He nodded, still not making a sound.

"I like that one too. Can I see the one you have in your hand?"

Obviously reluctant, Andy gave up the small black Pontiac Trans Am with flames painted on the hood.

She was accustomed to talking with anxious children, and knew a few tricks for establishing a sense of trust. "This one's very nice too," she said, quickly handing it back to him.

He clutched it to his chest.

"So which bed is yours?"

He walked to the lower bunk. "This one."

"It looks like a fun place to sleep, like having your own little room."

"I can climb this," he said, grabbing the ladder that led to the upper bunk. In a flash, he began to demonstrate.

Lily shot up from her sitting position, readying herself to catch him. "Wow, you're a good climber, Andy."

They had finally broken the ice, and Andy spent the next half hour showing her how he could cross his eyes, balance briefly on one foot, and almost reach the top bunk when he clumsily jumped up from the floor. Next, he showed her his other pair of shoes, and the five T-shirts and two pairs of shorts in the bottom drawer of the nightstand.

Time flew as he entertained her in the crowded room upstairs. She was delighted that he had opened up, and thrilled to watch him show off. It was surprising to see him suddenly become subdued when John and Mary Beth appeared again in the doorway.

"We've been having a lot of fun," she said, still smiling at Andy, who had retreated to sit on his bed against the wall.

"We've been hearing all that fun," Mary Beth said in a tone that made it sound like an admonishment. Obviously, they had heard the jumping downstairs. "You haven't been climbing on the ladder, have you, Andy?"

He looked down without answering.

"Uh, that was my fault. I asked him if he could and he showed me. Sorry, I didn't know he wasn't supposed to do that." She didn't want Andy to be punished, especially since he was only showing off for her.

"Andy knows he's not allowed to do that. Don't you, Andy?"

He nodded solemnly.

Fortunately, that reprimand was his only punishment, and Lily shot him a quick wink and a smile to lessen the blow.

"I need to be getting back to my office, Lily. Are you about ready to go?"

Lily wasn't at all ready to leave. She had enjoyed every moment of her time with Andy, and found herself strangely moved by the connection she felt. She ducked under the top bunk to say goodbye. "I have to go, Andy. Do you think I could have a hug to take with me?"

"Oh, he doesn't really like physical contact that much. That's probably from being abused when he was with his mother."

Lily flinched at the mention of possible abuse, but was more annoyed that the foster mother had said something so insensitive in front of Andy. Her protective instincts were on high alert. She coaxed him one more time. "Would it be okay if I gave you a hug?"

Slowly he crawled to the edge of the bed, rising up on his knees to wrap his small arms around her neck.

Lily's eyes quickly filled with tears at the tender gesture, and she hugged him fiercely to her chest. "Maybe I'll come back to visit you again sometime. Would you like that?"

Andy nodded and Lily slowly stood. She looked back one last time at his bright green eyes—eyes like hers—whispered her goodbye and started down the steps.

John was quiet in the car as they pulled away, probably aware that she was working hard to compose herself. Finally, he broke the silence. "So are you satisfied?"

"Satisfied with what?"

"Satisfied that he's doing okay. That's what you came to check on, isn't it?"

"He seems to be relatively healthy, except for the asthma she mentioned."

"His last checkup was pretty good. And the Shulls take pretty good care of the kids that stay there."

"But he doesn't seem to be particularly happy. I guess that's not all that unusual for kids in foster care, is it?"

"Yeah, he might do a little better if there were fewer kids there. The Shulls are only certified for two children, but they've had four at a time for most of the last year."

"And the other boys are so much older. You always worry about the little ones getting bullied, or picking up bad behaviors from the older ones. Isn't there somewhere else he could go?"

"You know what it's like. We just don't have enough beds for the kids that need them. All in all, the Shulls are doing a pretty good job."

"She seems nice enough, but you've got to admit she's a little severe. There were four children in the house, and the only toys they had were the little cars hidden under the bed. And Andy acted like he was afraid of her when she said that about him climbing on the ladder."

"Lily, I understand what you're saying, believe me. Our house looks like a toy box in every room. But a lot of these kids come into foster care with absolutely no sense of order or rules. It isn't such a bad thing to have them learn a few boundaries."

"But they're still kids, John. And I didn't like how she talked about Andy being abused with him sitting right there in the room."

He shrugged noncommittally.

Here in south San Francisco, they were only minutes from the airport. "Would it be too much trouble for you to drop me at SFO?"

"No problem." He crossed traffic to get into the turn lane for the freeway. "Will you be coming back?"

"I can't say anything for sure, but I hope so." She needed to explain all of this to Anna, to make her understand her sense of responsibility. "Could I ask you a huge personal favor? Will you just keep me posted on how he's doing?"

Moss never took his eyes from the road. "I will if you'll do something for me."

"What's that?"

"Will you go home and think about taking him in?"

Lily's stomach fluttered at the suggestion. When she felt Andy's arms go around her neck, she had been ready to scoop him up and take him home right then. "That's not a decision I can make by myself. I have to talk to Anna about it. I just don't think this is a good time for us." The excuse sounded feeble, but Anna was entitled to her reservations. Besides, Andy wasn't just any child. He was a child who had been abused and neglected, and he probably would have a lot of emotional difficulties to overcome.

"But it's a good time for Andy. He's doing okay, but I think he'd thrive if he got the right attention, especially if he was the only child in the home." John steered the small car into the departure lane. "What's your airline?"

"United," she answered, picking up her folders from the floorboard and hooking her handbag over her shoulder. She already had a boarding pass and could go straight to the gate. With luck, she could walk onto an earlier flight than her five o'clock departure.

John maneuvered in front of the United Airlines section and pulled to a stop. "How about as a temporary shelter?"

Maybe she could convince Anna to let him come just for a while, especially if it improved his chances of getting permanently placed in the right home. "Could we do it without Karen Parker finding out? I don't want any contact with her, and I don't want her to know where I live."

"She'd probably find out eventually. Her lawyer would be right on top of it."

"I don't want that woman in my life, John." The prospect of Karen knowing her business was repugnant. Lily stepped onto the curb but waited to close the door. "I'm sorry. I'll help you however I can to get what's best for Andy, but this isn't something I can do right now. I really appreciate all you did today."

"Please think about it, Lily," he pleaded, not even trying to conceal his disappointment.

She sighed deeply and looked away, knowing that, despite her words to the contrary, it would be all she thought about.

Chapter 5

Anna was glad to see the silver X3 already in the garage when she got home, but from the short turnaround to San Francisco and back, she guessed Lily would be disappointed. She couldn't possibly have had time to actually see Andres.

"Lily?" Anna strode into the family room, stopping briefly to pet Chester, who met her faithfully at the door.

"In here."

She continued into the kitchen, where Lily was running a garlic press over a buttered split loaf. Something smelled delicious. "Hey, baby. When did you get back?"

"About two hours ago." Lily tilted her head, allowing Anna to kiss her neck from behind. "I walked onto an earlier flight. How's your headache?"

"Gone, thank goodness." The table was set and the salad was tossed. When Lily opened the oven to put the bread in, Anna spied a dish of lasagna. "Cooking your fingers to the bone?"

"Nah, I picked it up at Whole Paycheck."

Anna chuckled at Lily's nickname for the premium

supermarket. "Tell me about your day."

When Lily turned, it was obvious she had been crying.

"Honey, what is it?"

"I saw him," she said, her chin quivering.

"And?"

"He stole my heart, Anna."

"That's too bad, because your heart belongs to me. He's going to have to give it back," she said, trying to sound playful, though her stomach was doing flips.

As they waited for dinner to warm, Lily described the Shulls' crowded home. Borrowing Anna's silverware, she laid out a model of the small bedroom, showing where the bunk beds were, and where she found him hiding.

"What did he look like?"

Lily's face took on a dreamy expression. "He was beautiful. He's small for his age—Mary Beth says he's a picky eater—and he's got curly, light brown hair, and big green eyes like mine."

"Like yours?" Anna was a sucker for Lily's eyes.

"And he's really bashful, but he finally opened up and started to play with me. He's very sweet. Oh, and guess what he likes to play with most? You'll love this."

"I have no idea."

"Cars. He loves those little Matchbox cars. He has a bunch of them that he hides under the bed so the other boys won't get them." Lily went on to tell about various tricks Andy did, and how he showed off for her until the other adults returned. "He was adorable. And when I had to leave, he gave me a big hug." She crossed her hands over her heart as if reliving the moment.

"I'm really glad you went, sweetheart. It sounds like he's doing okay. Was that the impression you got?"

"Yeah, I guess. I just wish..." Lily set down her fork and sighed. "I wish that he were...I don't know, happier. Foster care can be a cruel system sometimes."

"What do you mean?"

"It's just the nature of the beast. They move these kids around so much that they actually discourage the foster parents from trying to bond with them because it can cause separation problems for some of them when they have to leave."

"I guess that makes sense."

"Yeah, so Andy has a safe place to stay, and a bed, and he gets his meals and his bath. But he doesn't get to laugh and play very much, and I don't think he gets any affection at all. I think I might have been the first person to hug him in I don't know how long."

"That's too bad." Anna knew from her Kidz Kamp outings how much some of the kids craved adult attention. "So how long do you think he'll be there?"

"It's hard to say. John wants to find him a permanent home."

"You mean get him adopted?"

Lily nodded. "But you're not going to believe this. He said Karen Parker asked for custody."

"You've got to be kidding."

"My words exactly." She went on to explain Moss's theory about a wrongful death suit.

"Surely they won't put him there. That woman's already proven she can't take care of kids."

"That's what I said, but I know how the court system is here. They always lean toward placement with a relative when it's possible. John asked me to think about having him stay with us for the time being."

Inexplicably, Anna picked that moment to drop her fork and send it clanging across the tile floor.

They looked at one another in awkward silence before Lily finally spoke. "Don't sweat it, Amazon. I told him it wasn't going to happen." She got up to serve their dinner. "So tell me about your day."

Anna officially felt like crap—but not enough to relent.

"...and I'll keep my cell phone with me, Lily. You call me anytime you need to talk."

"Thanks, Virginia." Lily closed her phone and set it on the poolside table. In the two years since she had stopped drinking, today was the first time she had felt the need to contact her sponsor for support. It wasn't that she was tempted to drink. Rather, she found herself battling the same feelings of loss and helplessness she had experienced after her mother died.

Chester barked to announce Anna's car in the driveway, and moments later she came through the back gate. "Hey, baby."

"Are you talking to me or him?" Lily asked.

"I only have one baby. The other one is a worthless hound dog."

Lily took her briefcase and purse and set them by the door to the kitchen. "I need to talk with you about something important."

Anna followed her to the table by the pool, but they didn't sit down. "Sounds serious."

"I got a call this afternoon from John Moss in San Francisco." It was the first time she had mentioned anything related to Andy since their talk three nights ago, though the child had rarely left her thoughts.

"The social worker?"

Lily nodded. "They're getting ready to move Andy again. The other three boys in that house go to school during the day, and his foster mother decided she wants some time to herself."

"Where will he go?"

"John says he's worried the court might go ahead and award custody to Karen Parker, because she's the only one who's asking for him." Lily could feel the tears pooling in her eyes. "I can't let that happen, Anna."

"Can't you fight it? You can offer to be his guardian *ad litem* and argue for something better. You do that all the time for kids here."

Lily pushed back the tears on her cheeks. Surely Anna understood that just being Andy's advocate wasn't enough. "I'm afraid to take a chance like that. Anything could happen. He's such a sweet little boy, and Karen Parker will turn him into a…a street urchin just like his mother. He won't stand a chance with her."

Anna reached to comfort her, pulling her into an embrace. Several seconds passed before she spoke. "We won't let anything bad happen to him, sweetheart."

"He deserves a good home," she said, sniffing. "Anybody who saw him would fall in love with him."

"Maybe we can do what you said, bring him here for a while. Would they let us do that?"

Lily heard the trepidation in Anna's voice, but she didn't care. No matter how qualified the offer, she would seize it. All that mattered right now was keeping Andy out of the clutches of Karen Parker. "That's what John wants, Anna. That's why he called me, so he'd have another option."

"Then let's figure out how we can do that." Ever the businesswoman, Anna immediately slipped into management mode. "How are we going to take care of him with both of us working? What will you do about him during the day?"

"I can take some vacation time…maybe get him enrolled in a preschool program for part of the day. It would be good for him to be around other kids." It occurred to her that she sounded like a child promising to take care of a puppy.

"And what? You'll try to find him a family or something?"

"I will," she said, acknowledging her agreement to the boundaries. Anna wasn't saying yes forever, but her willingness to do this was at least a glimmer of hope.

"This is great, Lily," John said over the phone. "Whatever we can do to head off Karen Parker's quest for custody will buy him some time."

"I want to do more than that. I want to eliminate that possibility once and for all." Lily kicked her office door shut. She didn't want Tony to know about this until she was ready to ask for time off. "What's our first step?"

"I'll start the paperwork to get you certified as a foster parent. I need to hook up with a social worker in LA who can handle the preliminaries. They'll have to do a home visit and interviews with all the adults in the house. I know someone in that area. I can ask her to call you next week for an appointment."

"Would it be all right to use someone I know? I have a lot of friends in child services."

"It's all right by me, as long as it's somebody that's qualified to handle it."

Lily gave him Sandy Henke's name and number, assuring him that, though they were friends, Sandy could be trusted to do a professional job. "She's first-rate. I would actually put the two of you in the same league."

"If she's your friend, I'll take that as a compliment. Let me see what this says…" He was silent for a moment. "Okay, I'll need to run a background check on both of you, and you have to be fingerprinted. It's just routine."

She cleared her throat nervously. "You're going to find out I got a DUI a couple of years ago."

"I see." By his voice, he wasn't pleased at all. "Is that something that's a problem?"

"No, just a one-time thing. I swear. I lost my mom—my adoptive mom—and I didn't handle myself very well. But I got into a program, and I'm sober now, two years. It's not a part of me anymore."

"Okay, I appreciate the heads-up. I don't think it will be a problem." Papers rustled in the background. "Can you fax me a copy of your birth certificate? I'll probably need to prove you're Andy's aunt. And there's a good chance you'll have to come back up here to appear in court."

"What for?" Foster placements didn't generally require a court appearance.

"Because Karen Parker's lawyer will probably contest this move."

The last thing she wanted was to face Karen Parker in court. There were ways around it, things she did for her clients to avoid such showdowns. "If I can, I'd like to file a separate motion and testify in chambers."

"Okay, if it comes to that, we'll see what we can do. I'll have to talk to our attorney."

"I do it all the time, John. We just need to file a petition that separates our action from hers. In other words, we're not fighting against her getting custody. We're fighting in favor of our own, and the judge chooses. We can't lose."

"Whatever, but I'll still have to run it by our attorney."

She checked over her list. "I'll send the birth certificate out this afternoon and tell my friend to expect your call. Is there anything else you need?"

"I can't really do anything else on this end until I get the papers back. I'll try to get this packet out to your friend today, but it will probably be tomorrow. She should have it by Monday or Tuesday. When she gets it all filled out and sends it back, I'll walk it through."

Lily could feel the excitement building. "Is there any way you could send the packet overnight? We might be able to take care of it all over the weekend and get it back to you by Tuesday."

"Sure, I'll give it a shot. Why don't I just send it to your house?"

"Perfect."

"Thank you, Lily. I like that you seem so eager to do this. I have to admit I had my doubts when you left here the other day."

"So did I, but I talked it over with Anna. We both want to help."

"I have a feeling this is going to be really good for Andy."

Lily chuckled nervously. It would be great for Andy. The bigger question was how it would be for Anna.

Anna stood on the landing that separated her office from those of her two vice presidents, smiling as she witnessed the chaos unfolding in Hal's office.

"Well, isn't this a surprise!" He looked up from his desk as Kim pushed the overloaded stroller through the office door. Jonah followed closely behind, breaking into a run when he spotted his dad. "Hi, big guy!" Hal caught the boy as he rounded his desk. Then he kissed his wife and nuzzled his three-week-old daughter.

"Hi, handsome."

Hal's forehead wrinkled immediately. "So did you come to have lunch with me? How did you get that stroller up the stairs?"

"Brad and Danny carried it," Anna answered, waltzing in to drop a large white paper bag on his desk. "Roast beef on wheat for you, grilled cheese for Jo-Jo, chips and cookies."

"Is someone going to tell me what's going on?"

"Gotta have a talk with my sister. You get to babysit, Daddy-o." Kim planted a quick kiss on his cheek and set Alice's carrier on his desk. Then she followed Anna into the corner office and closed the door.

"I got you tuna," Anna said as her sister plopped down on the leather love seat.

"Tuna, schmuna! What's this all about?"

Anna spread out her lunch on the coffee table. "Lily's making arrangements to bring her nephew down to stay with us awhile."

Kim's expression went from confusion to wide-eyed excitement. "Anna, that's fabulous. I'm so proud of you."

"Don't be. It's just temporary, until Lily can find him a permanent home." She shook her head. "I can't believe I'm doing this, Kim. He's barely four years old."

"I can't believe you're doing it either. But it sounds like great news."

"What do you mean great news? The fact that I'm going to have a heart attack is great news to you?"

"Anna, come on. It sounds like Andy really needs a good home. You and Lily can give him that."

"It's just going to be for a while."

"What if you like it?" She smirked. "You're great with Jonah. I bet you'll enjoy this more than you think."

The debacle of Jonah's last visit was still fresh in Anna's mind, though he seemed to have forgotten it, showing nothing but his usual excitement at seeing her again. "Lily and I agree that Andy needs to be adopted by a family."

"Aren't you a family? Wasn't that what the ceremony on the beach in Malibu was all about?"

"You know what I mean."

"No, I don't." Kim leaned back and crossed her arms, proffering a challenging look. "Are you absolutely sure Lily wants this boy to be adopted?"

"She's going to do the work herself."

"But are you certain that's what she really wants?"

Anna should have known better than to expect her sister to take her side. If anything, Kim seemed to be enjoying her misery. "All I know for sure is that Lily doesn't want this boy—Andy—to end up living with his grandmother." She explained the likelihood that Karen Parker, the woman who had neglected Lily and her sister as children, was trying to adopt Andy in order to sue the police for wrongful death.

"I'm sure the fact that she wants him here in LA has a lot to do with not wanting him to end up there. But you're kidding yourself if you think she's looking forward to finding him a different home. He's her family."

Anna folded the paper around her sandwich, her appetite gone. "I don't think I can do that, Kim. I'm not any good at it."

"There's nothing to it, you big baby. You just follow them around twenty-four hours a day so they don't hurt themselves, teach them to have a conscience and hope they don't talk about your family's private moments in front of other people."

Anna recalled Jonah's declaration about his daddy's pee-pee. At least she didn't have one of those to talk about.

Sandy attached the form to her clipboard and clicked her mechanical pencil. "I just need to go through the house and check these things off."

"Lead the way," Lily said, clearly excited to have the process underway.

"I can't believe you two are really going to do this."

Anna bit her tongue before answering that she couldn't

either.

Lily put her arm around Anna's waist. "I have to admit, I was a little surprised when Anna agreed. But we both felt it was the right thing to do."

Anna found herself nodding mindlessly.

"This is all pretty straightforward." Sandy glanced around at things in the kitchen, taking a closer look at the pantry. "You might want to think about moving your cleaning supplies to a higher shelf. By the way, I liked John Moss. He seems to know what he's doing."

"He's a good guy," Lily answered.

They walked through the dining room and Sandy stopped to look around. "He asked me if your house was big enough for a child and I told him my whole house would fit in your dining room. He said he hadn't gotten that impression, that all you told him about Anna was that she sold cars. I wish I'd been able to see the look on his face when I told him she sold cars at the four dealerships she owned in Beverly Hills and Palm Springs."

"Did he have a problem with it?" Lily asked.

Anna stopped in her tracks as the others started up the stairs. "Why would he have a problem with that?"

Lily turned on the steps to explain. "They usually try to place kids in the types of settings they're used to so they don't have adjustment problems when they go back home."

"I told him you guys were pretty down-to-earth," Sandy said. At the top of the stairs, she turned toward the three small bedrooms opposite the master suite. "Which bedroom did you have in mind?"

With all eyes on her, Anna realized she was being handed the decision. She pointed to the one in the corner, farthest from their bedroom. "That one?"

"Not this one?" Lily gestured to the one directly across the hall from theirs.

"It has the door out to the balcony," Anna said. "I didn't think that was a good idea for a kid so little. That leaves the other two, and the one in the corner has more windows."

Sandy marched toward the corner room. "That's using your head, Anna. This room isn't all that far away. You'll have your privacy and still be able to hear him if he needs something."

Until that moment, Anna hadn't grasped the full implications of having a child in their home. It was one thing not to be able to run through the house naked, and quite another to lose all of their freedom and spontaneity. No more lying around in bed on a Sunday morning or making love on the couch in the family room. Her only consolation was that the arrangement was temporary.

Sandy looked around and made some notes. "Let's go back down to the kitchen and run through this list."

They dutifully followed and sat at the table in the breakfast nook.

"I recommend a few changes to the bedroom, but you don't absolutely have to do them. A child as small as Andy will be more comfortable with smaller furniture. Think about putting that double bed in storage for now and maybe getting a twin."

Lily waved her hand flippantly. "That's just the old bed from my apartment. Early Attic. As far as I'm concerned, we can give it to the women's shelter."

"Okay, that does it for the house. That leaves the biggie."

"The pool," Lily said.

"Right. I hardly ever place kids this young in a home with a pool. You have to secure it."

"What if we put flip locks at the top of all the doors?"

"That should work." Sandy looked around and chuckled. "Let's hope he doesn't try crawling through Chester's doggie door."

Anna opened her mouth in response and felt a kick beneath the table. "Ow."

Lily ignored her. "We'll have someone come in tomorrow and fix those locks. And I'll run out and find a bed." She turned to Anna. "I should get him some clothes, and maybe a few toys. He doesn't have very much."

Sandy closed her folder. "You might want to hold off until John has a chance to look this over. I'm pretty sure this will go through, but you can't always tell for sure. Sometimes we get all these things together and they go to some crotchety judge for approval. Anything can happen."

"I'm not taking no for an answer. Karen Parker is not getting her hands on Andy."

"That reminds me. Do you still have that child services report from when you were taken away from her? It wouldn't hurt to put a copy in there."

When Lily went into her office, Sandy lowered her voice. "Are you okay with all this, Anna?"

"I know it's important to Lily."

"That's not what I asked. If this is going to cause you a problem, you need to let me know."

She shook her head. Though she couldn't feign enthusiasm, she wouldn't sabotage what Lily wanted. "We'll work it out. I'm just a little nervous about it."

"When I talked to John the other day, I told him this was all new ground for both of you. I made him promise if we did this and it didn't work out, he needed to hustle and find a better placement. He agreed to do that."

She felt both relief and guilt that Sandy had bargained for a safety net. "Thanks."

"But between you and me"—she squeezed Anna's hand—"I think this is going to be the best thing that ever happened to Andy Parker, and I wouldn't be at all surprised if it turned out to be the best thing that ever happened to you and Lily too."

Lily returned with the papers, saving Anna from having to reply. The more she envisioned a small child in the midst of their daily lives, the less she shared Sandy's optimism.

Lily typed her final notes on Andrea King, who had completed the court-ordered parenting class, allowing her to regain custody of her two-year-old. It was a tenuous return, one that social workers would monitor aggressively, but at least Andrea was motivated to practice good care. These were the success stories that made Lily's job at the Braxton Street Legal Aid Clinic worthwhile.

Not so with the file on her desk, another case from the overflow of the public defender's office. Tameka Johnson, who had been arrested a month ago for bringing a gun to school, was back in jail on a probation violation after being picked up with her friends for shoplifting. As if theft wasn't enough, police had discovered a knife and two marijuana cigarettes.

Lily stopped by the receptionist's desk on her way out. "Pauline, would you call Azalie Johnson and ask her to meet me at the jail? Her number's in Tameka's file. I'm going to go talk to both of them and see if there's any reason Tameka shouldn't go to juvie hall this time." She was tired of giving her word to the judge that her charges would stay out of trouble and having them undermine her promises by going back to the same gangs and behaviors that had gotten them arrested in the first place.

Getting into the jail with Azalie Johnson was an hour-long ordeal of standing in line to be searched not once, but three times before they finally were shown to a small, dingy conference room. Lily held her tongue while Azalie reduced her daughter to tears of shame.

"All right, now that Tameka understands what a stupid thing she did yesterday, let's talk about where we go from here. What do you expect to happen now, Tameka?"

Tameka shrugged her shoulders.

"Answer the woman!" her mother said sharply.

"I don't want to stay in jail."

"The problem," Lily said earnestly, "is that you were already on probation, so the judge isn't going to give you more probation. You've shown him that you aren't reliable."

Tameka sniffed loudly and jutted out her bottom lip.

"And now you'll have to answer for the gun charge too. I'm not sure there's a way to keep you out of jail this time. We have to figure out what's going to motivate you to stay out of trouble. Do you have any ideas?"

"I could stay home and not do things with my friends."

"Tameka, staying home isn't going to help you out of this.

72

The kids that are going somewhere are either hitting the books so they can go to college, or they're working already. You're not a little girl anymore. You have to start taking responsibility."

"That's right," Azalie echoed.

Lily respected Azalie for holding down a full-time job as an appointment scheduler for a plumbing company in order to provide for her family, but it was obvious to anyone that Tameka needed more supervision. "I think you have one chance of staying out of jail this time. You need to plead guilty and tell everyone how sorry you are. Then ask the judge if he'll let you do community service after school and on Saturdays." Lily was already thinking about the strings she could pull to get the girl into a program near her house.

"They'll make me clean the bathrooms at the park," she wailed.

"I did that when I was in high school, and I was good at it. The next year they let me work with the grounds crew, and the year after that I went to college." She laid her pen down and folded her arms. "Your call, Tameka. Do you want to make something of yourself, or do you want to be in and out of jail all your life?"

She began crying again. "I want to make something of myself."

"Good. You can start by making friends with the kind of people you want to be, not the ones that keep getting you arrested. And when you're not out there working, you need to be at home cracking the books so you can get your grades up. The next time they catch you with drugs or weapons of any kind, there won't be anything anyone can do to keep you out of jail."

When Tameka returned to her holding cell, Lily explained to Azalie what she would do to arrange a community service schedule, provided the judge approved. With luck, they would have her daughter out of jail by five o'clock.

On her walk back to the office, she grudgingly admitted that her criminal work had its rewards for the struggling families she sought to help, especially when she had a chance to set a delinquent youth back on the right path. It was harder and usually more frustrating than custody cases, but the end goal was the same—to give kids their best chance to succeed.

When it came to doing what was best for kids, Andy was never far from her thoughts. Catching him at four improved his odds of staying out of the kind of trouble Tameka couldn't seem to escape, to say nothing of the fate of his parents, who had died too young. It wasn't at all ironic that Lily found herself in a position to help him. Her own experiences had shown her the importance of making wise decisions when a child's future was at stake. Andy needed a loving family, and a strong role model for overcoming his past.

Anna put the last of the dishes in the dishwasher and wiped her hands on a towel. "Was Tony surprised when you asked him for the time off?"

"I'm not sure surprised is the word I'd use. Panicked is more like it, but I suggested he might want to go ahead and hire someone full-time instead of just picking up an independent contractor to catch the overflow. We're getting busier every day."

"But you didn't tell him about your other offer?"

"Not yet. Maybe if he brings someone else on board now, he won't miss me so much come November."

Anna appreciated that Lily seemed to be leaning toward taking the director's job, because it meant she expected Andy to land a permanent placement within the next six weeks. She had convinced herself she could survive anything in the short term. "I sort of thought we'd hear from that social worker today."

Lily shrugged. "The hearing was late this afternoon. Sometimes the judge just takes everything under advisement and goes home to dinner."

A knock on the side door set Chester to barking.

Anna hurried through the family room. "I forgot to tell you Holly was coming over." She opened the door for her friend and coworker.

Lily pulled Chester back so he wouldn't jump. Since Holly was their regular dog-sitter, he always greeted her with excitement.

"Hi. We haven't seen you in a while."

"She's come to take Chester home with her for a few days."

"Oh, yeah? Looks like he likes that idea." She let him go and he went straight to Holly for attention.

"Did Anna tell you we got a Labrador puppy from the pound? He's driving us crazy, so we thought if we borrowed Chester for a week or so, he would calm down a little. If this works out, we may go back to the shelter and pick out an older dog too."

"Just the dog? You don't want Anna too?"

Anna laughed and retrieved his leash, wondering facetiously what Lily would think of her living with Holly and Jai for six weeks while Andy was there. "Just make sure the learning process only goes one way, Holly. We don't have any use for a basset hound that acts like a Labrador. If you ruin him, you keep him."

Chester happily dashed out the door to the waiting convertible.

"That dog has no loyalty at all," Lily said. The phone rang, and she excused herself.

Anna walked Holly to her car. "You heard Lily. You and Jai better not spoil this dog. He's already rotten enough."

"And you're the one who made him that way," Holly said, grinning as she backed out the driveway.

Lily was waiting at the door, her face a mask of giddy delight. "That was John Moss. He'll meet us at the foster home on Sunday."

Chapter 6

Interstate 5 was a desolate stretch of highway, especially from the bottom of the Grapevine to the cutoff for 101. Anna had driven this route with Lily to visit her mother in San Jose, and it usually seemed like a much longer ride. Today, it was as if they had gotten here in no time at all.

"Boy, this is a long drive, isn't it?" Lily asked, reaching across the console of the X3 to lay her hand in Anna's lap. "Seems like it's taking forever today."

Anna almost snorted at the juxtaposition of their thoughts. Lily was obviously eager to get there, while she was filled with dread. On their return trip, they would have a small child in the backseat, one who was coming to live with them and change their lives. It had seemed like a good idea at the time. Now, she wasn't so sure. What if they were unable to control his behavior or meet his needs? Anna had witnessed a number of behavior problems among the children at Kidz Kamp. Lily had explained that most of these youth had poor role models at home, and that being with other children in foster care often brought out the worst in even the best kids. What if he didn't like her? And what if he cried for hours the way Jonah had?

"I told John I'd call when we got to San Jose." Lily dialed the number as Anna drove past the city on their way up to San Francisco. "Hi, John. It's Lily. I guess we'll be there in about forty-five minutes. You still want us to come straight to the house?"

Forty-five minutes...the last minutes of freedom.

"I remember how to get there...Yeah, I picked up a few things for him yesterday."

That was understatement. Moss had called back on Friday with Andy's sizes, sending Lily into a shopping frenzy with Martine. The two of them had a field day buying clothes, enough to dress him in something different every day for a month. Lily was proudest of the bedroom slippers, which looked like racecars, right down to the headlights that flashed with each step.

Then came the toys. They went heavy on the cars, buying a dozen Matchbox cars, a plastic dump truck and a long red fire truck with moving ladders and hoses. To service those vehicles was a gas station and garage, to go along with thirty feet of plastic segments Andy could snap together to make roads and intersections.

At Martine's suggestion, Lily also picked up three toy boats— "bath toys," she had said. To top it all off, she bought a teddy bear dressed in a Dodgers jersey.

"Just follow the signs toward Candlestick Park...or whatever it's called this year." It seemed that corporate sponsors changed the name on a whim. "Just go to Candlestick Point. That never changes."

At Lily's direction, Anna followed the street that ran along the San Francisco Bay and pulled into a parking space behind a Honda Civic.

"That's John's car." Lily unhooked her seatbelt and opened her door. "You ready for this?"

"Ready as I'll ever be."

Lily grasped her hand and kissed it. "I love you. I hope you know how much it means to me that you're willing to do this."

Despite her trepidation, Anna couldn't help but smile. Seeing Lily happy was its own reward. "What are we waiting for?"

They crossed the street and climbed the steps to the second-floor entrance, where a stout, gray-haired woman met them at the door. "Welcome back."

"Thank you. This is my friend, Anna Kaklis. Anna, this is Mary Beth Shull, Andy's foster mother."

Friend? Anna couldn't remember the last time she had been introduced by Lily as a friend. "Pleased to meet you. I came along to help Lily drive."

Lily gave her a sheepish look. "And this is John Moss."

From the kitchen doorway, a slender man in jeans and a sweatshirt took two large strides across the living room, holding out his hand to Anna.

"Hi, John. I've been looking forward to meeting you. Lily and I both really appreciate your hard work." Anna's eyes darted around the room, where three young boys sat quietly in front of the TV. None of them matched Lily's description of Andy.

"It's my pleasure. I've been looking forward to meeting you as well. Would you like to go upstairs and meet Andy, or do you want me to bring him down?"

Before they could answer, Mary Beth handed Anna a brown paper grocery bag, folded down over halfway. "Here's his stuff. John said you'd gotten him a few clothes, so I won't worry about sending the other things. I'll keep those on hand in case I get another one that doesn't have anything."

Lily intercepted the bag and opened it. "Is his favorite T-shirt in here? The blue one with the racecar on it?"

"No, I threw that one in my rag pile. It's faded and it has a hole in the side. I practically had to hide it to keep him from wearing it every day."

"Would you mind if we took it? I don't care if it's dirty. I just want him to have something he's comfortable in."

Mrs. Shull left to retrieve the dirty shirt. Moss had started up the stairs.

"I'm sorry about the friend thing," Lily whispered. "I just

didn't want this woman to know our business."

"It's okay."

"You want to come up to see Andy or wait here?"

Anna looked about anxiously. "Do not leave me alone."

Lily chuckled. "Calm down. We'll be out of here and on our way soon." She took Anna's elbow and steered her upstairs to a small bedroom.

From the doorway, Anna could see two small feet swinging from the edge of the lower bunk. As she followed the others into the room, Andy came into full view. He was every bit as beautiful as Lily had said, and in his hand was a small Matchbox convertible. From his red-rimmed eyes, she guessed he had been crying.

"Hi, Andy," Lily said. "Do you remember me?"

Anna watched his face light up, and Lily's as well. It was obvious they had a special connection.

"Surprised to see me, huh?"

He nodded, never taking his eyes off her smiling face. He was dressed in dark blue gym shorts, with a white T-shirt and tennis shoes. A small scrape on his knee had scabbed over.

"So I guess John didn't tell you the big news. I'm going to take you home with me today. Would you like that?"

Andy's eyes darted to John.

"That's right, buddy. You're going to go for a long ride in a pretty car. Won't that be fun?"

Anna held her breath waiting for the boy to speak, but the only sign he understood what was happening was the worried look on his face. Lily had said he might be anxious, and that it wasn't unusual for kids to be afraid when the things they had grown used to suddenly changed, even when their current circumstances left a lot to be desired.

Lily squatted down to eye level. "Andy, do you remember when I told you that a friend of mine liked cars? Well, here's my friend. This is Anna, and she knows everything about cars. How about that?"

Andy shifted his eyes to Anna for the first time, then back to

Lily.

"Hi, Andy." Anna squatted alongside, gently touching the boy's shoulder to say hello. She wasn't sure which one of them was more apprehensive.

"Are you ready to go? I have your clothes ready downstairs, including your blue T-shirt with the racecar." She stood and held out her hand.

"I have a few papers for you to sign," Moss said. "And Mary Beth has written up a few things about this young man here that might help you get to know each other over the next few days."

When they reached the bottom of the stairs, Anna's worst nightmare came true. Lily, John and Mary Beth disappeared into the kitchen and she was left alone by the front door with Andy. She looked down to find him standing only a few inches away, his head tilted upward to stare at her face.

Her mind raced for a way to end their awkward silence. "Andy, do you like dogs?"

He shook his head quickly, his wide eyes a sign he was clearly frightened by the prospect.

She was beginning to wonder if he would ever speak. Lily hadn't said anything at all about him having a language problem. "Big dogs are scary, aren't they?"

Andy nodded along with her.

She knelt alongside him. "Especially dogs that are this big." She held her hand even with the boy's chest.

Again he nodded.

"But dogs that come up to only here aren't all that scary, are they?" This time, she held her hand just below his waist and shook her head no.

Obviously conflicted, Andy didn't answer.

"We have a dog named Chester, and he likes to play with everybody. You know what he does? He licks you right on the face." Anna quickly trailed two fingers across the boy's cheek, causing him to squeal and cover his face with his hands. She almost melted to see his first smile.

"What's going on in here?" Lily came in, grinning broadly.

"Nothing. We were just talking about dogs…licking you on the neck." This time, she tickled Andy's neck and he dissolved in giggles, reaching out now to tickle her too.

"Andy, you know this is not a playroom," Mrs. Shull said sternly.

Stunned by the harsh reprimand, Anna abruptly stood and held out her hand to the boy. "Andy, why don't you tell Mrs. Shull goodbye, and we'll go on out to the car?" Anna needed to get away from this woman before she said something rude.

"Bye," he answered—his first word—without even turning to look at his foster mother.

"Thanks, Mary Beth," Moss said as he and Lily followed them out. When they reached the car, he fished a pill bottle from his shirt pocket. "Here's his asthma medicine. You know how to file the claim to refill this, don't you?"

Lily had explained that all his medical services would be paid for by the state. "You know that isn't going to be a problem for us, John."

"Right." He pushed his hands into his pockets and rocked back on his heels. "I'll be in touch with Sandy at least once a week. If you need me for anything, you have my number."

"I think we're going to be fine," Lily said, mussing Andy's hair.

Anna opened the back door of the SUV and motioned toward the backseat. "Do you want some help, or can you climb up there by yourself?"

Andy seemed eager to show off his climbing skills. He gripped the car frame with one hand and the door with the other, pulling himself onto the running board. From there, he scampered easily onto the floorboard, then knee first into the seat, where he turned to face the front.

"Nice job." Anna patted the booster seat Lily had bought yesterday. "Sit here so you can see out the windows." He complied and she pulled the seatbelt across his tiny body and clicked it in place, double-checking the security with a firm tug. Her promise that he would be able to see was undercut by his size—he practically disappeared from view when she closed the door.

Lily stopped her as she reached for the driver's door. "Oh no, you don't. You drove all the way up here."

Anna continued to her place behind the wheel, snapping her own seatbelt into place. "You know what they say about possession being nine-tenths of the law."

Lily rolled her eyes, thanked Moss one last time and walked around to the other side.

Anna peered at Andy in the rearview mirror. He squirmed as he burrowed his shoulders into the plush leather of the seat. She pulled away from the curb and executed a tight U-turn.

"Andy, this car is called a BMW. Can you say that?"

From the look on his face, he was genuinely interested in this piece of information, and Lily helped him repeat the name.

"And now this—BMWs are the best cars on the road."

Lily smiled and repeated it herself with animation, then helped Andy with the phrase. His formal education on cars was officially underway.

Thirty minutes out of San Francisco, Andy had barely said a word. From her vantage point, Lily could see the fear and doubt on his face. "Is something wrong, Andy?"

Immediately tears sprang to his eyes, but still, he didn't speak.

"Are you afraid, honey?" She reached between the seats and patted his leg. "It's all okay, sweetheart. We're going to our house, but we have to drive a long way."

Anna said, "Where's the BMW dealer in San Jose?"

"Is something wrong with the car?"

"No, but I have an idea."

"What?"

"It's a surprise."

"Did you hear that, Andy? Anna has a surprise for us. Wonder what it is." She gave directions to the dealership and soon they were squeezing into a tight space between a customer's car and a brand new 335i with its hood up.

"I won't be but a minute if you want to just wait in the car." Anna got out and disappeared into the busy showroom.

Lily watched Andy stretch his neck to see all the cars on the lot. "Have you ever seen so many pretty cars before?"

She took a moment to peruse Mary Beth's handwritten notes about Andy while he was in her care. His last physical was in January, but she had taken him to the doctor three times during his relatively short stay in their home. One of the visits was asthma-related, and Mary Beth had concluded that the persistent coughing was—at least partially—attention-seeking behavior.

What a load of crap! Lily fumed as she thought again about Andy being exiled to the sofa at night because of his difficulty breathing.

She flipped through the pages quickly to find out what the other two visits were for. The physician's word jumped off the page—*enuresis*. Bedwetting. Not a big surprise, she thought. He was only four, and given how much he had bounced around, it was a wonder he was even toilet trained. Mary Beth was convinced that wetting the bed was Andy's passive-aggressive response to her demands for discipline.

Anna emerged from the showroom with a white plastic bag and a salesman carrying a large box. She opened Andy's door and unbuckled his seatbelt. "Why don't you scoot over to the other side for a minute, Andy?"

The salesman removed the bulky piece from the box, stripping away the plastic wrap to reveal a car seat. He demonstrated how it melded into the seat, and secured it with the seatbelt. Anna adjusted the shoulder straps for an older child, and held them back while Andy crawled in.

"Looks like a perfect fit to me," the salesman said. "When you said he was already four, I thought it might be too small."

"The other one was too low. He couldn't see anything outside." She thanked him and climbed back into the driver's seat. "Andy, do you remember what the best cars are?"

Lily helped him by whispering.

"BMWs," he answered.

"That's right. This one's called an X3. Can you say that?"

"X3," he said plainly.

"Good. This is Lily's car. My car is different. My car is called a Z8. Say it."

"Z8," he repeated clearly.

"Atta boy." She reached into the bag she had brought from the showroom and drew out a small box. "This is what my car looks like." It was a model Z8, just like the custom imported convertible that sat in their garage.

Lily opened the box and passed him the car. His delight was obvious as he studied the toy carefully. "Do you remember what Anna said it was?"

"Z8."

"And the best cars on the road?"

"BMWs."

Anna pulled into the driveway and pressed the button to open the garage door. She was exhausted, but no more so than Lily, and especially Andy, who had fallen asleep in his car seat soon after they had stopped for dinner near Bakersfield.

"I'll come around and get him," Lily said, keeping her voice low so she wouldn't wake him.

The day had turned out far better than she had imagined. When Andy first began to cry in the car, she had feared another episode like Jonah's. But unlike her nephew, who had been inconsolable, Andy had responded immediately to the car seat and toy. Soon after, she was able to distract him with a game of naming the colors of each car that passed them on the freeway, though he knew only red, blue, white and black.

Lily unbuckled the shoulder harnesses and gently lifted him from the SUV, where he fell limply against her chest. With one arm firmly tucked underneath his buttocks, she used her other hand to guide his head to her shoulder, and he promptly returned to dreamland.

Anna unlocked the side door, and forged ahead to turn on

lights. When they reached the newly-furnished bedroom, Lily knelt down to seat him on the edge of the bed.

"Andy? I need you to wake up for a little while so you can change into your pajamas and go to the bathroom. Can you do that?"

He opened his eyes and took in his new surroundings. He was clearly intrigued by the presence of another bed in the room. "Whose is that?"

"That's for a little boy named Jonah when he comes to visit," Anna said. "But it's just you tonight. Is that okay?"

He didn't answer. His eyes continued to roam the room, which Lily had decorated with posters of cars and comic book figures. The new furniture, all in knotty pine, consisted of the beds, a small desk, a chest of drawers and a bookcase, already stocked with stories a little boy might enjoy.

Lily opened the top drawer of the chest and took out a pair of pajamas. "Andy, why don't you go to the bathroom? When you're finished, wash your hands and face and I'll get your bed ready."

Anna flicked on the bathroom light and stepped aside as Andy went by her to the toilet, where he raised both the seat cover and the seat. She was intrigued at seeing Lily in a parenting role, especially since she had always been adamant about not wanting children of her own. Thanks to all of her work with families, motherhood seemed to come to her naturally.

"Stay here with him. I'll be right back." Lily rushed downstairs and returned with two large trash bags.

"What are those for?"

"I read the notes from Mrs. Shull on the way down. She says Andy sometimes wets the bed. I can go tomorrow and get a plastic liner for the mattress, but these will have to do for tonight."

Hastily, they stripped the sheets and spread the trash bags, finishing just as Andy emerged from the bathroom. From his wet shirt, it was clear he had at least tried to wash up.

Lily guided him back to the bed, which they had turned down. "Andy, can you change into your pajamas while I get your toothbrush ready? Then you'll be all set for bed."

Anna was ready to slip away when Lily caught her eye.

"Will you help him with the buttons?"

She knelt to help tug the T-shirt over his head. "Here you go, pal." The pajamas were made especially for youngsters, and she helped him close the three large buttons down the front of the shirt.

When he finished with the shirt, he sat on the floor and tugged off his shoes and socks. Anna collected the pile of clothing as he exchanged his shorts for pajama bottoms.

"Here you go, Andy." Lily held out his toothbrush. "Let's do this last thing, and I'll read you a story before you go to sleep."

Anna retreated into the master bedroom to call Holly, thinking it would be best to give Andy a few days to adjust before bringing Chester back home. When she finished, Lily was standing in the doorway holding Andy in her arms. Again, she was moved by Lily's maternal manner and the way Andy seemed to accept it. "Is something wrong?"

"No, I'm just showing Andy where we sleep." She walked him in and back out onto the landing. "If you wake up tonight and need something, just come into this room. But be careful right here. I don't want you to fall down the stairs."

Anna was coming out of the bathroom when Lily returned to their suite. "Did you get him settled down?"

"Yeah, but he was so excited when I started reading to him. He said no one had ever done that before." Lily hurried through her ablutions to get ready for bed. "Isn't he adorable? My heart just wells up every time I look at him."

"I was surprised by how small he was."

"Runs in the family."

"And I was really glad to see him calm down so quickly in the car. I hope he has a good time while he's here."

Lily's face hardened instantly.

"What's the matter?"

"Nothing…just"—she banged a drawer with obvious irritation. "He just got here, Anna. Can we not talk about him leaving already?"

"I wasn't—"

"I know." Lily threw up her hands. "I'm sorry. Forget I said that."

Anna caught her elbow as she walked past. "I'm sorry too. I didn't mean anything by it." She drew Lily into a hug. "I love you."

"I love you too. And I really appreciate you letting me bring him here. I promise I'll get to work on finding a family for him. He has too much to offer to end up with somebody like Karen Parker."

For Lily's sake, Anna wanted to relent and offer to have Andy stay as long as it took to find just the right home, but her reservations were stronger. They had no idea what they were getting into, and with Lily on the verge of taking a new job and Anna running for vice president of the Chamber, they would barely have time for each other. Besides, it wouldn't be good for Andy to stay too long, since it would make it harder for him to adjust to a new home.

She watched as Lily donned a nightshirt, a long purple tank top with a hole in the side. "I guess I need to find something to sleep in, huh?"

"Just for a few nights. I told him to come on in if he had any problems. Later on, I'll teach him about knocking on doors and waiting for permission." She raised her eyebrows twice and grinned. "Then we can sleep naked again and rub our bodies all over each other."

"Let's hope he's a fast learner."

Chapter 7

Lily was surprised to find Andy already awake. "Hey, sweetie." She sat on the edge of his bed and smoothed his hair. "Did you sleep okay?"

He pulled the covers to his chin.

She tugged at the blanket gently. "Let's go downstairs so we can have breakfast with Anna before she leaves for work."

He recoiled as if afraid.

"Are you worried about something, Andy? Did you wet the bed last night?" she asked, doing her best to keep any sign of rebuke from her voice. Tears rushed to his eyes and she quickly added, "It's okay if you did, honey. Those things just happen."

"I didn't mean to."

"I know. But you can't help it because you're still little. When you get older, it won't happen anymore." She pulled the covers down and found the bed soaked. "Let's clean you up a little bit and find something nice to wear, okay?"

Andy followed her into the bathroom, where she helped him out of his wet things. He didn't seem to mind when she pulled off his underwear. Gently, she washed his legs and buttocks with a washcloth, and then handed it to him. "Can you wash this part yourself?" She gestured to his private area. "You shouldn't let other people touch you there, okay?"

"It's private," he said.

"That's right." Lily was relieved to see that he had already gotten some early training on that. Many of the children she encountered in her work were not so lucky.

She helped him into a pair of denim shorts and a Spiderman T-shirt. His smile as he dipped his chin to study the appliqué was all the sign she needed that she had made just the right choices.

"Let's go see Anna."

They took the stairs slowly at first, with Andy holding onto the rail. As his confidence grew, he quickened his steps, finally jumping over the last one.

"You really like to jump." She thought of Mary Beth and her rigid rules.

Still showing off, he jumped three times toward the kitchen, where Anna looked up from her breakfast.

"Good morning, Andy."

Lily could feel his tiny hand squeezing hers as he oriented himself to seeing Anna again. "Can you say hi to Anna?"

"Hi," he said meekly, scooting behind her leg.

"Somebody's feeling bashful this morning." She guided him toward the table. "Go sit with Anna and I'll bring you some breakfast."

Anna moved the newspaper from the padded bench that bordered the bay window.

His eyes went wide as he climbed up on the seat and spotted the swimming pool. "What's that?"

Lily brought his cereal and juice and followed his pointing finger to the pool. "That's a swimming pool. Do you like to swim?" From his blank reaction, she guessed he had never been swimming before. "We'll give it a try later, but I need for you to promise me something, okay? The pool is really fun when we can go together, but you must never go out there by yourself, not even on the sidewalk. Promise?"

He nodded vigorously.

Anna checked her watch and stood. "I need to go to work. You two have a good day." She glanced at Andy and gave Lily a quick peck on the lips.

Lily tugged her shirt as she started to leave. Being prudent about sleeping in the nude didn't mean they couldn't show affection. "I know you can do better than that."

Anna smiled and gave her a proper kiss.

As she pulled away, Lily stopped her again. She jerked her head discreetly toward Andy, whispering, "Tell Andy bye."

Anna hesitated before leaning over and planting an awkward kiss on the top of Andy's head. "Have fun today."

Anna breathed a sigh of relief as Kim rolled the stroller into the showroom. "Hal, your kids are here."

He came out of his office to the balcony and waved as Jonah started gleefully up the stairs. "I had a feeling they'd be coming by one of these days. You've been hiding in your office all week brooding about something."

She scowled at him before heading downstairs to enlist help from one of her salesmen to carry the stroller to the top. Kim followed, cradling baby Alice.

"Your boss is having another bad day," Kim said to her husband. "And that means you get to babysit again, but just with Jonah. Your little girl's hungry."

Hal caught his jubilant son and cooed at his infant daughter. "Did you bring my lunch too, Alice?"

"Pizza's on the way," Anna said. "Hi, Jo-Jo."

He squirmed down from his father's grasp to give Anna a hug.

In that instant, she was suddenly struck by the difference between her reaction to Jonah and to Andy. With her nephew, the show of affection was clearly automatic. She never had to stop and think about what she should do. It just came naturally. With Andy, she weighed her words and touches, questioning at each juncture how to interact.

Kim got situated on the couch in Anna's office and opened her shirt for Alice.

Anna moved closer to watch her sister nurse. It always moved her to see this intimate bond between Kim and her babies.

"So you have a little one in your house now, eh?"

"Yeah, we brought him home Sunday night." Three days, sixteen hours and nine minutes ago.

"How did it go?"

"Okay, I guess."

"Then why were you hyperventilating this morning when you called me?" Kim was clearly amused at Anna's discomfort. "I can't wait to meet this little guy. I've only seen you rattled twice, and the last time was when you realized you wanted to have sex with Lily."

"I'm not rattled. I'm just"—she rolled her eyes at her sister's recall—"I'm not good with kids."

"You're great with Jonah."

"Until something goes wrong. Then I'm useless."

"No, you aren't. It just takes a little practice. Jonah would have been fine with you if he hadn't been so worried about us giving all our love to Alice. He was jealous. Did I tell you he wanted to nurse again? He screamed so loud I almost let him. I hate to think what the neighbors must have thought."

As much as she hated to admit it, she found it comforting to know Kim had suffered through a tantrum as well. "Andy adores Lily, but he acts like he's scared of me."

"And you probably act like you're scared of him too."

Anna shrugged. "Maybe I am a little."

"What are you afraid of?"

"I don't know. Doing something wrong?"

"Like what?"

"Like making him cry…causing him to get hurt…scaring him." She started pacing as her greater fear came to light. "I'm more afraid of doing something wrong with Lily."

"With Lily?"

"Lily—she wants this kid, Kim. I can tell by the way she looks at him. She's in love with him already."

"I know that feeling." Kim ran her finger through the black fuzz on her daughter's head. "It comes over you out of nowhere and there's nothing you can do about it."

Anna could feel her frustration mount. "This is freaking me out. It was just supposed to be temporary, but what am I going to do if she asks me to let him stay?"

"What would be so awful about that?"

"I'm not ready for this." That was the easy answer, and the only one she could share, even with her sister, who knew her better than anyone. The deeper truth was that she didn't feel drawn to Andy the same way Lily did. He was cute, and it was obvious that he needed a loving home, but that didn't mean she wanted to share her life—or Lily—with him. "So how do I tell Lily that without making her resent me for it?"

Kim closed her shirt and drew Alice to her shoulder. "I'm not sure you can," she answered, sounding nothing like her usual teasing self. "Andy isn't a puppy from the pound that you can take back and trade for one you like better. He's her sister's child, and she feels a bond to him. Whatever it is you're stuck on, you're probably going to have to get over it."

"In other words, I don't have any right to my feelings."

"Of course you do. But you have to ask yourself if your feelings are more important than hers, because there isn't a compromise, and Lily can't change how she feels."

Anna sighed dejectedly. The risk in asking for advice was getting that which she didn't want. "At least she's handling all the mother stuff."

"Maybe that's why she's bonding with him and you aren't."

"It's not my thing. Besides, she likes it."

"Sit down here and listen to me." Kim patted the seat beside her. "This attitude of yours needs to go. Do you want Andy to feel like Lily cares about him and you don't? Because I guarantee he'll see right through it. So will Lily, and no matter how long he stays with you, she's always going to remember that you let her down on this."

"I haven't let her down." She briefly thought about feigning a headache so Kim would go easy on her. "But I will if I screw this up."

"The only way you're going to screw up is to pretend you're not a part of it. I love doing things for my kids. But I want Hal to do them too, because sharing those experiences makes us closer. Not only that, my kids learn that they can count on their daddy to be there for them."

In all her life, Anna could never recall getting such serious advice from her wisecracking sister. Why on earth had she thought Kim would be her ally on this? "You know what I've just realized? All of you like Lily better than you like me."

"That's because she's a far better person than you."

Alice spit up on the cloth on her mother's shoulder.

"You deserved that for saying something so mean," Anna said.

"See how much fun kids are."

Anna wiped Alice's mouth with the cloth and held out her hands. "I'll take her now that she's gotten that over with. I'm a fair-weather auntie."

"You'll miss out on the fun stuff."

"Like vomit? I'll take my chances."

"So when are you having us all over for a cookout this Sunday around noon?"

Anna frowned and ran the words through her head again before realizing that Kim's question was not a question at all. "I was thinking maybe Sunday...noon-ish?"

"Great idea! I should have thought of it. Do you want us to bring some of Jonah's toys?"

"Sure. We got a few for Andy already. You know what he likes best? Cars."

"That's an omen if I ever heard one. You'd better get used to having him around."

Anna nuzzled Alice and savored the baby smell. "Why don't I just steal this one?"

"Seriously, Anna…if you don't feel close to Andy, at least go through the motions for his sake and for Lily's. You might even find out you like it. Kids need a whole lot, but something magic happens when you give it to them." She stood and smoothed her pants. "Now, if you'll excuse me, I'm going to let you hold her while I go to the bathroom all by myself. I may even lock the door and read a book…maybe *War and Peace*."

Anna relished the chance to cradle Alice for more than just a minute or two. The baby was barely a month old, and already Anna felt bonded to her. That had to be what Lily felt for Andy, a connection that transcended time. Instant love.

Anna looked over her magazine at Andy, who, with Lily's permission, had taken several books from her office to use as buildings in the make-believe town he was building on the floor of the family room. He had snapped together all of the plastic segments to make a winding road for his cars, and was placing stop signs and railroad crossings at strategic locations. She was impressed with his grasp of symmetry and spatial relations, and when he began to distribute the Matchbox cars to the various "houses," she couldn't resist joining him on the floor.

"Andy, do you remember the car colors?"

He looked at the one in his hand. "Red."

"That's right. That red car is a Mustang."

He repeated it and picked up another.

"That one's called a Porsche, and it's silver."

One by one, he named the cars and colors, and when Lily joined them from her office, he showed off by correctly identifying almost half. Each time he struggled, he held the car up to Anna for a clue. Then Lily helped him break down his little city and put the toys back in the box they kept next to the couch. It was time for his bath and story.

Anna relaxed on the couch and flipped through a few channels before settling on a finance show. Kim would be proud of her tonight, and she had to admit she felt somewhat less awkward about having Andy around after playing with him on the floor. It was a far cry from being comfortable, something she hadn't been since he got there, but it was better than sulking in her room.

Lily returned after a half hour and stretched out beside her on the couch. "You were so sweet to play with Andy."

"As much as he likes cars, I figured he'd like to know their names."

"How did you learn car names when you were little?"

"My dad would quiz me all the time. By the time I was eight, I was quizzing him."

"Why am I not surprised?"

"I was watching him while he played. He's really smart."

Lily tossed her head haughtily. "Of course he is. He has my genes."

"Not to mention your love of hotdogs and ice cream. What I was noticing was how careful he was with all of his streets and buildings. I bet he grows up to be a city planner or an architect, something that lets him design things."

"If he's going to design things, something tells me it will be cars. He's every bit as fascinated as you are. Maybe you can take him down to the dealership someday and show him around. Wouldn't he like that?"

Andy might like it, but the thought of having Andy on her own unnerved her. "Maybe you two can come visit me some afternoon. I'll take him into the garage and let him see the guts of a couple of cars."

"Then he'll want a car he can take apart."

"Speaking of taking him somewhere, Mom invited us over for dinner tomorrow night. They want to meet him before the cookout on Sunday, but since we usually keep Fridays to ourselves, I told her you'd call."

"I think it's a good idea for him to meet them early. He's going to be so overwhelmed on Sunday." She picked up the portable phone. "But we'll have to do it early because I want to get him home in time for bed at eight. He sleeps so well, I'd hate to mess it up."

Anna nodded as Lily went into the other room to call. She

had wondered how Lily would respond to the invitation. Friday nights had always been their special time, a night to go out together, or to relax at home and kick off the weekend. Having Andy changed everything.

Lily was thrilled with how easily Andy had adapted to being in their home. With Anna pulling a few strings, she had gotten him enrolled in a half-day preschool program in nearby Westwood Village, where they would do some tests to determine if he had any special needs. He was set to start on Monday, and had three days to settle into his new routine before her vacation ended.

Anna was meeting them after work at the Big House, which was what she called her parents' mansion-like home in Beverly Hills. "Look, Andy. Anna's here already. There's her car."

His wide-eyed amazement as they drove through the gate made her recall her first visit to this house almost four years ago, in which her future father-in-law had insulted her with his bigoted remarks. How far they all had come, she thought.

She helped Andy out of his car seat and held his hand as they walked to the front door. Anna and her mother met them in the foyer, where Martine crouched low to say hello.

"Who's this little fellow?" George bellowed as he stormed into the room. "Have you brought someone for me to play with?"

Andy took cover behind Lily's legs while Anna persuaded her father to tone down his voice. Gradually, Andy came around, smiling as George admired his Spiderman T-shirt.

"Come on, Andy. Let's leave these women and go have a cigar."

"Dad!"

George ignored his daughter's scolding and took Andy's hand to lead him into the den. Lily knew from their family gatherings at the Big House that George had amassed quite the collection of toys to keep Jonah engaged. Andy was sure to be fascinated by another set of cars.

"He's very small for a four-year-old," Martine said. But then she poked Lily in the side. "It runs in the family."

"That's not the only thing," Anna said. "They both like junk food and ratty clothes."

As Martine put the finishing touches on dinner—the meatloaf recipe that was Jonah's favorite—Lily and Anna went to check on "the boys."

"I can't get over seeing my father like this," Anna whispered. "He loves this grandpa business."

Lily smiled at the association, wondering if Anna really saw him as Andy's grandfather, or if it was only a reference to his rapport with children. Regardless, she had her own memories from her mother's funeral of George telling her the Kaklises would be her family. It was hard not to hope they were now Andy's family too.

Martine and George were clearly excited about meeting him, and peppered him with questions all through dinner about his favorite foods and toys, and how he liked his new room.

Andy seemed wary of being the center of attention. He didn't speak much, but he ate well and answered most questions with a nod, a shrug or a shake of his head.

They caravanned home, where Anna met Lily at her car door. "I'll carry him upstairs." They were a few minutes late getting home, and, in just the short trip from Beverly Hills, he had fallen fast asleep in the backseat.

"Good thing I gave him his bath already." Lily was pleasantly surprised by the offer of help, as much as she had been when Anna had played with him the night before. That had been Anna's first overture toward him since the drive home when she bought the car seat and Z8. Though she had been supportive overall, she had seemed content until now to step back and allow Lily to handle all of the caretaking chores.

Lily helped Andy into his pajamas and read three pages of a story before he fell asleep for good. The fact that he slept well gave her peace of mind for more reasons than one.

"Did you just lock the door?" Anna asked.

"Uh-huh." Lily gave her a seductive look.

"And Andy knows he's supposed to…?"

"Uh-huh."

"So we can…?"

"Uh-huh." On her way to the bed, Lily pulled off her sweater and tossed it carelessly on the floor.

Anna wasted no time in stripping off her own clothes. "I've missed you."

They fell together on the bed, a tangle of writhing arms and legs.

Lily fretted only a moment about being overheard before losing herself under Anna's heated touch.

Lily looked up from the grill, where burgers and hotdogs sizzled. The backyard scene was as idyllic as any she could imagine. Anna, Hal and George tossed Andy and Jonah about in the pool as the youngsters squealed with delight. Martine and Kim cheered excitedly from beneath the umbrella, where they sat with baby Alice. Suzanne sunned herself in the chaise lounge, while Sandy conducted her home inspection for John Moss.

Lily had been thrilled with Anna's idea of a poolside cookout, especially her eagerness to have Andy and Jonah play together. Though reluctant to read too much into it, she harbored a faint hope that Anna was getting used to the idea of Andy being a part of their family.

After a week of having Andy in their home, Anna's feelings were still tough to read. She mostly kept her distance, especially when it came to Andy's bath and bedtime, but had loosened up since mid-week. When Chester returned on Saturday from his visit with Holly, Anna had enlisted Andy's help with feeding and walking him. And now, she seemed as comfortable in the pool with Andy as she did with her nephew.

"I'm happy to report you've passed inspection," Sandy proclaimed, dropping her clipboard on the umbrella table. "Are you sure he's never been around a pool before? He looks fearless out there."

"We played with him a little yesterday," Lily answered. "He

was scared at first, but then he relaxed and let Anna lead him around." Like Jonah, he wore water wings to stay afloat, but he didn't seem to mind being submerged. He would be swimming on his own in no time if he stayed with them, she thought.

"He and Anna seem to be getting along."

"Hmm...I think the jury's still out on that. They have moments like this, and the next thing you know, they act like they're scared half to death of each other."

"It takes a while to sort things out, but it looks like they're headed in the right direction."

"Yeah, I guess." Her optimism was more guarded than Sandy's. "I sometimes wonder if she's just making the best of it, trying to hang on until we can find Andy a family."

"So that's definitely decided? You guys aren't going to adopt him?"

"We haven't talked about it anymore, but it's what I promised her."

"And how do you feel about that?"

Lily felt tears sting her eyes. "Like it would cut out my heart to lose him."

Sandy glanced briefly at the action in the pool. "So why aren't you asking for permanent custody?"

"I can't do that to Anna. She's not comfortable with this."

"But surely she can see—"

"It's a big decision, Sandy. I can't force it on her. She doesn't feel like I do."

"Have you heard anything from John?"

"I got an e-mail Friday. He said Karen Parker's attorney called him wanting to know about Andy's current placement. He stonewalled him...said he couldn't release it without a court order. John thinks the attorney will drop it if they run into a lot of resistance, especially if we can get Andy into the pipeline for an adoption by somebody who hasn't already had two kids taken away by the state."

"You think there's any chance at all Karen really wants Andy?"

Lily snorted. "No way. I looked up her attorney. He's an ambulance chaser. He smells money from the city for Kristy's death, and the only way a jury will give it to him is if she's raising the poor orphan."

Sandy rolled her eyes and nodded. "Just what I'd expect from her kind. Where do things stand on the adoption front? Does John have any prospects?"

"He's meeting with some Catholic group next week." She lowered her voice. "I told him to take his time."

"So you're going to work on Anna?"

She shook her head. "No, I just want to buy us some time and see if she comes around on her own. What matters in the long run is that Andy ends up in a good home…and I wouldn't mind it if I could find a way to be in his life, like maybe through an open adoption."

Sandy grasped both of Lily's shoulders and turned her toward the pool. "Can Andy end up in a better home than this one?"

Looking at the way they all laughed and played together, it was hard to imagine a better life for Andy. Lily doubted he had ever had this much fun before, or had ever been around people who really cared about him the way Anna's family did. That alone gave her hope he would grow on Anna, and that she would realize that no one could give him what they could.

Suzanne joined them, eyeing the meat on the grill. "I like my burger medium rare."

Lily spun back around and proceeded to flip the burgers. "Why don't you call everyone to lunch?"

Suzanne walked to the water's edge and made the announcement. She offered her hand to Hal as he started up the ladder, and found herself sailing headfirst into the deep end.

Anna guided Andy to the side of the pool where Hal lifted him out. Then she turned to lend a hand to Suzanne, who was flailing and sputtering dramatically. "By the way, Lily should have warned you about Hal. He can't be trusted."

"Now you tell me."

Anna climbed out and grabbed a towel from the chaise. "Come here, Andy." She removed his water wings and toweled him off. "Was that fun?"

"Yeah! Did you see me swim?"

"I sure did." She loved seeing him so excited, and she patted herself on the back for the progress they had made together since she decided to take Kim's advice and do more things with him. Though she still left the care and feeding to Lily, she had tried to build a rapport by helping him with his toy cars, walking Chester and playing in the pool, and it seemed to be working. "You were like a little fishy. Go ask Lily if she saw you swim."

As he started down the pool deck, he stumbled and landed sharply on his knee. Anna watched in alarm for several seconds as he processed his mishap. Then he let out a squall.

She darted to his side to find his knee skinned and bleeding, and in that instant grasped the magic Kim described when her children needed her. "Poor Andy. Come here and let me fix it."

He looked at her momentarily through teary eyes, then pushed her hands away and ran the length of the pool to Lily.

Stung by the brush-off, she watched as Lily carried him inside.

Hal handed her another towel. "Don't take it personally, Anna. Jonah would have done the same thing to me."

For the rest of the afternoon, she chatted with Suzanne and Sandy about their remodeling project, and took a turn holding baby Alice. Andy and Jonah returned to the pool after eating, this time with George and Lily. As the sun faded, the air grew chilly, and their guests packed up to leave.

Anna carried the diaper bag to Kim and Hal's car and waited while Alice was strapped into her seat. "I'm glad we did this."

"Me too. Andy's adorable. If you and Lily don't adopt him, Hal and I will."

She smirked, weighing whether or not to call her sister's bluff. "He and Jonah were fun together."

"I can't believe Andy's four. They're practically the same size."

"Lily says he probably didn't get the proper nutrition when he was a baby, but she thinks he might catch up with his peers if he eats right."

Hal came through the gate carrying Jonah, who was worn out from playing in the pool all day. "Somebody has a new best friend."

"So we'll come to your house next weekend," Anna said.

Kim looked at her skeptically. "Love to have you. Come early, and bring cleaning supplies and food."

Anna waved as they backed out the driveway. It had been a nice day for everyone, up until Andy fell. Though she understood his natural inclination to run to the one who bathed him, fed him and put him to bed, she couldn't help but feel hurt by his rejection.

Chester met her at the side door, ready for his walk. The water running upstairs was a sign that Lily was giving Andy his bath.

"Looks like it's just you and me, hound dog."

Their normal route was out to the median and back, but Anna crossed the street and started down the next block. Between the bath and a bedtime story, Lily would be tied up for at least another half hour. Chester would enjoy the extra walk, though probably not as much as he seemed to like walking with Andy, who skipped ahead and clapped his hands for Chester to hurry.

More important, Anna had an excuse to make herself scarce, which is probably what she should have been doing all along. It made no sense to try to bond with Andy, not for the short time he would be with them. It was clear he wasn't any more comfortable with her than she was with him, and it wasn't healthy for either of them to be so ill at ease.

Lily shuffled her folders on the couch, satisfied she was caught up and ready to return to work. She was due back tomorrow, but planned to ask Tony to let her work half-days through the next couple of weeks. If Andy adapted well at preschool, she could put him on the waiting list to go all day. Her other option was to hire a sitter to pick him up at noon and keep him until either she or Anna got home. That was the most practical option, but she hated to subject him to another stranger.

From the way their criminal caseload had grown, she had a sinking feeling a move to part-time would be in paycheck only. Even at part-time, the criminal work could tie her up in court past time to pick Andy up. Martine had offered to step in for emergencies, and that was a relief, but Anna hadn't spoken up at all.

To her great disappointment, Anna had withdrawn somewhat over the past three days, ever since the cookout, heading to their room with her briefcase after dinner instead of spending time with Andy in the family room. She said she was working on her campaign speech for the Chamber of Commerce, but it wasn't like her to bring work home.

Lily had decided to ignore it, since anything she said might force the issue. If Anna had misgivings about her decision to let Andy stay with them, she didn't want to know.

"Lily?"

Startled by Andy's soft voice, she gathered the folders to clear a space on the couch.

"Hi, there. Did you have a nice nap?"

He nodded, obviously still sleepy.

"Come up here and sit with me."

He climbed up to sit beside her, but her urge to hold him was overwhelming, and she pulled him into her lap.

"Do you like living here, Andy?" she asked, her chin resting on top of his head.

"Yes."

"I thought so. What do you like about it?"

"I like my room, and my toys and Chester."

"Uh-huh. What else?"

"I like the swimming pool."

"Anything else?" She hoped he would volunteer how he felt about her and Anna. "Do you have a good time when you play with Anna?"

"Yes."

"And do you like when I read you a story at night?"

"Yes."

She allowed for the possibility that he was just trying to please her with his answers, but at least he hadn't hesitated. Children with Andy's past often held back affection out of insecurity it wouldn't be reciprocated. "You know what I like? I like you. I think you're a very sweet boy, and I'm glad you live here with us."

That got her a bashful smile, which in turn, earned Andy a fierce hug.

"Let's go to the store and get something good for dinner, okay?" His appetite had improved considerably since his arrival in their home, a fact Lily attributed to involving him in the menu planning. His favorite food by far was macaroni and cheese, an ironic choice, since it was at the very bottom of Anna's list. He didn't care much for vegetables, but what child did? At least he tried a few bites every night at dinner.

John Moss had been pleased to hear Andy was eating well and especially that he hadn't had an asthma attack since coming to LA. Not only that, he hadn't wet the bed since the first night. All of it, he said, translated to a healthier, happier, well-adjusted child, which was what he would write in his file. He asked again if she and Anna would consider adoption, a question she deflected with one about whether he had heard more from Karen Parker's attorney.

Lily knew she couldn't put off the subject of adoption with Anna much longer, especially since she had promised she would work hard with John to find Andy the right home and to date, she had done nothing at all. But first, it seemed that another conversation was in order, one that got to the bottom of Anna's misgivings.

Chapter 8

Lily's desk phone beeped to announce a message from Pauline, the clinic's secretary.

"Lily, Tony just got back from court. He's in his office."

She had been waiting all morning to catch her boss, and growing increasingly nervous by the minute. He had been more than accommodating in allowing her to take vacation on such short notice, but he wasn't going to like her next request. They were swamped with work, and Pauline said no one had time to process the applications they had received.

She stuck her head in the door of his office and knocked gently. "Hey, got a minute?"

Tony slumped into his chair and sighed. "That depends on what you need. I have forty minutes to eat and go through my inbox before I have to head back to court."

No, he wasn't going to like this at all, but she had no choice. "I won't beat around the bush. I need to cut back on my hours until we get things sorted out with Andy. I was thinking maybe seven to noon." That meant dropping Andy off at six thirty, but his preschool opened early.

He ran his hands through his hair. "You couldn't have picked a busier time, you know."

"I didn't pick it, Tony. Andy needs me right now."

"I know. It's just that we've got a backlog of cases. I've talked to three applicants, but I haven't had time to follow up."

"I can do that," she said eagerly. "I can check references from home this afternoon. I'll pull everything together in a report and have it for you tomorrow."

"And what about your caseload? What happens if you have to be in court all day?"

"I have a fall-back plan for emergencies. Anna and Martine will help out, but Andy needs as much stability as I can give him right now."

"How long are we talking?"

She wished he hadn't asked that, not because of Andy, but because of the guardian *ad litem* post. "I don't really know. Maybe…" It wasn't fair to Tony for her to hedge on this, especially since she was ninety percent sure she would be leaving within the next two months. "Look, I wasn't going to mention this until things were definite, but I've been talking with the board of directors about Wes McLean's job."

Tony shook his head and groaned. "Why didn't you say something? I know you hate the criminal work, but I had no idea you were that unhappy."

"It isn't that—though I do hate the criminal work," she admitted. "I didn't go looking. They recruited me. They got referrals from some of the judges in family court, and my name kept coming up."

He muttered something under his breath.

"What?"

"Nothing, I was just cursing. I don't blame you for being interested. That would be a fantastic job for you, and I don't know anyone who could do it better."

She swelled with pride at his praise. Tony's opinion of her mattered more than almost any other. "They haven't officially offered me the job, and they probably won't decide for at least another month."

"Still, I'm going to need a new attorney right away, and maybe another one later."

"So…does that mean you want me to start the vetting this afternoon?"

He came around the desk. "Be on the lookout for a fresh face right out of law school, somebody who's optimistic and eager to right all the wrongs in the world. Someone who's going to stand up for mothers and their kids."

Lily felt tears spring to her eyes as she realized he was talking about someone like her. "I'll find the right one, Tony."

Anna strode through the showroom of the Volkswagen dealership, admiring the new vehicle display. It had taken almost a year to straighten out the mess she had inherited from the previous owner, but now they were turning a tidy profit. Having her father come out of his retirement after only a few months to take over the reins had been a godsend.

"Hi, Anna." It was Marco, the youthful sales manager she had plucked from the ranks at the BMW dealership.

"I like the way you've rearranged the showroom. Is Dad in his office?"

"Last I saw him, he was in the garage."

Anna wasn't in the mood to get her hands dirty today, but she couldn't resist seeing what had piqued her father's interest. She found him bent over the engine of a black Karmann Ghia convertible. "New toy?"

"Isn't she a beauty?" he exclaimed. "She's older than you are."

"Lovely." Anna and her father both enjoyed the chance to work on older cars. The younger mechanics in their shop depended almost solely on the computer for diagnostics and recommended repairs, which weren't available for the classic models, especially those so old the engine was in the back. "Wish I had my grease monkey outfit."

Her father called out to the service manager, who disappeared and returned with a brand-new jumpsuit. She slipped it on and pushed up her sleeves. "I bet I haven't done this in a year."

"You need to get your hands dirty more often. That's what makes the car business so much fun."

"I brought something else that makes it fun. You won a Chamber of Commerce award for your first year sponsoring Kidz Kamp. It's in that box I brought." Premier BMW had given money every year to fund the community program that enabled youth in foster care to go camping with volunteers from child services. As head of the VW dealership, George had signed on as co-sponsor last year.

He wiped his hands and opened the box to examine the plaque. "Isn't it funny how things work out? We all got involved with Kidz Kamp because of Lily, and now she's brought us our own foster child."

She was surprised to hear him speak possessively of Andy. "I'm glad we've been able to help him out. He's a good kid."

"Are you and Lily thinking about making it permanent? She must feel close to him since he's her nephew."

Anna felt enough pressure from Lily without adding her family to the mix. "That's not our plan."

George pried the spark plugs from their sockets and handed them to one of the mechanics. "See if you can find me four of these." He returned to clean the sockets. "I got the impression from Martine that Lily had other ideas."

She definitely didn't want to have this discussion. "It's news to me. I don't think I'm ready for kids. We're just keeping him so he won't end up with his crazy grandmother."

"Lily's mother?"

Anna had come to share Lily's vehemence about Karen Parker. "No, Eleanor was her mother. That lady just happened to give birth to her, but the mothering ended there."

"Right, I didn't mean anything by it."

She realized from his obvious contrition that her voice had sounded sharp. "It's okay. That woman doesn't deserve to be called a mother. Lily was lucky to escape all that."

He nodded. "Let's just hope Andy's that lucky. We like him a lot. If you two change your mind, I'll have somebody else to play with."

She bit her tongue to mask her growing frustration. "I need to get back to my office," she said, shrugging out of the coveralls. "And speaking of play, thanks for the jumpsuit."

"I'll call you next time I get one of these in. It's cars like this one that make us appreciate what all the new ones can do."

She drove back to her office and closed the door, vowing to stay there until she knew Andy would be in bed. No one seemed to care that this didn't feel right for her.

The glare of headlights flashed across the ceiling in Andy's room, the signal that Anna was home from work. Two nights in a row she had phoned to say she was working late on her vice president campaign speech, one she hoped would convince her peers that their businesses would thrive only if their whole community did.

Lily closed the book and smoothed Andy's hair. It was good for everyone that he fell asleep so easily, especially since it gave her and Anna their own time after eight o'clock. She tiptoed out and went downstairs to find Anna in the kitchen fixing a sandwich. "I made spaghetti."

"Hey, baby. A sandwich is fine." Anna dropped the bread and pulled Lily into an embrace. "How did your day go? Did you hire your replacement?"

"I have it narrowed down to two, but it's Tony's decision. The way our work has picked up, he might want both of them." She took the knife and peanut butter jar from Anna. "Have a seat and I'll bring it to you."

Anna kicked off her shoes and sat at the breakfast nook. "How was Andy's day?"

"Good. He drew this." She gestured to a picture on the refrigerator. "Clearly, it's him and Chester."

"Of course it is. Anyone would know that."

Lily poured a small glass of milk and took it, along with the sandwich, to the table. "I need for you to watch Andy for a few hours tomorrow. Can you do that?"

Despite her obvious effort to remain calm, Anna's face showed signs of panic. "I was going to tell you I need to go into—"

She put her hand on Anna's forearm to stop her. "I wouldn't ask if it weren't important. It's just that I need to see Virginia. I've talked to her on the phone, but I haven't been to a meeting in over three weeks."

Anna acquiesced immediately, as Lily had known she would. "Sure. I can do it for a few hours. Maybe we'll ride over and visit Jonah."

"I bet they'd both like that." Lily saw through Anna's plan to avoid being alone with Andy, but she didn't care. Every little bit of progress mattered. "Can you eat faster? There's something else I haven't done in a while, and it involves you."

"Is that so?"

"It is. Our bathrobes are hanging on the back of the door in the powder room."

"The hot tub?"

Lily nodded.

"I take it Andy's asleep."

"Very. And it's Friday night. This is our time."

Anna rewarded her with the biggest smile she had seen in ages, and when they slid into the tub, it was like old times.

"Come sit on my lap," Anna said. She pulled Lily close and sought her lips.

Lily felt her passion surge as their tongues danced. She needed this intimacy, and apparently, so did Anna. "I love you."

Anna tipped her chin upward. "Is everything okay? You're not worried about anything, are you?"

"No, not at all." Though she had never come close to a relapse as far as her drinking was concerned, Anna was ever vigilant about making sure things were under control. "Virginia says I need to learn to recognize certain emotions and head them off."

"You mean like when your mother died?"

"Yeah, and when I started feeling alone." It was never easy to talk about those times. "That wasn't your fault, you know. It was just baggage I carried from when I was a kid."

Anna cupped her cheeks to look her straight in the eye. "You'll never be alone again, Lily, no matter what. I promised you that."

"I know." Lily also knew that her anxiety about losing Andy was as fierce as any she had ever felt. "I just need to get back down to earth. Andy's really thrown me for a loop."

Anna nodded ever so slightly, as if showing understanding, but not agreement. "What do you need from me?"

"Just look after him tomorrow. That's all." What she wanted most was for Anna to fall in love with him as she had.

"I can do that. You don't have to worry."

"And come home from work and spend more time with us."

Anna looked away, then drew in a deep breath and nodded again. "I just…I thought it would be easier on him if he didn't have to share you."

"That isn't his choice. It's mine, and I want you here."

"Okay."

After a long silence, Lily began to stroke Anna's sides, allowing her thumbs to brush the sides of her breasts. She pushed off Anna's lap to the far side of the hot tub and coaxed her to follow. "Suppose you sit on my lap for a while."

As Anna lowered herself, Lily met her center with two fingers.

"I love feeling you inside me." She rested her forehead against Lily's and rocked her hips slowly against the pressure.

As they came together in a kiss, Lily felt Anna's hand between them as she massaged her own clitoris. The instant she gasped, Lily felt a clenching around her fingers and she reveled in the pulsing wake. Then she gently touched her other hand to Anna's chest. "I'm always inside you…right here."

Anna felt guilty about barging in on her sister during the weekend when Hal was home, but not enough to turn down Hal's invitation to Andy to come over and help Jonah make a fort in the backyard. It was the best way she knew to spend several hours with Andy without actually spending several hours with Andy.

She helped him out of his booster seat, the smaller one they had gotten for the X3 when they went to San Francisco to bring him home. Lily had suggested keeping it in Anna's car for those times when she would be needed to drive him somewhere. Today was the first occasion for that, and Andy had been excited about his first chance to ride in her sports car.

"Do you remember playing with Jonah in the pool?"

"Uh-huh." He surprised her by taking her hand as they walked into the backyard, where they could hear Jonah and Hal already working on the fort.

Anna greeted them and waited until Andy started playing with Jonah. Then she went in search of her sister, who was folding cloth diapers from a rack in their laundry room, while Alice watched from her baby seat. "Need some help?"

"Hey! Did you bring food and cleaning supplies like I told you?"

Anna chuckled. "Nope, just me and Andy. But I'll be happy to play with Alice while you do your Cinderella shtick."

"Very funny. Can you imagine how far behind I'd be if I didn't have Consuela twice a week?" They shared a housekeeper, who also cleaned the Big House. Anna and Lily had her only once a week.

"What do you want me to do?"

"Just sit with me and talk about something besides pooping. How did you end up with babysitting duties?"

"Lily wanted to go to an AA meeting. She hasn't had time since Andy got here."

"She doing okay?"

"Yeah, but I think some of this business with Andy is putting pressure on her. I wish we could get it settled."

"If you ask me—and I know you didn't, but if you did—I think you could settle it in the blink of an eye by deciding to adopt him. It's obvious that's what she wants."

Anna was tired of being bombarded from all sides. "But it isn't what I want, Kim. Andy doesn't even like me."

"That's not true. I saw how he played with you in the pool."

"And did you also see how he pushed me away and ran to Lily after he fell? Why would he do that if he liked me?"

"Because he sees Lily as his mommy. If she hadn't been there, he would have been all over you. Kids do that all the time."

That's what Hal had said. "What does that make me? I don't know how to be a daddy."

"It makes you a parent," Kim said sharply. "I don't pretend to know how two women are supposed to handle all that, but Andy has his own ideas about what a mommy does. Maybe he ran to Lily because she deals with things like that. It doesn't mean he doesn't need you too. At four years old, he needs something from everybody he meets."

Anna was growing increasingly exasperated. "Does it matter to anybody that I don't want this? Andy's a cute kid, and I know he needs things, but I don't want to spend the next fifteen years feeling like I'm on the outside of the circle." She got up to stand in the doorway of the laundry room, just in case a certain little one came within earshot. "I had other plans for my life with Lily. We have careers, and we both want to travel."

"You think just because Hal and I had children that it means we're giving up all of our dreams?"

"That's exactly the point. You and Hal had children together. You planned it that way. I didn't."

Alice began to fuss at the commotion and Kim picked her up.

"You're going to be pissed when I say this."

Anna rolled her eyes. "When does that ever matter?"

"I think you're jealous."

"I am not!"

Alice squalled.

If she thought she could handle Andy on her own for the next two hours, she would have collected him and left. "Why doesn't anyone care what I think?"

Kim swayed gently with Alice on her shoulder and answered in a soft, even voice. "Because you're thirty-five years old, and no matter what happens here, you're going to land on your feet. Who knows where Andy will land if he loses this chance? And if you think Lily's going to just pick up and carry on after he leaves, you're not paying attention. She needs this little boy as much as she needs you."

Anna walked over to the kitchen window and watched as Andy played. He was undeniably content, and seemed to genuinely enjoy the company of Jonah. Perhaps she was making too much of Andy's reaction last weekend.

There was no escaping the truth of Kim's observations about Lily. Not once since Andy had come to live with them had she talked about her plans to find him another home. The only way she would do that was if Anna insisted, and Anna couldn't do that, not when doing so might send Lily on another downward spiral.

"So how do I do this?"

"You keep reaching out to him. You can't expect a four-year-old to take the lead. You're new and scary. Just be there for him when he really needs you, and he'll eventually come around."

"And if he doesn't?"

Kim leaned close enough so that Alice could drool on Anna's shoulder. "He will. You're one of the kindest, sweetest people I know, and I'd say that even if I wasn't about to ask you to watch her while I go take a long bath."

For the ride home, Anna lowered the top on her convertible and took a side trip through Topanga State Park, which thrilled Andy. "What's the best car on the road?"

"BMWs!"

Of all the meetings she could have chosen, why this one? They were supposed to be there to help each other, but Lily had no words to offer Diane, who was starting fresh after her third relapse. Rather than be encouraged by Diane's renewed commitment, she was disheartened by the reality that people fell every day.

More than once in the past week, Lily had found herself thinking about a drink—not that she wanted one, but that she feared she would break down and have one. That would be devastating, not only to her, but to all of the people who had placed their faith in her.

Virginia seemed to sense her discomfort and patted her hand.

At the end of the meeting, they joined hands for the Serenity Prayer, and Lily heard herself mouth the words, "Keep coming back!" She knew she needed to make time for this. If Diane had kept up the meetings, she wouldn't have fallen off the wagon.

"You want to talk about it?" Virginia asked as they walked out.

Lily sighed. "I'm freaking out about things at home."

"About Andy?"

She nodded. "I don't want to give him up. It'll tear my heart out."

"Have you and Anna talked about it? Really talked?"

"No, but that isn't really the problem. If I tell her how I feel, I know what she'll do. She'll give in, even though raising Andy is probably the last thing she wants to do. It's just the kind of person she is. But then this big wall will go up between us, and next thing you know, she'll be working late again, and—"

"You don't know that for sure. Give her a chance."

"I do know, because it's already started. I had to practically beg her to keep him today so I could come to a meeting."

They reached Lily's car and Virginia leaned against the hood casually. "And this is freaking you out because you're afraid of losing Anna?"

Lily shook her head. "No, I'll always have Anna. I'm sure of it." She twirled the band on her left hand as her tears built. "But I've asked so much of her. I couldn't stand it if she gave me this and it made her unhappy."

"And if you lose Andy, then you'll be unhappy."

"So either way…"

115

"Are you worried about this affecting your sobriety?"

"Wouldn't you be?"

Virginia bobbed her head from side to side in question. "I suppose some people would. But I think I have a lot more faith in you than you do in yourself. You can go in any direction you want, but drinking only takes you down."

"I'm not tempted to drink. But I'm worried about what we talked about last time, about having all those negative feelings and regrets. I'm afraid of dancing too close to the edge."

"You're always going to have challenges in your life, Lily, and you can't face them if you're drunk. I know you know that. But if you're really worried about it, maybe you should talk to somebody."

Lily chuckled and looked around the emptying parking lot. "I thought that's what I was doing now."

"I'm just a substance abuse counselor. If you're grappling with feelings you can't handle, maybe you should think about seeing a psychotherapist."

"I don't think what I feel is all that different from what we all go through. Maybe it's just that these feelings bring back all those bad memories about when I bottomed out."

"I wouldn't doubt that's a big part of it. The other part is that you feel vulnerable because you've been missing meetings. I think you should do whatever it takes to get to a meeting at least once a week. You need to stay in touch with this, and keep working the steps. Get a babysitter if you have to, but don't slip away. That's what Diane did, and it cost her."

Lily nodded. "You're right."

"And go home and talk to Anna. The sooner you get things settled, the sooner you can stop worrying about it."

Or start worrying about it even more. "Thanks, Virginia. I appreciate how you're always there for me."

"That's what sponsors are supposed to do." She held out her arms to give Lily a hug. "Everyone has fears and doubts about their recovery, but I can tell you this from the years I've worked with people in the program. You're doing all the right things.

Alcoholism never goes away, so you need to keep working the program, even more when you feel challenged, because every single victory makes you stronger."

Driving home, Lily savored Virginia's praise and encouragement. No matter how difficult the situation with Andy, the stakes were too high for her to let go and lose control. She needed to be honest with Anna about what she wanted and hope they could talk their way to a solution both of them could live with.

She arrived home to find only Chester, and she followed him into the backyard and stretched out in a chaise lounge to enjoy the last few warm rays of sun. Within minutes, the garage door went up to announce Anna and Andy's return. "I'm back here!"

They entered through the back gate and Anna nudged Andy from behind. "Go tell Lily what you did with Jonah."

It was a jumble of words, but she gathered they had built something in the backyard that had windows.

Anna relaxed in the chair beside her. "Basically, Hal cleaned out his garage and they built a fort out of everything that wasn't toxic."

"It sounds like you had a lot of fun, Andy."

He nodded. "And we rode in the car without it no top."

She looked at Anna, who was chuckling at his description. "Did you like riding in the car without it no top?"

"Uh-huh."

Lily was delighted to see them both smiling. "I want to hear about your fort. Did you—"

"That's the phone. I'll get it," Anna said.

"Did you have fun with Jonah?"

"Uh-huh. We used a hammer to hit a stick, and we drank juice in the fort."

"Lily, it's for you," Anna called. "It's John Moss."

"On a Saturday?"

Anna shrugged and handed her the phone.

"Hey, John. What's up?"

"I'm afraid I've got some bad news. I just got served a summons to Superior Court on Monday to explain why we placed Andy in LA when there's an active adoption petition by a relative."

"You've got to be kidding. How did they even know where he was?"

"They got a court order. And apparently, they looked up your address on the property tax rolls and don't like the idea of Andy living in such a ritzy place."

Anna guided Andy to his toy box in the family room and leaned against the kitchen counter to listen.

"Has anyone even called you to ask how he was doing? No, let me answer that. Karen Parker doesn't care, because this isn't about Andy, it's about the money."

"Andy has a guardian *ad litem*, an attorney by the name of Tom Greene. I faxed him a copy of the summons, so he'll be there to argue our side. I really think you should come up for the hearing."

"He's just starting to get used to his preschool. What happens if we can't come?"

"We don't need Andy. In fact, I don't want to risk having him here if there's even a remote chance they award Karen Haney custody. We'll need time to appeal without handing him over."

She glanced at Anna—who would have to care for Andy by herself—and started to pace. "Do you honestly think any judge in his right mind would grant her custody of a child?"

The sound of toys clattering to the floor sent Anna into the other room.

"I don't think so, but I don't want to take a chance. We need to hit back hard, and one of the best things we can do is have you tell the judge how well Andy's doing. And it won't hurt for him to see you in person because the comparison between you and Karen Haney will be pretty stark."

"God, I don't think I can be in the same room with her without throwing up."

"One thing you're not going to like..." He rustled papers in the background. "She's claiming to be Andy's only living relative."

118

She knew where he was headed. "No way, John. I'm not going to tell her who I am. In the first place, I don't want her to feel like she's off the hook because I turned out all right. And in the second place, I don't ever want her to think of me as her daughter because that ended the day I walked out of court with Eleanor Stewart."

"Hmm...well, it's your call."

She dropped her head straight back and stared at the ceiling, resigned to make a trip to San Francisco. "What time on Monday?"

"Nine a.m. Superior Court on McAllister."

Tony wasn't going to be happy, but he was the least of her worries. Anna was going to freak out completely.

Lily walked into the family room and leaned in the doorway.

Anna was helping Andy sort his toys so he could build another town on the floor, but she followed Lily back into the kitchen so they could talk. "What was that all about?"

"Karen Parker's lawyer filed an objection to Andy's temporary placement here," she said, her voice low. "They're arguing that it's not good for him to be in a place like this because he's going to have trouble adjusting to his permanent home, which she obviously thinks will be hers."

"That's ridiculous. Does she really think a judge is going to give her custody?"

"Apparently."

Anna huffed and shook her head. "Unbelievable. Did I hear right? You have to go back up there?"

She nodded. "John thinks the judge needs to hear from me how well Andy's doing. Her attorney is arguing that Karen Parker is Andy's only family. She doesn't know Andy is with me."

"And don't you want to keep it that way?"

"Yes, but not if there's a chance in hell she'll get custody."

"So you and Andy have to go back to San Francisco."

"Not exactly." She lowered her head, drew a deep breath and then met Anna's eyes with a pleading look. "I can't take Andy. If the judge rules against us, I need time to file an appeal."

"But that means"—her stomach dropped—"you'll leave Andy here with me."

"I won't be gone that long. I can catch the last flight on Sunday and be back in time for his bath on Monday night. All you'll have to do is take him to preschool and pick him up." She picked up the phone again. "Never mind. All you have to do is drop him off. I can call Martine. She said to call her if I ever got hung up and she'd go get him."

Anna paced anxiously on the landing outside Andy's room. Lily had Andy in her lap and was rocking him to calm his wheezing, which had started almost the instant she told him she was going away overnight.

She looked in again to see if the situation had improved. "Can I get you anything?"

Lily nudged Andy. "You want Anna to get you some juice?"

He nodded, but never made eye contact with Anna.

She went down to the kitchen and filled a plastic cup with grape juice. This was exactly what she feared most about Lily leaving her alone with Andy—that something would happen and she wouldn't be able to fix it. She would never have known about the rocking chair, and even if she had, it was doubtful he would have responded to her the way he did Lily.

After more than an hour of rocking, Lily put him to bed without his bath.

"He's a little upset about me going off tomorrow."

"That makes two of us."

"He'll be fine. We talked about it. I told him I had to go talk to the judge so he could stay here with us instead of moving somewhere else."

Anna stretched out on the bed and propped up on her elbow. Two hours ago, she had been ready to tell Lily to go ahead with making this arrangement permanent, but all of that changed with Andy's asthma attack. Now more than ever, she was convinced that he needed to be in a home where he felt less anxious. "What are you going to say?"

As if demonstrating the gulf between them, Lily opted to sit in the armchair rather than join her on the bed. "I'll say whatever it takes to keep Andy from being placed with Karen Parker."

Anna reluctantly acknowledged the unspoken message. If necessary, Lily would challenge Karen Parker's adoption by petitioning for her own. "What do you think the options are?"

"The most important one is for John to prove—actually, it's not John. It's a guy named Tom Greene. He's Andy's guardian *ad litem*. How's that for irony?" She continued without looking up. "Tom has to make the case that Karen isn't fit to raise Andy. If he can do that, I may not have to say anything at all, unless the judge feels like Andy shouldn't be here because our house is too big."

"And if he does?"

"Then I'll tell him how well Andy is doing here. I wish I could have said he hadn't had an asthma attack."

"Have you thought any more…"—Anna hesitated, knowing her question would be upsetting—"about what kind of home would be best for Andy in the long run?"

Lily stared at the floor, her face growing red. After a long silence, she said, "I can't talk about that right now, Anna. Please don't ask me to."

With her question, Anna had hoped to press the issue, to get their cards on the table once and for all. If Lily was open to finding him a better home, she felt strongly they should do that. It wasn't anything against Andy, but her doubts about what sort of parent she would be. Conversely, if adoption was ultimately the only solution Lily could accept—and especially if her feelings about Andy were tied to her alcohol issues—then they needed to acknowledge that and figure out how to make it work for all three of them. The stress and uncertainty wasn't good for anyone.

Later that night, Anna scooted up behind Lily in bed and wrapped an arm around her waist.

Lily grasped her hand and kissed it.

"I never even asked you how your meeting went."

"It was kind of a downer, but I'm glad I went. I need to keep it up." She rolled onto her back so they could look at each other in the faint light that came through the window from the street. "Anna, I don't ever want you to be unhappy."

Anna's mind worked to connect those two things, Lily's need for support and her concern for their happiness. It could only mean she thought they were headed for a conflict of such proportion that she would be tempted to return to drinking. Anna would never let that happen. "I won't ever be unhappy as long as I'm with you."

"And what about Andy?" Her voice was barely a whisper.

Anna drew a deep breath. "I just told you. What really matters is that I have you."

Chapter 9

"Lily, I don't think I can do this." Anna was following her around the bedroom as she finished packing.

"Of course you can. We've been through everything, and I even wrote it all down. It's only until tomorrow night, and Martine's going to pick him up tomorrow after school." She zipped up the roll-on bag and set it by the door.

"But I don't..." Anna was clearly frantic. "What if he has another asthma attack?"

That was Lily's chief worry also, that Andy's stress about her being gone would trigger an attack like last night's. "I told him everything was going to be okay. He's had his bath, he's ready for bed. All you have to do is read him a story, drop him off at school in the morning and pick him up at your mother's after work."

"But—"

"If he starts wheezing, just sit with him in the rocking chair like I did until he calms down. Just don't let him get excited."

"I don't understand why you have to be there. Can't John take care of this? He has all the information."

"Because I can answer the judge's questions better than John can. If we don't make a strong case, he might transfer Andy into Karen Parker's custody on a whim. I won't sit by and let her ruin Andy's life."

Anna had sulked all day, all through Lily's instructions on dressing, bed changing and emergencies.

"But you know this is going to be hard on Andy."

Lily couldn't stand it any longer. She thought after their conversation the night before that they understood each other, even if Anna still had reservations. "I have to go, Anna. I know you're scared to do this. I know you'd rather I stayed home. But I don't really feel like I have any choice. Please don't make me feel guilty about it."

Anna chewed her bottom lip in obvious frustration. "I'm sorry. I just…" Her voice trailed off as she slumped onto the end of the bed.

"Why are you so worried about this?"

"I don't know. What if…? Suppose he…?"

Lily took pity on her as she floundered about, trying to articulate her fears. She sat beside her on the bed and took her hand. "Talk to me, sweetheart."

"It's just that I'm worried Andy will get upset and I won't be able to deal with it."

"You mean like Jonah did that time?"

She nodded. "I'm not worried about me. I'm worried about him. What if I can't reassure him? I'm not good at this like you are."

"Honey, you're better than you think. Andy likes you. He loves it when you play with him. I can see it. His whole face lights up when you get down on the floor with him."

Anna smiled faintly at her cajoling.

"Honey, right now Andy's afraid too, and he needs for you to be there for him. I need it too. You have been wonderful about all this, and I love you more than you could ever know. But I need you to hang in there with me and get us through this."

"Of course I will." Anna put her arm around Lily's shoulder

and pulled her close. "I'm sorry for being such a jerk."

Lily was silent but returned the hug, burying her face into Anna's neck.

"You're supposed to say 'Oh, you're not being a jerk.'"

"Oh, you're not being a jerk."

"Good morning, Anna. Flat tire?" Hal asked as he passed her in the showroom.

Anna grunted and stormed up the stairs to her office, where she slammed the door and closed the blinds to the window that looked out over the people milling about below. She always kept a change of clothes behind the door, just in case the temptation to take a motor apart proved irresistible.

She ripped off her tan jacket and ivory top, both of which now sported greasy black smears. The navy top she kept for emergencies clashed horribly with her dark green slacks, which were wet at the knees, so she was forced to change into her tan skirt. That move necessitated hose, which she kept in her bottom drawer, and heels, which she did not. The first person who commented on her casual brown shoes would be fired.

The morning had been less than ideal, to say the least. Though Andy had made it through the night without having an asthma attack, his anxiety about Lily being gone had kept him awake until nearly eleven. As a result, he was very difficult to rouse. Twice, Anna had returned to his room to find he had gone back to sleep.

When he finally got up, he and his bed were soaking wet. She helped him wash and directed him to the clothes Lily had laid out for school. However, when he joined her several minutes later in the kitchen, he was wearing the ragged T-shirt with the hole in the side. She sent him back upstairs to change, but when he returned, his mood had worsened. It didn't help that she poured for him the same bran cereal she always ate for breakfast, which he didn't like at all. After watching him push it around in his bowl for a while, she relented and dumped it out, discovering to her chagrin that they were out of the sugary flakes he usually ate. With no more cereal options, she smeared peanut butter and jelly on a piece of bread and folded it half. Andy protested that sandwiches were lunch food, but he ate it anyway, dropping a large blob of jelly on his clean shirt and pants.

Anna thought seriously about sending him on, but remembered her mother was picking him up. She wouldn't be happy to hear he had made this mess before leaving home. So back upstairs they went to find something new to wear. Anna then threw the sheets and all the dirty clothes into the washer and steered him out the door into the drizzling rain ten minutes late.

As they were climbing into the car, Andy suddenly remembered his favorite toy, the model Z8 she had given him on the ride down from San Francisco, which he took with him everywhere. After ten more minutes of searching, she found it underneath the couch in the family room. Chester, seeing her crawl on the floor, assumed she was playing and climbed onto her back, leaving a dirty footprint in the middle of her crisp white shirt. She quickly changed to the ivory top and jacket, and finally headed out the door for good.

When they reached Andy's preschool, she hustled him out of the car, which caused him to drop his little Z8, and it rolled underneath the big Z8. Seeing him on the verge of tears, she ignored the wet ground and crawled underneath the car to retrieve it.

The intercom beeped announcing a message. "Anna, Dave Cahill is here to see you."

Dave Cahill…she had forgotten about their meeting to discuss the Chamber elections. "Send him on up." Would he notice if she were barefoot?

Lily checked her watch and noted grimly that her prospects for getting back to LA in time for Andy's bath were nil. An emergency had pushed their placement hearing into the afternoon, and threatened to postpone it until the next day.

She had made the most of her downtime, calling clients and

writing briefs on her laptop, but now was caught up. Had she known they would end up sitting in the hallway so long, she would have brought a book. John was absorbed in paperwork, as was Tom Greene, whom she had briefed about how well Andy was doing in LA.

At the far end of the hallway was a thin, almost gaunt, middle-aged woman who had spent nearly an hour cleaning the bright red polish from her nails. Lily knew her at once as Karen Parker, the woman who had brought her into the world and left her to languish in foster care until age seven when she had been rescued by Eleanor Stewart. Karen had changed very little since Lily's trip to Oakland two years ago, where she had discovered the woman working as a cocktail waitress in a hotel lounge. If anything, the simple frock Karen wore made her look older.

Beside her was a man of about forty, presumably her attorney, dressed crisply in a navy blue suit with a blue and yellow tie. Lily sized him up as an adversary, noting the well-worn briefcase that said business was good. He didn't strike her as an ordinary ambulance chaser. His filings on this case, which John had faxed to her hotel last night, were concise and well-stated…even if they were a pack of lies. Tom, who worked a number of cases like Andy's, had never encountered this firm in a family court case. Their specialty, he said, was injury and wrongful death.

More than once, she felt Karen's eyes on her, and she willed herself to focus on her work. After seeing the mug shot of Kristy on the news, she knew she bore a striking resemblance to her sister, but her short blond hair—as opposed to Kristy's long brown hair—and her professional attire posed a considerable contrast.

Today's hearing was run-of-the-mill for continuation of foster care, with Karen Parker taking on the typical role of the parent wanting custody of her child, and social services arguing that the circumstances warranted an out-of-home placement. It was unlikely the court would address Karen's adoption petition, but the judge would take seriously a family request for custody unless John and Tom made a solid case that Karen was unfit. John had not shared with either Karen's attorney or the judge that Lily was Andy's aunt. As far as they knew, she was here only to bolster the state's argument that Andy's current placement was ideal for his needs.

Several times, she had been tempted to tell John and Tom that she and Anna had agreed to adopt Andy. Each time, she recalled the anguished look on Anna's face as she left for the airport. Though Anna had given her tacit permission to proceed, Lily wasn't convinced it was the right move for all of them.

John closed his folder, a sign he too was caught up with his work. "I wonder what's taking so long."

Lily shrugged. "Emergency hearings in family court usually mean somebody spent the night in jail. Now they have to get all the restraining orders in place and make sure everyone understands the new rules." She had been involved in dozens of cases like that.

"I don't think that's what's happening here," Tom said. "I saw a couple of attorneys go in earlier, and neither one of them was wearing a suit off the rack. If I were guessing, I'd say somebody's in the middle of a very messy divorce."

John snorted. "Great, so while we're all sitting out here burning the taxpayers' money, they're in there fighting over the Picassos and the French poodle."

"That's about the size of it," Tom said. "If they don't call us soon, we'll be coming back tomorrow."

Lily dreaded making the call to Anna, but she was holding out hope it would just be news that she was getting in late—not that she wouldn't return until tomorrow.

Suddenly the door opened and people began exiting. From what Lily could see—an impeccably-dressed woman with her attorney and a scowling man with his—Tom's prediction had been right on the mark. She breathed a sigh of relief that things were on track to get home tonight, though definitely not in time for Andy's bath. Anna would probably be so grateful to see her that it wouldn't matter what time it was.

The bailiff stepped into the hall. "Parties for Andres

Parker?"

Lily fell in behind Tom and John, taking a seat in the row behind the defendant table on the left side of the courtroom. She averted her eyes from Karen, who followed her attorney to the plaintiff's table. As if they hadn't waited long enough, they sat another twenty minutes before the bailiff called them to their feet and introduced Judge Max Cruz, a heavyset man of about sixty with a faint accent Lily pegged as Central American.

Cruz looked over his reading glasses as he apologized for the delay. Next he apologized for not having read the complaint prior to entering the courtroom. Then he frowned at the file before him, removed his glasses, and apologized again—for deferring their case to the next morning.

Lily seethed with frustration, but she knew better than to rile a judge with a show of petulance.

Karen Parker did not, prompting her attorney to stage a sudden, loud coughing fit to cover her indignant sigh.

On her walk back to the hotel, where she now needed a room for tonight, she placed a call to Tony, bracing herself for his disappointment. "Tony, I've got some bad news. We got delayed until tomorrow. I probably won't make it back to the office before Wednesday, but I have some files I can e-mail later on the Washington case. It's a first offense, so probation's a no-brainer if you can get Lauren to hammer it out with the DA's office."

"Sure, or I can do it. I don't have to be in court tomorrow." He sounded so cheerful, she wondered at first if he was being sarcastic. "Anything else?"

"Uh, no. Did you see the report I sent on the two applicants?"

"Sure did. I think I'm going to hire both of them."

"Tony?"

"We just got a community action grant for a quarter of a million dollars."

"That's fantastic!"

"Yep, so don't give me any more bad news. It's a great day and I'm keeping it that way."

She closed her phone and smiled—for about three seconds. Then she called Anna.

Anna wiped the counter and turned out the kitchen light. Thank goodness Lily had left macaroni and cheese in the refrigerator in the "extremely unlikely" event she didn't get back in time for dinner.

Andy sat on the floor of the family room with his toy cars lined up to visit the gas station. His mood sullen and uncertain, he had mostly kept to himself through dinner.

"Andy, I need to go upstairs and take a shower. I won't be gone very long. Will you stay here with Chester?"

He nodded without looking up.

"I'll play with you when I come back. Okay?"

He shrugged.

It was hard not to be hurt by his obvious distrust. She had done everything Lily had said, from reading his story last night to getting him off to school. Still, he had said barely a word to her since she picked him up from the Big House.

Besides her responsibilities with Andy, the day had taken its toll at work as well. After her meeting with Dave Cahill, the service manager had popped into her office to let her know about a car they had just taken in for service, a 1959 507, BMW's timeless roadster. Mindful of her father's advice to savor such rare opportunities, she had changed into her jumpsuit and spent the rest of the day in the garage.

Under other circumstances, she would have preferred a soak in the hot tub, since her neck and shoulders ached from bending over the classic engine all afternoon. At least the pulsating showerhead helped the hot water penetrate her pores. Another five minutes of—

Andy was staring at her from the doorway of the bathroom.

Anna nervously wiped a circle of condensation from the glass to see him clearly. How was a woman supposed to respond to a four-year-old boy seeing her naked? "Is something wrong, Andy?"

"Can we go swimming?"

He wanted to go swimming. It was the first time he had shown an interest in anything at all since Lily left, and it had to be while she was in the shower. "Andy, would you mind going to sit on my bed until I'm finished? I'll be out in just a minute and we'll talk."

"Okay."

She couldn't make out his features through the steamy glass—which meant he probably couldn't make out hers either—but she saw him disappear from the room. She hastily dried off and wrapped herself in an oversized towel so she could retrieve her robe from a hook on the back of the door.

Andy sat obediently at the end of the bed.

"Thanks for waiting out here, Andy." Anna cinched her robe and hesitantly joined him. "When you get a little older, you'll start taking baths all by yourself. For older people—like me, for example, or like Lily—taking a bath or a shower is private. Do you understand what I mean by that?"

Though he nodded, his confused expression suggested he wasn't making the connection.

"I guess what I'm trying to say is that you shouldn't come into the bathroom when an older person is taking a bath or a shower, okay?"

"But the door was open. Lily said I had to knock when it was closed."

"Right...right. I forgot and left the door open."

"Are you mad at me?" He looked as if he might cry.

"No, of course not. You didn't do anything wrong." Remembering the stern, aloof woman he had lived with in San Francisco, she smiled and reassured him with a gentle shake of his shoulder. "You've never done anything that made me mad."

"I peed in the bed two times."

"You can't help that, Andy. Lily didn't get mad at you, did she?"

He shook his head.

"I didn't think so. It's silly to get mad over something that's an accident." She patted his knee. "Now what was it you wanted to ask me?"

"Can we go swimming?"

She was stirred by his sweet voice, and hated to say no when he asked for so little. "I don't think we have time tonight. It's almost your bedtime, and I should be getting your bath ready."

"But if I went swimming, I wouldn't have to take a bath."

Anna chuckled. "No, it doesn't work that way. Baths are with soap. That's how you get clean. Swimming is just water—no soap."

Andy nodded as though he understood, but he was noticeably disappointed about not going swimming.

"Tell you what. I'll try to come home early tomorrow. Lily should be back by then, and we'll all go swimming together before dinner. How does that sound?"

"Like fun."

"That's right. It'll be fun." She was thrilled to see his mood brighten. "Now that we've got that settled, you go brush your teeth and I'll get your bath ready."

She dressed quickly in sweatpants and a T-shirt and followed him into his bathroom. Lily had explained the bath routine over the phone. Anna's preference would have been to get the bath over with as expeditiously as possible, but she said Andy enjoyed his time in the tub when he got to play a bit, especially with bubbles.

Anna bent over the tub to pour two capfuls from the pink jug of bubble bath into the running water. After disappointing him about the pool, she couldn't begrudge him a little playtime. She added two more capfuls, thinking if bubbles were fun, twice as many would be twice as much fun. "You ready for your bath?"

He eyed the growing white mass excitedly. Without a trace of modesty, he discarded his clothes and placed them in the hamper behind the door like Lily had shown him. Then he carefully crawled into the tub, where the bubbles now surpassed the rim.

"I think I made too many bubbles."

By the happy look on his face, he didn't agree.

Despite her reservations, Anna found herself having fun too. First, she piled bubbles on top of Andy's head, even fancying a beard and moustache as she helped him wash his face. When the bubbles started to fade, she helped him scrub his neck and ears, then his back, chest and arms.

"How about poking that filthy foot out here?" she asked in a teasing voice. She scrubbed and tickled first one then the other, all the way up past his knees. It was reminiscent of the time she and Hal had played in the pool with him and Jonah. That day, she had felt confident and relaxed until Andy fell and ran past her to Lily. Maybe tonight was a turning point for them. She hoped so. But not as much as she hoped Lily would hurry home.

Lily entered the courtroom at a quarter till ten, relieved this morning's emergency hearing hadn't turned their day into a repeat of yesterday. She took her seat behind Tom and John and studied Karen Parker from behind. Today's dress was a blue print, knee-length with a belted waist. A far cry from the miniskirt and fishnet stockings she wore slinging drinks.

"We're here to discuss Andres Parker," Judge Cruz said, peering at the file as if seeing it for the first time.

Lily's tan suit and blue silk top were brand-new, off the rack at Nordstrom just before closing last night. She chose it to match the navy pumps she had worn with yesterday's suit. Her goal was to look responsible, like an appropriate caretaker for a four-year-old boy, something Karen Parker could never do.

"I have a petition from Karen Parker Haney, maternal grandmother of Andres, to award temporary custody in anticipation of legal adoption. I have a counter-motion from the state of California to retain current placement in Los Angeles County with Lilian Kaklis. Are all the parties present?" He acknowledged Tom Greene and Parker's attorney, James Lafollette. "Let's get this show on the road."

Lafollette took the podium. "Your Honor, my client is here today seeking custody of her grandson, her only remaining connection to a daughter who was tragically killed last month."

"Excuse me, counselor. This is a placement hearing, not a custody hearing."

"Yes, of course, Your Honor. She has filed an adoption petition and requests the court grant her temporary custody to facilitate bonding with the child. The longer he remains in institutional foster care, rather than with his family, the more difficult it will be for him to adapt to his new home, particularly since the home in which he currently resides is a multi-million-dollar..."

Lily groaned inwardly as he put forward his list of absurdities. Nothing he might say could compare to Tom's arsenal—namely, that both of Karen Parker's children had been removed by the state.

"...his last remaining blood relative. For that reason..."

She shuddered at the words. This miserable excuse for a mother, as Anna had called her, would never get Andy in her clutches as long as Lily drew breath.

"What say you, Mr. Greene?"

Tom spread his notes on the lectern and pushed his hands into his pockets. "Your Honor, as the child's legal advocate, I wish to make two points. First, I'd like to address Mr. Lafollette's concerns regarding Andres Parker's current placement."

She liked Tom's relaxed demeanor. John said he was a regular in Judge Cruz's court, another fact that was on their side.

"Andy is presently living in a very safe and comfortable home, where he has his own bedroom. He is enrolled in preschool and is making new friends. According to the reports provided by his foster mother, Lilian Kaklis"—he pointed her out to the judge—"his appetite is good. He sleeps well and interacts appropriately with others. Best of all, Your Honor, his asthma, which was reported as a frequent problem by his previous foster mother, now seems to be under control."

"I'm sure Ms. Kaklis is doing a fine job, Mr. Greene, but it's usually the court's opinion that kids belong with their families. Why aren't we making that effort here?"

"That's my second point, Your Honor. The state of California has a file on Mrs. Haney. When she was Karen Parker, the state removed her older daughter from her care due to neglect, drug and alcohol abuse, and criminal activity, and subsequently severed parental rights. Eleven years later, after confirming neglect and continued drug use, the state removed her second child, Kristy Parker, Andres Parker's mother, and placed her in foster care. The state is convinced that Karen Parker Haney lacks parenting skills and cannot be entrusted with the care of another child. As Andy's advocate, I'm inclined to agree."

Judge Cruz rubbed his chin and turned back to Lafollette. "Got an answer for that?"

"We do, Your Honor." He was on his feet immediately and back at the podium. "Mrs. Haney admits that she was unprepared for motherhood years ago, that she fell in with the wrong crowd and took desperate actions to support an unfortunate lifestyle. But that is not the woman here today asking for her grandson. Mrs. Haney now holds a full-time job with retirement benefits at the Holiday Inn, and her husband works as a sanitation engineer for the City of Oakland, a job that includes family health insurance. They have lived at the same address for eight years and have ties to their community. If it pleases the court, she'd like to speak."

Lily could barely believe Karen Parker had the nerve to stand before the judge and proclaim herself a fit guardian for a child.

Karen meekly took her place behind the podium and waited while Lafollette lowered the small microphone that was mounted on the front. When she spoke, her voice was shaky and uncertain. "I'm ashamed of my past life, Judge. I have no excuse for being the horrible mother I was. I loved my girls…both of them. I just didn't know how to take care of them. If there's anything in my life I regret, it's how I let them down." Her lower lip quivered. "I can't change that, but I can tell you that I've turned my life around. I went after Kristy when I found out she was on the streets and I tried to get her to come home with me, but she wouldn't. I believe she ended up there because the foster care system failed her. I can't let that happen to Andres the way it happened to her. I know I don't deserve a chance with my grandson, but I've learned my lessons. Please give me this, Your Honor. You won't ever be sorry."

It was all Lily could do not to curse aloud and spit on the floor. Other than her admission that she had been a horrible mother, there wasn't a word of truth in anything Karen Parker had said.

Tom jumped to his feet again. "Respectfully, Your Honor, it is doubtful the state of California would ever approve Karen Parker as a foster parent. In fact, on Andy's behalf, I plan to challenge her adoption petition. Andres's placement with Ms. Kaklis is proving to be the best possible living arrangement, and in only two weeks, he is thriving more than has ever been documented."

Cruz folded his hands and looked down from his perch, pointing a finger at John. "You represent the state in this, right?"

John abruptly stood. "Yes, sir."

"How long do you plan to leave Andres in this setting?"

"We aren't certain, Your Honor."

He looked past Tom and made eye contact with Lily. "Ms. Kaklis, do you have any plans to adopt this boy?"

Lily gulped and looked desperately at John, knowing full well he couldn't save her from answering. "Not at this time, Your Honor."

He closed his folder, his decision apparently made. "Seems to me Andres Parker needs a home. I'd like the state to show me what it's doing to facilitate that, and I'm also ordering a full assessment of Mrs. Haney's home to determine its suitability as a permanent placement. And Mr. Moss"—he pointed a finger at John—"I expect an objective assessment."

"Your Honor, if I may?" Lafollette was on his feet. "We'd like to ask for the court's consideration on the matter of current placement as it relates to visitation. Given her work schedule and modest income, Mrs. Haney is unable to travel to Los Angeles in order to get to know her grandson. We ask that the state find a temporary placement here in the Bay Area."

Lily's stomach dropped as Cruz began to nod. "It does seem curious that this boy was placed in La-La Land. Why was that,

Mr. Moss?"

"I can answer that." She was shocked to find herself on her feet and speaking. "Andy is staying with us because I'm his aunt... Kristy Parker's sister." She could feel Karen Parker's eyes on her but she refused to meet her gaze. "I'm the first daughter, Lilian. I found out about Andy when Kristy was killed and I called Mr. Moss. When he said Karen Parker had petitioned for custody, I knew I couldn't let that happen."

The silence that followed lasted only a few seconds, but the air crackled with suspense.

"I see."

Lily could feel her face burning as she held her gaze firmly on the judge.

"And you're not seeking custody?"

"Not at present, but we are open to the possibility if Andy continues to adjust well."

He shocked her with a small smile. "I'd say that changes the playing field a bit. How long do you think it'll be before you know whether or not he's adjusted?"

"It's difficult to say."

"A month? A year?"

"I don't know, Your Honor. There are other factors, but I promise you that Andy's well-being is our top priority."

"Other factors." He nodded slowly. "Mrs. Haney is offering him a permanent home. Isn't that what you want for him?"

"Not with her. I want him to have better than that. Andy needs a home like the one I was lucky enough to find. When I was seven years old, I was adopted by a loving mother—someone who knew what being a good mother meant. If not for her, I might have ended up like Kristy. I promise to keep Andy safe and healthy until we can find him a home like that, whether it's with me or with somebody else, but not with Karen Parker. The only reason she wants him is so she and her lawyer can sue the city for—"

Judge Cruz cut her off with a slap of his gavel. "This court is concerned about the welfare of Andres Parker. Other matters belong in other courts."

Lily had spent enough time in front of a judge to recognize a scolding tone when she heard one. Judges rarely appreciated advice.

"All right, I'm not going to let this little boy blow in the wind while the state figures out what it wants to do with him. I want all of you back here on Friday morning. We're going to try this again with all the puzzle pieces. I expect to see a report on Mrs. Haney's home, and I want an answer from Ms. Kaklis about what she has in mind for this boy, and when." He slapped his gavel and exited to his chambers.

"Lily?" Karen's eyes were wide and her hand covered her open mouth. "I can't believe it's you."

Lily looked at her coldly and said, "Here's something you can believe. If you ever get custody of Andy Parker, it'll be over my dead body." She spun and stormed out of the courtroom, relaxing only when the elevator doors closed and sealed her escape.

Chapter 10

When Anna first saw it was Lily on the phone, she had hoped to hear that her plane had landed back in LA. Instead, she found herself suppressing a groan as she spun in her desk chair.

"I'm really sorry, Anna. Please don't be upset."

Upset wasn't the word Anna would use. More like over a barrel. "What is it you have to do tomorrow?"

"I'm going along with John to meet with the adoption agency. We need to go back into court on Friday and show that there are lots of better options than Karen Parker."

She was shocked to hear Lily mention the adoption agency. Though her agreement to do whatever was needed had been far from enthusiastic, she had expected Lily to forge ahead. Perhaps after thinking it over, Lily had realized for herself that Andy might be better off elsewhere. "And what about Thursday?"

"Tom asked me to work with him on making the case against placing him with Karen. I've done this kind of thing a million times. If I can get the court to appoint me as his actual guardian, even if it's temporary, Karen Parker will go away."

Anna was thoroughly confused about what Lily wanted. "I don't get it. What's the point of guardianship if Andy is in the pipeline for adoption?"

"It just gives me more leverage. And it sends Karen and her sleazebag lawyer a message that they might as well get lost." Her voice filled with contempt every time she mentioned Karen. "Can you handle three more days, Anna?"

"Sure." Anna looked at the clock. "I guess I'd better go pick him up."

She made arrangements to call back later in the evening and headed out. On the way to her parents' house, she phoned Martine and asked her to have Andy ready. As soon as she pulled through the gate, the front door opened and he appeared outside with her father.

"What are you doing at home, Dad? Don't you have a Volkswagen dealership to run?"

"Not when I get a better offer. Martine called me and said my playmate was here, so I packed it in and came home early."

Anna chuckled. She loved the way her father doted on Jonah, and she wasn't surprised to see him do the same with Andy. "Why do I get the feeling you missed out on having a son?"

"Nonsense. You've given me everything I ever wanted, even a daughter-in-law."

"Very funny." She opened the passenger door and held the seatbelt. "You ready to go, Andy?"

He started for the car, but turned when George called to him. Then he raced back for a fierce hug.

Anna felt a swell of jealousy. What was it about her that Andy didn't like? She had done everything she could think of to make him feel safe and cared for, but he hadn't shown her the tiniest bit of affection.

On the way home, she made small talk, asking him what he had done in preschool and what he had played with her father. His answers were short, almost sullen, a marked decline from the progress she thought they had made together last night in the tub. When his mood continued through dinner, she could stand it no longer.

"Andy, what's wrong?"

Her question caused his eyes to fill with tears.

"Are you upset because Lily didn't come home?"

He nodded.

Great, she thought. The one thing she couldn't do anything about. "Do you want to talk to her on the phone?"

All he managed was a shrug.

"She'll be home in a few days, Andy. We can have fun, you and me. Wouldn't that be all right?"

"But you said we'd go swimming when Lily came home."

Anna thought about their conversation the night before and realized the real reason he was disappointed. "We'll just have to go without her. Okay?" Her reward was his first smile of the day.

For thirty minutes she led Andy back and forth across the pool, finishing with a soak in the spa. He seemed to love the swirling water from the jets.

"This is like a bubble bath," he said.

"Not quite, because this one doesn't have any soap." She leaned over and turned off the jets, which caused the bubbles to die immediately. "See? If I turn off the jets, the bubbles go away. It's the soap that makes the bubbles stay."

He climbed out of the tub to look under the bush at the levers that controlled the heater and the jets. As he studied it, he began to shiver in the cool night air.

"Let's go inside, Andy. It's time for your real bath."

As they finished the ritual, the phone rang.

"Get your PJs on and pick out a book. I'll come right back." She took the call in the master bedroom. As expected, it was Lily. "We're running a little behind. I promised Andy we'd go swimming tonight, so we did that after we ate."

"What did you fix for dinner?"

"You don't want to know." Anna's lack of prowess in the kitchen was a running joke with everyone. "I had the good sense to pick up a pizza from Mulberry Street. Somebody loves pepperoni."

"Good choice."

Anna listened as Lily summarized her day in court. "Karen Parker's such a fake. I almost asked her how much she was going to sue for if she got Andy."

"I can't believe any judge in the country would even consider letting her adopt a child."

"But she's so sorry for everything, Anna," Lily said, her voice dripping with sarcasm. "She gave him this big snow job about how she tried to help Kristy, and she even blamed the foster care system for how Kristy turned out. And get this. She wants to be the one to keep Andy from a life like that."

"She said all that with a straight face?" Anna shook her head in disbelief as Lily told her of the judge's order to have Karen Parker's home evaluated just as theirs was before Andy was placed with them. "Is he serious?"

"I'm sure this judge wants to see Andy adopted. I think all the judges do, because otherwise these kids keep coming back into their courtroom. But I can tell he doesn't want it to be Karen. I think he wants it—"

"—to be us." Anna was surprised at how calmly she uttered the words.

"Yeah," Lily said quietly. "But I didn't say yes. I told him we were waiting to see how Andy adjusted."

Anna almost laughed. Andy wasn't the one they were waiting for. "Are we waiting?"

"Anna, you know I can't do this if you have doubts about it. You have to tell me how you really feel."

As her anxiety rose, Anna paced the bedroom. "Honestly?"

"Of course."

"It scares the shit out of me, Lily. I can hardly get Andy to talk to me. I want him to be happy as much as you do, but I don't think he's happy with me."

"That isn't true. He just hasn't gotten to know you as well because I've been there. I bet he likes you more since I left."

"I'm not so sure about that. I don't know what I did wrong,

but sometimes I think he's afraid of me."

"He's afraid of everything. You don't understand what it's like for kids like him. They get attached to people, and then the system yanks them out and drops them somewhere else. So they learn to hold back a little. It doesn't mean he won't learn to like you if he stays with us."

There was no mistaking Lily's plea. "If this is something you need, you know I'll support you."

"Anna, I would never force you into this. Andy's a person, not a stray puppy."

"You aren't forcing me. I'm making a choice. I'm being honest with you here, but you have to be honest with me too." She remembered Andy in the other room. "But not now. I need to go read Andy a story and get him to sleep. He's almost as hard to wake up in the morning as his aunt."

Lily laughed and Anna felt some of the tension dissipate. "I love you, Anna."

Anna already knew Lily wouldn't abandon Andy to his grandmother. Neither would she, though she realized that had more to do with her love for Lily than her concern for Andy. She could never live with herself if she denied Lily something and it caused her heartache. "We're married, Lily, and that's forever, no matter what. We'll do the right thing."

She returned to Andy's room to find him in bed with a book. Chester was curled up at his feet. "Do you like sleeping with Chester?"

He stretched out to pat the dog's head. "I like Chester."

"I'd say he likes you too." And Anna had to admit that Chester sleeping with someone besides her and Lily had a lot of appeal.

It was possible Anna was imagining things, but Andy seemed happier than usual this morning. She credited this breakthrough to the time she had spent with him in the pool, which had given them the chance to relax and enjoy each other. Maybe Lily was right about them bonding as they spent time together alone.

"I got some of that cereal you like," she said as they entered the kitchen, both of them dressed and ready for their day. "Do you want orange juice or apple juice?"

"Apple!" he sang.

"Boy, somebody's in a good mood this morning. What are you so—" Anna froze in her tracks as she turned, looking past the bay window to the stunning sight in the backyard. A mountain of white filled her view. "What the—" She slapped a hand over her mouth to keep the curse word inside.

She released the deadbolt at the top of the French door and walked onto the patio, the grinning four-year-old right behind her. She could hear the pump of the hot tub, and the wheels turned in her head as she distinctly recalled turning it off last night.

"Stay right here, Andy. Don't move." The thick cloud of bubbles passed her knees and made it impossible to see where she was stepping. She carefully navigated the wet mass in the direction of the hot tub, being careful not to get too close to the pool's edge. Never in her life had she seen such a mess. She would have to call the pool service to clean it up and find out what had caused it.

Fortunately, the hot tub controls were located beneath the bushes, which made them easy to locate. She groped for the on-off lever and turned it, effectively shutting down the bubble machine.

Standing slowly, she looked across the mass toward the house, where Andy still grinned with excitement. He probably thought it looked like a giant bubble bath, and he was right.

A sinking feeling swept over her when her foot struck something…something that sounded ominously like a plastic jug skidding across concrete. She followed the sound and picked up the reason for all this mess—an empty container of bubble bath. "Oh, my God."

Andy was practically jumping up and down with glee.

"Andy? Did you pour the bubble bath into the hot tub?"

He nodded, rubbing his palms together excitedly. "Now we can take a bath in the swimming pool."

At least that settled the question of why. Now to answer the how and the when. Someone was going to be punished…as soon as she figured out the best way to do it without losing the meager gains she had made in the past two days.

"Temper, temper," she said under her breath as she marched closer to where he waited.

Her scowl must have sent out a warning, as his face fell and his eyes grew wide with apparent fear.

Suddenly her foot slipped off the edge of the pool deck, and her ankle viciously scraped the side as she fell headlong into the deep end. It was dark beneath the surface, but she located the ladder and swam toward it. When she climbed out, a clearly terrified Andy spun and dashed back inside the house.

As she limped toward the house favoring her bleeding ankle, she caught her reflection in the full-length glass door. The suds clung to her pantsuit and hair. It might have been funny had it been someone else.

She entered the kitchen door and kicked off her wet shoes, two-hundred-dollar Italian pumps. "Andy!"

He had vanished.

Anna started up the stairs, not yet clear on what would happen when she found him. With every step she asked herself what Lily would do.

"Andy? Where are you?" Her first stop upstairs was in the master bath, where she shed her sopping wet clothes, put on her robe, and wrapped her hair in a towel. Next, she used a washcloth to stop the bleeding from her ankle scrape, but that worked only as long as she held it in place, and she needed to find Andy.

When she entered his room, she almost laughed at the sight. His foot was sticking out from under the bed, and Chester lay beside him, thumping his tail wildly at the hiding game. Anna took a seat on the opposite bed and pressed the washcloth to her ankle again.

"Andy, I can see you under the bed. Will you come out?"

She could hear the sniffles from his apparent crying, but he didn't emerge. Instead, his protruding foot disappeared inch by inch. Obviously, his young mind didn't process that she still knew where he was.

"Come on, Andy. We need to have a talk. I promise I won't get mad, sweetheart. Come on out."

His response was mostly incomprehensible as he crawled out from under the bed crying, but Anna distinctly heard the words "beat my butt."

"Andy, no one is going to beat your butt. We don't do that here. Now sit on your bed. We have to talk." From his show of tears, he was already sorry, so it would serve no purpose to belabor that point. "Bubble bath is for the bathtub, not for outside. Do you understand that?"

He nodded solemnly, seemingly bothered by the sight of her scraped ankle.

"When did you do that?"

"At night," he spoke so softly she could barely hear.

"When I was asleep?"

He shook his head. "When you were talking on the phone."

So he went back outside right after his bath. It's a wonder the pile wasn't higher than the house.

"Andy, how did you get outside? The door was locked up high. Did you climb up there and unlock it?" She knew he liked to climb on things.

Again, he shook his head. "Through Chester's hole."

Anna raised her hand to her face immediately to hide her sudden smile. This was serious business. No child should be out by the pool alone, ever.

"I'm a little upset with you right now." She needed to make her point, but not at the expense of breaking his heart. "Do you know why?"

"Because I put bubbles in the pool?"

"That was wrong, but you didn't know that, so it wasn't your fault. The reason I'm upset is because Lily and I told you that you were never to go out to the pool by yourself. Do you remember that?"

"But I didn't get in the water."

"That doesn't matter. We didn't say don't get in the water. We said don't go out to the pool alone. Isn't that right?"

"I guess so."

"And the reason we told you not to is because you're too little to be out there by yourself. What if you had an accident and fell in and there was nobody there to help you? Anybody can have an accident, Andy. I even had one today."

"I'm sorry."

"We don't want anything to happen to you because we care about you very much. We'd miss you if you weren't here, and we'd be very sad if you got hurt."

"Are you going to tell Lily?"

That Lily's reaction was his biggest concern shouldn't have surprised her, but it was disappointing nonetheless. "I have to tell her, Andy. It's pretty serious. She's going to be worried because something could have happened to you."

His lower lip jutted out.

"Now let's go get breakfast. You're going to be a little late for school today because I have to get dressed again."

He hung his head in shame as he walked behind her.

Anna couldn't let him worry all day. She squatted and caught both of his shoulders. "Andy, it'll be okay." She touched his cheek, hoping it would cheer him up. "I'm glad you didn't have an accident, and I hope you won't go out by the pool by yourself ever again."

He shook his head.

She smiled. "Good. That's all that matters." That, and getting a pool crew in to clean up the mess.

John Moss held the door for Lily as they exited the offices of St. Mary's Adoption Services. "What did you think?" he asked.

She shrugged. "I'm always a little concerned when families say they'll take a four-year-old, but they prefer an infant."

"There were a few who were looking for an older child."

"Right, but those are the ones who want a playmate for their other child. What happens if the kids don't get along? I think most people favor their biological children in those cases, and I wouldn't want Andy to feel like second-best."

"Face it, Lily. There's only one home that's right for Andy, and that's yours."

She tried to suppress a smile, but couldn't. "I think Anna might be coming around."

"Seriously?" They reached his car and he gallantly opened her door. "Will you tell the judge that on Friday?"

"If it comes to that, but I hope it doesn't...at least not on Friday."

"You're not making any sense. Why not just go ahead and put your cards on the table?"

Lily wasn't normally one to discuss personal things with people she barely knew, but she felt a kinship with John. "Let me put it this way. Suppose we found an adoptive family where the wife really wanted Andy, but the husband wasn't too keen on the idea. Let's say he was just going along with it to make his wife happy. I wouldn't want Andy in a home like that."

"Is that what Anna's doing?"

"I think that's where she is now. In her heart, she'd rather I found the right home for him somewhere else, but she's worried I'll hold it against her down the road for not really wanting him." As she put her worries into words, she remembered her promise to Anna to be honest about her wants, and vowed to have this very conversation with her later. "A part of me wants to take advantage of that, but I don't want her to look back on this later and resent me. If I can just buy Andy a little time, it'll give them a chance to bond."

"How are they doing this week?"

"I think the jury's still out on that. I had a message from her this morning that I wasn't going to believe what he'd done, that I'd laugh my tail off. That sounds like they're having fun."

"Yeah, it does." He pulled up in front of her hotel. "I know you know this already, but I think Judge Cruz would like nothing better than to place Andy with you and Anna. I just hope he doesn't feel like Karen Parker is his only choice."

"Believe me, if it comes to that, I'll speak up."

"I know, but he has to know you really mean it. If you wait until the last minute, he'll see through it."

He was right, she knew. It was risky saving this as a trump card to play only in case the judge seemed inclined to move Andy from their home. But she had to make sure Anna was really on board.

Anna settled into the rocking chair and pulled Andy onto her lap. She had skipped his bath tonight, opting instead to wash him quickly with a cloth so he could get into his pajamas and try to relax.

His coughing had started shortly after dinner as a mere tickle in his throat. It had worsened, however, as he played on the floor with his cars, to the point where he couldn't catch his breath.

"Does that feel better?" She rocked him slowly and brushed his bangs off his forehead. Lily said the rocking helped to soothe him and make him sleepy, especially with the lights off in the room. As a last resort, Anna could give him the medicine, but it had a stimulant effect, which would make it hard for him to fall asleep.

He leaned forward and coughed again. When he settled back against her chest, his fingers came to rest on her left hand, where he traced the strands of her woven wedding band. "It's like Lily's."

"Shhh…that's right. Try to go to sleep."

He stroked her ring for several more minutes before his hand went still.

Anna strained to hear if he was wheezing, but the rattle in his chest had gone. Ever so slowly, she cradled him in her arms and carried him to the bed, which was already turned down. He barely stirred as she laid him down and drew the covers to his chest.

Chester jumped onto the foot of the bed and curled up in his new spot.

She waited at the bedside to make sure Andy was down for

the night, and after several minutes had passed, she tiptoed out. Having him get sick had been her worst fear, but at least Andy had responded to her when it counted, allowing her to comfort him. That didn't mean she wasn't ready for Lily to come home and take over.

She fell into the chair in her bedroom and kicked off her shoes. Lily was expecting her call, but Anna needed to collect her thoughts first so they could finish the conversation they had started last night. Was she willing to take on the responsibility of raising a child? She had said the idea terrified her, but helping Andy through his asthma attack had given her confidence a much-needed boost.

So if she took that issue off the table—because she could learn to be a good mother—the other issues were less intimidating. Sure, she was worried it would disrupt their lives, that having Andy around would take away their privacy and the freedom to do things at the drop of a hat. But it didn't have to mean they would never be alone again, and she and Lily could find ways to adapt.

Her other concern was that she would feel left out of the bond Lily and Andy might create with one another, but that didn't have to happen either, not if she made the effort to stay involved. It was the pinnacle of immaturity to be jealous of a four-year-old.

The bottom line was that all of her doubts added together were small when compared to Lily's need to have Andy in her life. Given all that Lily had lost and all she had overcome, she deserved to have this. Anna wouldn't be able to live with herself if she told her no.

She rang Lily and gathered her nerve to make the second biggest decision of her life, next to asking Lily to marry her. "Hey, baby."

Lily gazed out at the city from Tom Greene's ninth-floor office on Hyde Street. "I really appreciate the workspace."

"No problem," he said, looking up from his desk. "You and

your spouse just saved me about two days of work."

"That remains to be seen. I never dreamed in a million years Karen Parker's home would have passed a county assessment."

"Me neither, but her lawyer probably helped her get things in order."

She had spent the morning drawing up the petition for adoption. Anna had faxed her signature on the preliminary forms after calling last night to say she was willing to raise Andy as their son. She said she understood the stakes, and that nothing mattered more than giving Andy the same chance Lily had gotten with Eleanor Stewart.

In a perfect world, agreeing to raise a family would have been a joyous proclamation. Instead, Anna's had been a solemn resolve, typical of when she turned things over in her head and reached what she thought was the right conclusion. It wasn't exactly what Lily had hoped for, but it would have to do.

She had barely slept the night before, toggling between excitement about Andy and guilt about taking advantage of Anna's kindness. Anna had given so much during their few short years together, and had asked for so little in return. It wasn't fair to put this on her, but Lily had no choice. It wasn't just about keeping him from Karen Parker. It was about Andy, and the gaping hole she would feel if she lost him.

She scooped up her papers and placed them in her briefcase. "I guess I'll go file these at the courthouse."

"I can have one of our paralegals do that if you want."

"No, that's okay." Lily had another errand in mind, something that had been in the back of her mind ever since learning about her sister.

Outside, she cinched her raincoat against the mist and opened her umbrella. The folks at Nordstrom knew her name by now, after outfitting her with three suits and accessories, a pair of shoes, a raincoat, and assorted lingerie.

Lily walked two blocks to the courthouse and submitted her filings to the Unified Family Court so Judge Cruz would have an opportunity to review them before they reconvened the next day.

Then she walked into the Clerk of Court's office and filled out an information request.

After a ten-minute wait, the clerk returned with an envelope. "Here you are. This is that woman that was killed by the police, isn't it?"

Lily nodded and took the document, Kristy's death certificate, and stowed it in her briefcase. Only when she reached the shelter of the deserted bus stop bench did she dare open it. A wave of sadness passed over her as she realized this was all she would know of her sister.

Like Lily, Kristy had been born in Oakland, her father unknown. Last known address was a shelter in the Tenderloin District. Cause of death: GSW…gunshot wound. Lily shuddered at the brutality. As if getting by on the streets wasn't difficult enough. No wonder the homeless advocates were outraged. The online newspaper stories said the bank robber had grabbed her as she fished through a garbage can near the bank's entrance. When he brandished a gun, police opened fire, killing both Kristy and the robber. A miserable life…and a tragic death.

In the lower left-hand corner was the name of the mortuary that had handled her burial in an Oakland cemetery. Why, if Kristy was indigent, would she have been buried? Homeless people were cremated, unless—of course. James Lafollette had probably arranged for his "grieving" client to claim her daughter's body for a proper burial. It made their case against the city stronger.

Anna hung up the phone and grumbled as she grabbed her car keys from her desk. Her mother had called to say she had broken a crown and needed to make an emergency trip to the dentist. That meant Anna had to pick up Andy from his preschool and bring him back to the dealership for the afternoon. She was scheduled to meet with Premier's vice president for human resources, who was driving up from the office in Palm Springs. It was too late to postpone, as she was due there in less than an hour.

"I'll be back in a few minutes," she told Carmen, their

receptionist.

Andy was clearly surprised to see her at the door of his preschool. In fact, he didn't look particularly happy about it.

"You have to come with me today, Andy. Martine had to go somewhere, so we're going to spend the rest of the day at my office." She took his hand and led him out to her Z8, which had the booster seat on the passenger side. "You want a cheeseburger for lunch?"

His face lit up. "And french fries."

She smiled and shook her head. It was almost scary how much he was like Lily. She pulled into the drive-thru lane of the In-N-Out Burger on Wilshire Boulevard. "What do you want to drink?"

"A chocolate milkshake."

Lily had definitely trained him well. She ordered his combo and a grilled cheese sandwich for herself, and pulled to the window. She already felt sorry for Andy, who was in for a long, boring afternoon. Maybe this treat would make up for it.

"Here's our lunch." She put the bag of sandwiches and fries on the floor beneath his feet. "Should I put your milkshake in the cup holder, or can you hold it?"

"I can hold it," he said happily, licking his lips in anticipation.

"Okay, but use both hands and be very careful." The last thing she wanted was a sticky milkshake all over her classic car. Fortunately, it was only a few blocks to the dealership.

She eased into traffic, watching Andy from the corner of her eye. He was gripping the shake tightly, but leaning toward the cup holder as if he had changed his mind about holding it.

"Wait, Andy. Let me—"

"Uh-oh!"

It was too late to stop the disaster. The drink tipped from his hands, sending frozen chocolate goo all over the console and between the seats. It covered the leather-encased gearshift and for good measure splattered the instrument panel for the sound system.

"Uh-oh is right." A four-year-old holding a milkshake in a hundred-thousand-dollar sports car. How stupid could she have been? "Andy, I asked you to be careful."

He suddenly burst into tears.

"Don't cry! It was an accident." Showing her annoyance would only make matters worse, especially if it led to an asthma attack.

He calmed, but it was clear he was upset.

Bypassing her parking space near the side door, she drove around to the back where Javier and Rudy detailed the cars Premier took in on trade. "Hi, guys. I have a little emergency here. I need this cleaned before it stains."

"We'll get right on it."

She helped Andy out of his seatbelt and handed him the small bag with their lunch. They entered the office through the back door and stopped at the vending machines. "I'll get you a soda for now, Andy. You can have another milkshake later, okay?"

He had stopped crying, but he was far from happy about the turn his day had taken.

She led him into the conference room, where the others had assembled for their meeting. "Sorry I'm late."

"Hi, Andy. I didn't know you were going to be in this meeting too," Hal said. "I should have brought Jonah for you to play with."

Andy smiled shyly, apparently glad to see a familiar, friendly face.

"Mom had to run to the dentist this afternoon, so Andy's going to hang out here and help us with these benefits questions." Anna situated him in a chair at the far end of the conference table and spread out his lunch. "Shall we get started?"

An hour into their meeting, she noticed Andy opposite her, clearly bored. He had finished his lunch, and had absolutely nothing to do but listen to their discussion on health coverage and hiring policies.

"Will you excuse me for a minute?" She tossed the trash in the can by the door and held out her hand to him. "Come on.

Let's see if we can find something fun for you to do."

They walked down the stairs to the media room, where the two sales DVDs she had purchased played in an endless loop. "You want to watch some movies about cars?" She knew the videos that touted the BMW features were a pitiful alternative to the talking dog cartoon her mother said he liked to watch in the afternoon, but they had to be better than spreadsheets and numbers. "You can watch these and learn all about cars while I finish my meeting. Then we'll stop and get another milkshake on the way home, okay?"

"Okay." Andy settled against the back of the leather couch, his eyes already riveted to the screen.

"As its sleek, progressive design suggests, the new 760Li is a marvel of engineering. Inside, the cockpit invites you to sample the exhilaration of an advanced six-liter, four-thirty-eight horsepower..."

Anna paused at the receptionist's desk. "I know I shouldn't be asking you this, and I promise never to do it again."

Carmen waved a hand at her. "I'll watch him. He'll probably go to sleep."

"Thanks."

The meeting dragged on, but Anna made time to slip downstairs twice to check on Andy. Both times, he was paying close attention to the demonstration films. If anyone could relate to his utter fascination with cars, it was she.

"Wait here, please," Lily said to the limo driver. She had learned the limo trick from Anna—that private cars were almost as cheap as taxis on long trips in heavy traffic, and infinitely more comfortable. The trip across the Bay Bridge to the cemetery had taken almost an hour.

Hillview Cemetery was no Forest Lawn, but it was reasonably well-kept. The markers were flat granite, which made it easier for the mowers, and gave the place a uniform look.

Inside the paneled office, a young man sat behind a desk. Barely old enough to shave, he was dressed in a pressed white shirt with black slacks and a thin striped tie. Lily would have bet money Hillview was a family business, and this was the heir.

"Good afternoon. I wonder if you can help me find a gravesite. I'm looking for Kristy Parker. She died about six weeks ago."

He nodded vigorously. "Yes, Kristy Parker. Are you family?"

"I'm her sister."

He turned to an ancient file cabinet in the corner and pulled out a folder. "Hmm."

She noted his serious look as he flipped through the pages. How complicated could it be to point her to a plot?

"You wouldn't by any chance"—he rubbed his chin—"be here to make a payment?"

"Excuse me?"

He set the folder down and danced nervously from one foot to the other. "This is really awkward. The woman who contracted with us—a Karen Haney—made a down payment and financed the remainder. But according to our records, she missed her first payment last week."

Of course she did, Lily thought. Karen Parker only knew one way to get by, and that was to scam people. "And what happens if she fails to pay?"

"Unfortunately, we'd have no choice but to exhume the body and arrange for cremation. The vault could be—"

"How much does she owe?" Lily didn't need to know about the cemetery's recycling program, and she wouldn't have her sister's final indignity be being dug up for payment due.

"Uh…it says here she paid half, so that leaves five thousand two hundred. She was supposed to make payments of three hundred dollars a month."

Lily handed over her credit card. "Put the balance on this."

He seemed ecstatic to get the money, and when the paperwork was finished, he escorted her to a gravesite in the corner of the cemetery, near the gardener's shed. Already, the rectangular patch of sod showed signs of taking root in the uneven earth. Several of the nearby markers were concrete tiles, probably the least expensive option.

"I want a permanent marker, a nice granite one with her name and all the dates."

He left to draw up the order, which she promised to pay for on her way out.

Lily turned back to the gravesite and drew a deep breath. "I wish I could have known you, Kristy. My mom and I would have helped you climb out of that life Karen Parker left for us. You would have been my little sister." Her throat hurt as she suppressed her tears. "I want you to know that I have Andy. He's precious, and I promise you I'll love him like my own. He's going to grow up and go to college. Maybe he'll even be a lawyer like me."

The gravel crushed behind her as the limo pulled closer.

"I'm sorry you had such a hard life, but you can rest now. I won't let Andy forget you."

"Tell Lily goodnight," Anna said, holding out her hand for the phone. Then she nudged him off to his room.

Andy was already bathed and ready for bed. He had missed his nap this afternoon, and was barely able to hold up his head.

"He sounds beat," Lily said.

"Yeah, we both are. It was a long day." She held back the news about Andy's asthma attack the night before so Lily wouldn't worry. "I'm going to read him a story and go on to bed a little early tonight."

"I'll call you tomorrow after the hearing."

"Better yet, call me from LAX and tell me you're home." Anna returned the phone to its cradle and went back into Andy's room. "You want a story tonight or do you just want to go to sleep?"

He answered by plucking a book from the shelf.

"Okay, come get in bed." Anna scooted in beside him and propped up on his pillow.

Andy sidled up next to her so he could see the pictures. The story began in a small village, where a little boy...

She had no idea how long she had been asleep. All she knew

was that her neck was stiff and sore from the way it had slumped against the headboard. The bedside light was on, and the book had dropped to the floor. Andy was still cuddled into her side, with his arm wrapped snugly around her stomach. Her leg was wet.

Without moving, she looked down at the sleeping child. Whatever reservations he had about her disappeared in slumber. Only then could he reach out to her the way he did to Lily. Only then did he feel close enough to hug her.

She studied the soft lines of his face and wondered if her own face showed the peace she felt by having him snuggle close. This was it, the magic she had longed to feel.

It was never really Andy who had kept his distance, she realized. It was her. All this time, she had held him at arm's length, afraid to trust that he needed her too, every bit as much as he needed Lily. Looking now at the way he clung to her in his sleep, she knew for certain she wanted this feeling to last, not just for a few weeks, but for the rest of her life.

With a gentle shake, she called to him. "Andy. Sweetheart, wake up."

Groggily, he raised his head.

"We need to get cleaned up, okay?"

His eyes grew wider as he realized what he had done.

"Come on, honey." She went to his drawer and grabbed a fresh pair of pajamas. In the bathroom, she wet a washcloth and spread the soap.

Andy hesitantly joined her and peeled off his wet things. "I'm sorry, Anna."

"It's okay." She tried to keep her voice cheerful. "We'll get it all fixed up and you can go back to sleep."

"Lily says I can't help it."

"She's right." She rolled her neck to ease the kink and handed him the washcloth so he could finish cleaning himself. "I need to change your bed."

He came out of the bathroom a few minutes later in fresh pajamas, though his buttons were askew.

"Come here and let me fix your shirt. You almost got it all by yourself. That's because you're such a smart boy." She adjusted the buttons and helped him back into bed. "Do you want me to sit here until you go to sleep?"

He nodded.

She smoothed his soft hair. "Andy, when I woke up, you had your arm around me. You were giving me a big hug. That was very sweet, and it made me feel good." So did his smile, which she could see clearly from the light that streamed into the room from the hallway. "I like it when we hug."

His reply was so quiet, she almost didn't hear it. "George says I'm a good hugger."

"I bet he's right, but you know what? I don't think I've ever had a hug from you when you were awake."

"I can hug you now."

"I'd really like that, and I'll be a good hugger too."

He got up on his knees and threw his arms around her neck.

It was the sweetest sensation she had ever felt, and she squeezed him tightly. "I love you, Andy. I'm so glad you came to live with us."

Chapter 11

Lily kept to herself in the corner of the hallway as they waited for the bailiff to call them into the courtroom. She was kicking herself for not realizing that the outlet on her desk lamp worked only when the light was on. Consequently, her phone had failed to charge overnight and she had no way of checking in with her office or Anna.

She could hardly wait for Judge Cruz's reaction to her pending adoption filing. The official papers would be filed Monday morning after she and Anna met with Walter Kaplan, the Kaklis family's longtime attorney. But the affidavit she submitted yesterday served notice of her intent, which would make it easier for Judge Cruz to rule against Karen Parker.

Mostly, she wanted to see the look on Karen's face as she came to grips with her crumbling case of negligent homicide against the City of San Francisco. Lily had no doubt that the multi-million-dollar settlement was all that mattered to Karen and Lafollette, and it gave her special satisfaction to know they were out thousands of dollars in time and expenses. Karen would fold her tent and go back to work in her seedy dive, and Lafollette would find another victim to exploit.

The bailiff called their group to the courtroom, where they waited for the judge to appear. From the corner of her eye, Lily could see Karen stealing glances her way. It must have come as quite a shock to learn that the daughter she had neglected and abused had returned for the ultimate payback.

After twenty minutes, Judge Cruz entered and took his seat on the bench. He was juggling several folders, most likely motions from Lafollette, her filings and John's assessment. "I see you've all had a busy week."

Lily smiled to see him nod in what appeared to be satisfaction as he paged through the documents. Then her stomach dropped as he suddenly frowned and looked directly at her before returning to his papers.

"Let me just run down this list. I have a certification from Mr. Moss that the Haney home is in compliance with state foster care standards. I'm assuming Mr. Lafollette won't contest that, so we'll enter that into the record." He handed the filing to the clerk. "I have a request from Mr. Greene that Lilian Kaklis be designated Andres Parker's legal guardian until his adoption is resolved. I'd like to table that."

Lily shifted uncomfortably on the wooden bench.

"I have an affidavit from Ms. Kaklis that she intends to file a formal petition for adoption on Monday. We'll talk about that later too. I'd first like to address a motion from Mr. Lafollette calling into question the fitness of Ms. Kaklis to serve as either a guardian or foster parent. Mr. Lafollette?"

The attorney handed Tom a copy of his filing and took the podium. "Thank you, Your Honor. As you can see from our filing, we have several concerns. First, we'd like the court to consider the nature of the relationship between the two women in the household where Andres currently—"

"Don't even go there, Mr. Lafollette," Cruz said sharply.

Lily breathed an inward sigh of relief, though letting such an objection slide would have given them automatic grounds to appeal.

"Very well," Lafollette said, clearly chastened. "However, we'd like to make another point about the Kaklis household, that both adults in the home work full-time, which would mean Andres will require some sort of daycare, either in a program or under a babysitter. Mr. and Mrs. Haney, on the other hand, work opposing shifts, such that Andres will be in the constant care of a parent figure. If it pleases the court, we would like to submit these scientific studies into evidence, all supporting the benefits of parental care versus care for hire."

The bailiff collected the packets and distributed them to Tom and the judge.

"Along these same lines, we ask the court not to assign undue weight to the fact that the Kaklis family enjoys a life of financial privilege far above that of the average California family. Wealth is not a prerequisite for biological parenthood. Nor should it be required for adoption."

That wasn't much of an argument. Tom would counter it with the likelihood that Andy would follow their lead and go to college in order to pursue a rewarding career.

"Also, Your Honor, as you can see from our motion, we discovered some rather distressing news about Ms. Kaklis, a recent conviction for drunk driving. In light of the state's objections to my client based on her status over twenty years ago, I should think the court would be wary of placing a small child in a home where the likelihood he will be in harm's way is high."

John turned slightly to give Lily a small wink, though his assurance meant nothing if this sort of thing was a deal-breaker for Judge Cruz. Some judges—especially those like Cruz who were elected to the bench—were notoriously tough on drunk drivers. If his stern expression was any indication, this revelation could be trouble.

"Is there more, Mr. Lafollette?"

"Not at this time."

"Very well. Mr. Greene?"

Tom approached the podium. "Your Honor, studies about

child-rearing have shown many things, that working parents, same-sex couples and families of all economic strata are capable of producing responsible, well-adjusted young adults who can make meaningful contributions to society."

He went on to cite six different reports—all of which Lily knew by heart, because she used them too in her work—and promised to deliver copies to the court.

Judge Cruz held up his hand to stop the recitation. "Let me just apologize for not saying this earlier to Mr. Lafollette. I've been a Family Court judge for fourteen years, and I know this research as well as anybody. We're here today to talk about one child, Andres Parker. I'm satisfied that both families meet the threshold for adoption in the generic sense, but the specifics are still in doubt. I'd like to hear from Ms. Kaklis about her adoption petition, as well as this drunk-driving conviction."

Tom yielded the floor and Lily stepped up, reminding herself she was a witness here and not an attorney. It wouldn't do to take an advocacy position, no matter how much she wanted to talk about what a terrible mother Karen Parker had been. It was more important for her to convince the judge that their home was right for Andy, and her alcohol troubles were behind her.

"You had a very quick change of heart on this adoption matter, Ms. Kaklis. Are you certain you've thought this out?"

"Yes, Your Honor. I wanted very much to speak up on Tuesday when you asked me if we had plans to adopt. But I had to give my spouse a few more days to sort out her feelings. As you can imagine, it's a very big step, but we're both committed to it."

"So your spouse"—he checked his notes—"Christianna Kaklis, is in full agreement with you?"

"Yes, she is. She's caring for him this week at our home in LA." Where he filled their backyard with soapsuds and spilled a milkshake in her hundred-thousand-dollar sports car. "I'd also like to add that I've recently arranged to work part-time so that I can pick up Andy from preschool and spend afternoons with him."

"What sort of work do you do, Ms. Kaklis?"

"I'm an attorney for a legal aid clinic. I handle a lot of adoption and foster care cases, and I've served over a hundred times as a guardian *ad litem* for children in the system. I chose that kind of work because I knew firsthand the consequences of poor parenting." If that sounded like a testimonial on Karen Parker's mothering skills, it was.

"So what can you tell me about this DUI?"

Lily saw another opening to drive her point home. "It was a mistake on my part, Your Honor. I had recently lost my mother—and by mother, I mean Eleanor Stewart, the woman who adopted me and helped me become the person I am. In my grief, I was drinking more than I should have. I completed a residential treatment program, and I haven't had a drink in over two years."

He nodded slightly and looked toward Lafollette. "Do you have more?"

"Yes, sir. I would like to point out that, unlike the Kaklises, my client has been interested in the welfare of Andres ever since he was born. Lilian Kaklis's sudden appearance in this picture seems more about her capricious need to punish her mother than a genuine interest in this child's welfare."

Tom Greene leapt from his seat. "Objection, Your Honor. Ms. Kaklis has testified that her mother is deceased."

"Sustained."

Lafollette continued, "The one thing we haven't been able to measure in this courtroom is the capacity of Karen Parker Haney to love her grandchild. If you hold her up in comparison to her daughter—"

"Objection."

"Sustained."

"My point, Your Honor, is that if you compare the Haneys to the Kaklises, it's obvious who has the biggest house, the finest clothes and the newest cars. But we're not a society that allows wealthy people to buy children just by virtue of being able to provide them with the finer things. The Haneys are hard-working, middle-class people who will share their traditional American values with Andres, and raise him in the heritage to which he was born. We can't stand here in this courtroom and conclude that lawyers and car dealers make better parents than waitresses and trash collectors, or that every child must have a backyard swimming pool and go to private school. What we can say is that children belong with people who can give them love. My client has turned her life around, and she deserves to be rewarded for that. All she asks is that she be given the chance to make up for her past by raising her grandson right."

Lily couldn't believe he had the nerve to say such a thing, or that Judge Cruz was buying this middle-class shtick even for an instant. Andy was nothing more than a gravy train to them, their ticket to a windfall.

Tom Greene returned to the microphone to rebut. "Your Honor, as Andy's guardian *ad litem*, I'd like to see him placed permanently with his aunt, Lilian Kaklis, and her spouse, Anna Kaklis. That's also the recommendation of the state of California, represented here by Mr. Moss. While it may, in fact, be true that Mrs. Haney has turned her life around—Mr. Lafollette's words, not ours—Mrs. Haney has not demonstrated the skills necessary to care for and raise a child. Even in the short time Andy has lived with the Kaklises, he has thrived. He is—"

Judge Cruz slapped his gavel gently. "That's enough, I think. If the parties agree, I'd like to skip over all these other motions about temporary placements and emergency injunctions. We need to place this boy once and for all and quit yanking him around. I'd like to see all of you back here on Monday. Ms. Kaklis, if you want to be considered in these adoption proceedings, you'd best be certain your papers are in order. I want to see"—he peered through his reading glasses at the forms—"Christianna Kaklis and Charles Haney here as well. And I'd like to have a chat with Andres. Does anyone have a problem with that?"

Lily's heart sank. In any other court, this would have been a slam-dunk. Why on earth was he even considering Karen's bogus request? Was it actually possible that he believed her song and dance?

"...a county-wide campaign backed by the Chamber that would reduce the tax ratio for small businesses. If you elect me vice president, I'll make this my top priority."

Anna listened in admiration to Jose Peña's well-crafted appeal, aimed right at the wallets of the majority of members. She could only hope they were progressive enough to see that her priorities made more sense for the long term.

Geri Morgan, a close ally of incoming president Dave Cahill, took the podium to place Anna's name in nomination. As was customary, Geri ran down her business résumé, including her experience as the Chamber's treasurer and her committee work on behalf of the underprivileged community.

As she listened to Geri's introduction, she recalled the day she realized the importance of the Chamber taking a more active role in making the LA area a better place to work and live. It was the day of the earthquake, and the day she had met Lily. How far she had come since then, not only in her life but also in her outlook. First, she had gotten her "baptism by fire" on an outing with Kidz Kamp, and then followed that up by signing Premier Motors on as its primary sponsor. Over the next two years, she steered most of the dealership's charitable giving away from the arts and into area youth programs, the ones Lily said got the best results. And in her recent stint as chair of the Chamber's community development committee, she launched a program of job partnerships in low-income neighborhoods. Her business philosophy had been completely transformed, and she was ready to spell that out.

The room erupted in polite applause when her name was announced, and she stepped up to the podium, leaving behind her neatly typed speech. She didn't need it to make her point. The principles were as much a part of her as her accomplishments.

"Thank you, Geri. And thank you, Jose, for outlining your goals. I found them compelling, and I can certainly understand why many of the members would be inclined to support your candidacy." She joined the audience in a brief round of applause. "But while I understand the need for a tax break for small businesses, I also think it's a small piece of a larger mosaic. The bigger picture is that of the social and economic landscape of the whole community, which will have an enormous and lasting effect on our success and our quality of life. A tax break would have an immediate impact, but we need to look ahead, to what we want our businesses to look like five years from now, ten years, even twenty."

Heads bobbed in agreement around the huge ballroom.

"My goal will be to leverage our strength and resources to cultivate more customers, grow the tax base and secure a better-trained workforce." She methodically outlined how the Chamber could make a difference in the everyday lives of Los Angelinos by taking an active role in the community, especially with youth. Her voice rose with passion and resolve as she shared her hopes for her term as vice president, and in the following term, as president.

It was only when Geri tapped her watch that Anna realized she had been speaking for nearly twenty minutes.

"And finally, if you elect me your vice president, I promise not to talk this long ever again."

Laughter and dubious applause were her reward.

As she passed the exit for Endicott Avenue on her way to the dealership, Anna was reminded again of that fateful day almost five years ago, when she had detoured from a Chamber meeting in search of a book. She smiled to think how a last-minute change in plans had changed her life forever.

It had taken her a few days to realize it, but Andy would change her life too, and in much the way Lily had—it would be richer, sweeter and filled with love.

By her watch, Martine had already picked him up at his preschool, but that didn't mean she couldn't change her plans for the afternoon. She hurried back to her office to dispense with the stack of papers in her inbox. Then she darted home to ditch her suit in favor of jeans and sneakers. It was nearly four when she headed for the Big House.

Alerted by the gate opening, Martine met her at front door.

"What are you doing here so early?"

"I came to pick up Andy. I thought we'd spend a little time together."

"Is Lily back?"

"Not yet, but if she doesn't come home tonight, we're going to go up and get her." She followed her mother through the house to the den, where Andy sat on the floor in front of the television. "Hey, pal."

Andy whipped his head around in obvious surprise.

Taking a cue from her father, she had asked for and received a farewell hug when she left him at the school this morning. Now she signaled for another by dropping to one knee and holding out her arms.

He raced over to give her a hug.

"You want to go have some fun?"

His eyes grew big and he nodded. "Can we go swimming?"

"I think we still have a soapy pool. I have something else in mind." She helped him with his jacket and picked up his Z8. "Tell Martine bye, and you'll see her later."

"Bye. I'll see you later," he repeated. Then he gave her a hug and followed Anna outside. The top was already down on the Z8 and he let himself in to his seat and waited while she buckled the seatbelt.

"Have you ever been on a Ferris wheel?"

He looked at her in confusion.

"A merry-go-round?"

He shook his head.

The words in their abbreviated conversation were like any they had shared since Andy had come to live with them. The difference today was in attitude, both hers and his. They smiled. They touched. They trusted each other.

Lily huddled outside the courthouse with John and Tom. "Is he seriously buying all her bullshit?"

John seemed just as stumped as she. "I don't think I've ever gone into court with two more different placement options and had the judge drag his feet."

"It's the lawsuit," Tom said. "Cruz needs to get it right, because Lafollette will almost certainly appeal. If he rules in your favor, they're going to argue that he was in cahoots with the city in trying to steer off a multi-million-dollar settlement."

Lily seethed with frustration. "What happened to Kristy was wrong, and someone in the police department should be held accountable for it. But Karen Parker doesn't deserve to be a millionaire just for being such a bad mother that her kid ended up homeless."

Tom nodded. "I feel like Cruz wants to come down on our side. But we need to make our case as strong as it can be and give him some cover."

"Are you absolutely certain Anna's going to be convincing?" John asked.

"Not as certain as I'd like to be," Lily conceded. "She wants to do the right thing, but I'm pretty sure she's doing this for me, not Andy."

"Let's hope the judge doesn't see through that on Monday."

"I'll talk with her about it this weekend and make sure she knows what's at stake." Lily had no doubts Anna would come through for her in the clutch, but if Tom was right about the lawsuit, there wasn't much margin for error.

John dropped her at her hotel where she collected her bag and hailed a cab for the airport. It would be good to get back home. By this time tomorrow, for better or worse, she and Anna would be filing for adoption.

Anna took Andy's hand on their walk through the sparse parking lot at the Santa Monica Pier, making a mental note that Friday afternoon was a perfect time to beat the crowd. It was already apparent he was fascinated by the sights—the beach, the kites, the seagulls, and most of all, the giant Ferris wheel that towered in the distance.

She vaguely recalled the last time she had been here, about seven years ago when her college friend, Liz, had visited LA with her husband and their five-year-old daughter. It was a kid's paradise, not as grand as Disneyland, but fun and exciting just the same. Best of all, it was convenient and situated right on the ocean, where they would see a gorgeous sunset in about an hour.

As they crossed the street to the stairs, strains of organ music filtered down from the pier above. "So you never rode a merry-go-round, huh?" She stopped at the ticket booth and purchased two unlimited day passes, which they wore in the form of blue wristbands.

It was difficult to tell if Andy was more excited or intimidated by the boisterous, bobbing carousel. He clung to her hand as they climbed aboard, and with Anna's guidance, selected a black stallion that pranced up and down as they circled.

Anna stood by him at first, but after securing the leather safety strap around his waist, she stepped away to watch him. He was the picture of delight, his face fixed in a grin and his eyes taking in everything around him. She had no doubt he would stay there all day, but if her memory served her correctly, there were better things to come. "Let's go see what else is here. We can come back later if you want to."

Next stop was the arcade. Just as she expected, Andy was drawn immediately to the racecar simulators, most of which were too complicated for a four-year-old, but that didn't stop him from giving it a try. "I'm driving!"

"You sure are," she said as his simulator sailed over a cliff. "Let's go play Skee Ball."

He followed her to an alcove that held a row of ramps, where the object was to roll a ball up the incline and into a circle. She held his sweatshirt as he got the hang of things, and it seemed to work best when she helped him swing his arm with just the right force. Even with their teamwork, she fed almost five dollars worth of tokens into the machine until he scored enough points to win a stuffed baseball worth about fifty cents.

"Let me hold that for you. I think you're going to like what's back here." She led him out the back archway to the area called

Kids Cove, which boasted several rides for children Andy's size. Their first stop was the Red Baron, a circling plane ride. From there, he tried out the L'il Scrambler, the Crazy Submarine and his favorite by far, the Pier Patrol, a small truck that ran along a track.

"I'm driving!" he yelled each time he circled the track.

Anna waved and laughed at his obvious delight. She doubted he had ever had this much fun in his life, but if she had her way, today was just the beginning. She and Lily were going to show him the whole world. How on earth could she have been jealous when all she had to do was ask for his love?

"I want to do that one again," he said as he exited the truck ride.

"We can come back if you want to, but I bet there's another ride you're going to like even better."

He reached for her hand without any prompting and her heart nearly melted. Kim had been right about the feelings. Ever since last night when she woke to find his arm around her, things between her and Andy had been nothing short of magical. It wasn't only because she enjoyed being with him, but because that happiness clearly ran both ways. Her jealousy had been silly. If he wanted Lily to tend to his skinned knees, that was okay. What mattered was that he knew he could count on her too.

"Look, Andy. It's a car you can really drive."

He watched in amazement as a boy and a girl rammed one another in bumper cars made just for children his size.

The operator who was running the ride shut it down and told the children in the cars to stay put. "You want to drive one?" he asked Andy.

Anna couldn't have held onto him if she had tried.

He raced immediately to the small blue car, where the operator strapped him in and showed him the pedals that made the car go forward and back. He squealed with utter joy as the car lurched forward. Content just to drive in circles around the track, he didn't concern himself at all with the other children, who were ramming one another repeatedly.

Anna wished she had remembered her camera. She did the next best thing and took a photo with her cell phone, and promptly sent it to Lily. It was curious that she hadn't heard from Lily all day, but at least she was due home tonight.

A half hour passed before Andy tired of the bumper cars. The sun was gone and a chilly breeze came in off the ocean.

"Let's put your sweatshirt back on." She squatted and helped him into it, playfully pinching his nose when his head appeared through the hole. "How about some ice cream?"

"Chocolate."

"Of course." Definitely Lily's nephew.

They sat on a bench at the pier with their cones and watched the growing crowd mill around. The colorful lights of all the rides were enchanting against the night sky, but none more than those on the giant Ferris wheel. "Will you ride that with me, Andy?"

"It goes high."

"I know. But if you sit on my lap, I'll hold on to you. We can see everything from up there." She wiped his chin, hands and sweatshirt with a napkin. "Or we can go home and wait for Lily if you're ready to leave."

He pointed to the Ferris wheel. "I want to ride that."

She chuckled, recognizing his decision as an attempt to stay and play longer. Since she hadn't heard from Lily, there was no hurry to go home.

The pier was getting busier, but they made it onto the wheel after only a short wait. Lucky for Andy, who was obviously nervous, the seats were actually baskets with a bench that went all the way around, and they got a whole compartment to themselves. He huddled close and Anna drew him into her lap as they rose.

"Look, Andy. We can see everything."

His hands dug into her forearms, but he craned his neck nonetheless to see the ground below them. "We're up high."

"We sure are. See the beach?"

The roller coaster whizzed by their heads on the Ferris wheel's downward swing.

Andy inched closer to the edge, never letting go of her arm. "I've got you if you want to look. I won't let you fall."

Gradually, he relaxed enough to scoot to the other side by himself. He patted the seats all around him. "If we came back, Jonah could sit over here."

"Where would Lily sit?"

He patted the space next to him.

"And where would I sit?"

He grinned and slapped the space on his other side. "You and Lily can both sit beside me."

That was all the confirmation Anna needed. She congratulated herself for following her father's cue and taking the afternoon off to play with Andy. Now she needed to follow Lily's and start helping out more with things at home, like meals and baths... maybe not so much with meals. But whatever she did, she wanted to show Andy that she would always be there for him, just as Lily was.

"You ready to go home now?"

He cast a longing look over his shoulder in the direction of the Scrambler.

Lily's face fell when she saw the dark house. It was only six thirty—Anna often worked until seven—but she had hoped to find everyone home already after her long week away. She paid the cabbie and dragged her bag into the family room, where Chester met her with his usual exuberance.

When she turned on the lights in the kitchen, the open door to the laundry room caught her eye. A quick check confirmed her suspicions that Andy's sheets and pajamas were in the washer, along with a few of Anna's things. She moved them over and started the dryer.

Poor Anna had endured a lot this week, and Lily decided on the spot to keep Andy busy all weekend so Anna could have some time to herself. She deserved it after being such a trouper. In fact, Anna was so much more than a trouper. Her agreement to let her proceed with adoption was the most profound statement of love

173

Lily could ever have imagined.

"My cell phone!" she said aloud as she fished it from her purse and plugged it into the kitchen charger. Right away, she could see that she had three voice mails and a photo message.

The first was from Wes McLean, the retiring executive director of the guardian *ad litem* program, inviting her to lunch on Wednesday so she could meet two more of their board members and go over the compensation package. They were gearing up for their meeting in two weeks, when they would vote on a candidate to take over the program.

Over the last couple of days, Lily had concluded she would have to decline their offer. She couldn't take a full-time position with so much responsibility and still have time to tend to Andy. Even if they hired an in-home nanny for the afternoons, Anna would have to pick up the slack on long days. Lily didn't want to ask that of her. She was already going beyond what anyone could reasonably expect.

The second message was from Anna. "Call me."

The third was Andy screaming, "We miss you!" Odd…that had come at four thirty. So why weren't they home?

Chester barked to announce a car outside just as the photo materialized. Lily's jaw dropped at the sight of Andy waving from a bumper car. "What the—"

"Lily's home. Go give her a hug," Anna said from the family room.

Andy barreled into the kitchen with his arms open wide. His new red sweatshirt told her where he had ridden the bumper cars.

Lily scooped him into a hug. "You've been to the Santa Monica Pier."

"I drove the car and rode on the bear's wheel. And I rolled the ball and got a prize."

Anna was leaning in the doorway, wearing the adult version of Andy's sweatshirt, but in blue. "I called you all day." The look on her face was peculiar, like the proverbial cat that had swallowed the canary.

"My phone was dead. I just got home."

"We bought you a sweatshirt too. Yours is yellow." She handed over one of her plastic bags and gave Lily a peck on the lips. "Andy, tell Lily why we're both wearing new sweatshirts."

"'Cause I threw up on the Scrambler and it got all over us."

Anna nodded and held up the other bag, presumably their soiled clothes.

"Ew! That's icky."

Andy scrunched his nose in agreement.

Something was simmering underneath this conversation that Lily couldn't quite put her finger on, something unexpected or out of place. Anna had been through the wringer this week, but she didn't seem at all eager to disengage now that she could. "I owe you big time, Amazon. You name it, you got it."

"I don't know, I think we're all paid up." She held out her arms for Andy. "Come here, pal. Tell Lily what we talked about in the car."

Lily was stunned to see Andy fall into Anna's arms, where she shifted him to her hip.

"We all love each other," he said.

"Who loves you?" Anna asked pointedly.

"You do," he said, putting his finger on her chest. "And Lily does."

"That's right. And who does Lily love?"

"Me and you."

"And who do you love?"

"I love you"—he touched her chest again and then pointed to Lily—"and I love Lily."

Anna gave her a look that could only be described as smug. "So I definitely think we're all paid up. And I happen to agree with every single word Andy just said."

Lily blinked back tears of pure joy. She looked past Andy into Anna's smiling eyes. "What did I ever do to deserve you?"

Anna held out her free arm and pulled her into a group hug. "I think all three of us hit the jackpot."

Chapter 12

Lily laughed as Andy skipped ahead. "He looks like he knows exactly where he's going."

"That's because he does," Anna said, swinging open the glass door to the showroom. "We were here the day of the Great Milkshake Accident."

"Right." Lily followed Andy inside, where he made a beeline for a red sedan with its hood up. "I should have realized as soon as I saw how much he liked cars that you two would end up being best buds." She was still soaring over their turnabout, which Anna had explained last night as an epiphany. The moment she realized Andy needed her, she needed him just as much.

Andy darted from one car to the next, finally turning down a hallway. "Where's he going?" Lily asked.

"It's the new media room. I let him watch the sales DVDs last week." Anna chuckled at her stupefied expression. "Don't look at me like that. They're exciting."

"Says you."

"And Andy, obviously."

The weekend receptionist flagged them over to the desk and covered the mouthpiece on the phone. "Walter Kaplan's upstairs in your office."

Anna turned on the lights in an empty sales office across from the media room. "I think we should meet down here so we can keep an eye on Andy. I'll go get Walter."

Lily grabbed her sleeve. "When did you get to be so good at this?"

"You left us together for a week. It was sink or swim."

While Anna ran upstairs, Lily observed Andy from the doorway of the media room. He was sitting perfectly still on the big leather couch, mesmerized by the sales video showing off the features of BMW's largest luxury sedan. Occasionally, he would repeat words from the presentation, although his pronunciation left a bit to be desired. She could easily imagine Anna doing the same thing as a little girl.

Anna and Walter returned, and they all went into the small office. Walter was George's longtime friend and golfing buddy, and he handled not only the legal affairs of Premier Motors, but also those of the Kaklis family. Lily had met him only once, the day almost two years ago when she had—at her own insistence—signed a prenuptial agreement.

"Did you find everything in order?" she asked. She had sent all of the official adoption forms overnight from San Francisco, with the pertinent information on Andy already filled out.

"I did. If you ever need another job, come see me. I like your work." He spread out the papers and gestured for both of them to sit. "As you well know, Lily, adoption is a relatively straightforward legal procedure for married couples in California. Basically, we file the petition and get an approval from the state. That starts the clock, and in six months, we finalize. In some cases—and this one might be one of them, since Andy is being adopted by a relative—the judge can waive the waiting period, or set it lower. Normally, I would advise my clients to take the prudent course in the event they have a change of heart—"

"We won't," Anna said emphatically. "We're all making a

promise here."

Lily always loved the forcefulness of Anna's voice when she was certain of her convictions. However, they needed to prepare for the worst, a contested adoption. "There's a complicating issue, Walter. If the judge sides with us, Karen Parker's attorney will probably appeal." She went on to explain the wrongful death suit Lafollette would likely file if by some miracle they won custody.

"If that's the case, then this will probably take much longer, since you'll have to wait for that to play out in the court. But the other party will probably feel an urgency to move things along, because it works against them to have Andy placed with you during that time."

"They tried that already. The judge wasn't having any of it."

Walter nodded. "You never know who they might get on appeal, so it's something we have to keep in the backs of our heads."

"I wish there was a way we could close this right away," Anna said, in full business mode. "This being in limbo isn't good for anybody, especially Andy."

"The best thing you can do is get a definitive judgment on Monday. If you feel like you need representation, I'm happy to appear with you, but I spoke with Tom Greene yesterday afternoon and it sounds like you're in pretty good hands."

"I think we can manage," Lily agreed.

Walter turned the paper toward them and set out his Lamy pen. "Before you sign those, I want to make sure both of you understand the seriousness of what all of this means. Adoption is rarely revocable. Are you certain you've thought this over carefully?" Though his question was directed at both of them, his eyes were on Anna. "Andy will be your son and your heir. Is that what you want?"

Lily followed Anna's pensive gaze through the doorway, where she could see Andy's small feet bouncing at the end of the couch.

"Yes, it's exactly what I want. And something else." She folded her arms and crossed her legs, as if demonstrating her resolve.

"Lily signed a prenup before we were married. I'd like to void that."

"Anna, that's silly," Lily said. "This doesn't have anything to do with that."

"It's the principle of the thing. It was a crummy idea to begin with, and I never should have gone along with it."

Walter cleared his throat gently. "Should I remind you about the prenuptial agreement you signed with Scott?"

"And I bet it saved your ass," Lily said.

"Is my ass going to need saving again?"

"Of course not."

"Then let's get rid of it. Those things might have their place in a simple marriage, but once kids are involved, all bets are off."

Lily watched the silent face-off between Anna and Walter, a stubborn battle of wills on both sides. "Walter, could I have a few moments alone with Anna?" When he had gone, she gently kicked Anna's foot. "These are pretty big steps you're taking, and I wish you'd slow down."

"If you're worried I'll have regrets, don't. I told you how I felt, and that isn't going to change. I could no more give up Andy than I could give up this dealership."

"Premier Motors has been in your family for over fifty years. If something were to happen between us"—she held up her hand—"not that it will, but if it did, I could end up owning part of this business."

"Right. And you'll be Andy's mother, which means you'll pass it on to him. So either way, it ends up in the same place."

"And what about Kim's children? Do they have a stake in this?"

"We'll work that out. We can write a will that distributes our assets, but I want this place to go to someone who'll love it like I do."

Lily chuckled and looked again back into the other room. "You mean like him?"

Anna smiled. "What do you think?"

"And what if he grows out of it and decides he wants to be a rocket scientist, or a movie actor?"

"Then I'll support those dreams, just like you will." Anna leaned forward and took Lily's hands. "I know this is a big step. You remember the night I asked you to marry me?"

The night she had been caught crawling naked through Chester's doggie door. "Trust me. That isn't a night I'll forget."

"I wanted to ask you earlier and I kept putting it off because I was waiting for the perfect moment. I waited too long, and I almost lost you. I won't ever make that mistake again. We want the same things for Andy, so let's not drag our feet about it. Let's just get it done."

Anna put on a black cashmere blazer over her jeans and T-shirt. "I think I just heard Henry pull up. Are you ready?"

"Two more minutes," Lily said. "Will you help Andy pick out a couple of toys that will fit in the suitcase?"

"Sure." She hurried downstairs to find Andy dragging out the pieces to build his city. "We don't have time to play with the cars today, pal. We're going for an airplane ride. Why don't you pick out two or three cars to take with you?" She waved to the limo driver outside.

As expected, the Z8 was Andy's first choice. But then he pulled out six of the smaller Matchbox cars and lined them up on the couch.

"Just the Z8 and two of the little ones, Andy," she said. She pulled out the brown paper bag she had used to wrap her shoes. "Put them in here so they won't get our clothes dirty."

He dug in his toy box and produced the ball he had won at the pier, and his water wings. "Can I take these too?"

"We don't have room, pal. Those will be here when you get back."

His face suddenly turned red and his eyes filled with tears. "When will I get to come back?"

Lily walked in just as he let out a sob. "Andy, listen to me." She squatted and grasped both of his shoulders. "We have to go ask the judge to let you stay with us. If he says yes, then you never have to move again."

He stopped blubbering and wiped his runny nose with the back of his hand. "Can I keep my toys?"

"All of those toys are yours forever, no matter what happens."

He calmed down and selected two of the smaller cars. Then Lily told him to go to the bathroom one more time before they left.

"What was that all about?" Anna asked.

"It was the paper bag. That's the unofficial suitcase of the foster care system. Every time a kid gets moved, his things go in a brown paper bag."

"Andy thought he was moving again?"

"That's my guess."

Anna shuddered to think of how devastating it would be for all three of them if the judge ruled for Karen Parker. "Do you think there's any chance we won't win this?"

Lily looped her arm through Anna's. "I can't promise you there won't be a few bumps in the road, but I like our odds."

"Let's hope you're right."

"...and don't let him get too excited, because he might start wheezing," Lily said into the phone. She flashed the thumbs-up sign to Anna, who sat on a bench outside the courtroom. John Moss had arranged for another social worker to sit with Andy in the Children's Waiting Room so Karen Parker wouldn't try to talk to him. "We'll call you when Judge Cruz asks to see him." She pocketed her phone and positioned herself to block Anna's view of Karen.

"Is that her husband with her?" Anna asked.

"Charles Haney. Can't wait to hear how he feels about having a four-year-old to raise."

"Where's her attorney?"

Lily glanced around in search of James Lafollette. "I don't know."

"Maybe he's meeting with the judge."

Lily nodded toward Tom Greene, who was working on his laptop, and John, who was on his cell phone. "No, if he was meeting the judge, John and Tom would be in there too. None of the parties are allowed to talk to the judge alone."

"Then what the hell's taking so long?" she muttered.

Lily worried that Anna's irritability would lead to a migraine. She hadn't slept well the night before, despite Lily's assurances that their case for adopting Andy was solid. "What's eating you this morning?"

Anna rubbed her forehead. "Karen Parker."

"What?" She sat close so they could keep their voices low. "Why?"

"I just feel so much anger toward her. All she's ever done is cause you pain. It makes me want to go over there and rip her head off."

One of the things Lily had always admired about Anna was her even temper. This was a rare show of anger, and apparently, one that had been brewing for a few days. "She can't touch me anymore."

"She's touching you right now. That's why we're here," she said bitterly. "People like her should be locked away where they can't fuck up other people's lives."

Yes, Anna was definitely in danger of losing it. Lily sat on her opposite side and forced her to turn away from Karen. "Look, honey. I'm as angry as you are about this charade of hers, but you need to pull it together for Andy's sake. Judge Cruz isn't going to be impressed by you flying off the handle. He wants to see that Andy is in good hands."

Anna glanced over her shoulder and seethed. "So you don't think ripping her head off shows my protective streak?"

"You're showing it to me and I love you for it. That's all that matters."

The bailiff appeared and called them into the courtroom, but Lily held Anna in her seat until Karen and her husband went inside. Lafollette was not present, but Karen took her usual seat at the table on the right. Lily and Anna sat behind Tom and John on the left.

Judge Cruz appeared moments later, surprising everyone with his promptness. He looked over his glasses at Karen. "Mrs. Haney, I received notice that you've fired your attorney. Is that correct?"

"Yes, sir."

"You may or may not be aware of this, but Mr. Lafollette is an officer of this court. He is not permitted to discontinue his representation unilaterally." He looked at her pointedly. "That means he can't quit on you. I spoke with him by phone and he assures me this was your idea. Are you in agreement with that?"

"Yes, I fired him," Karen said flatly.

"Can you tell me why? Was he doing a poor job?"

Lily followed the lines of his questioning. If Lafollette had bailed on her, or if she was dissatisfied with his performance, she could claim poor representation as grounds for appeal.

"He wasn't interested in Andres."

"What do you mean?"

"I mean he didn't care how he was doing, or what was good for him. All he wanted was for me to get custody so he could sue the city for killing Kristy."

"Was that also your goal?"

"Never," she said emphatically. "But I couldn't afford a lawyer any other way."

It was a breathtaking admission, one that might now make it nearly impossible for Karen to win custody, since Judge Cruz no longer had to worry about how his decision would impact the pending litigation.

"Does this mean your primary interest is in what's good for Andres?"

"Yes, sir. I've always wanted that for Andres. When Kristy first told me she had a little boy, I tried to get her to move back home so we could help take care of him. She wouldn't do it, so I asked her to give Andres to me, to let me raise him. She said no, that having a little boy made the men leave her alone. The best thing that ever happened to him was the state taking him away from her. Otherwise, he might have been with her when she was killed."

Lily shuddered at such a horrible thought.

"Is this gentleman your husband?"

"Yes, this is Charles Haney."

Haney stood at the mention of his name, a move Lily attributed to the likelihood he had stood before judges before. He was clean-shaven and dressed in khaki pants, an open-collared white shirt and a tweed sport coat with wide lapels that were long out of fashion.

"And what's your primary interest in this procedure, Mr. Haney? Are you here because you also want what's best for Andres?"

"Honestly?"

"I certainly hope so," Judge Cruz replied, a quirk of humor in his voice.

"I do want what's best for him. But I'll tell you the truth. The main reason I'm here is because my wife asked me to come. I'm missing work for this, and I'm only doing it because she wants this in the worst way. That little boy's just about all she's talked about since he was born."

Lily would have written off every word as bogus if not for the fact that Anna might have answered the same way last week. She couldn't deny that his words had sounded sincere, even as she resisted the notion that Karen genuinely cared about Andy.

Judge Cruz shook a finger in Haney's direction. "Thank you for your frankness. I'm going to come back to this side in a minute. On behalf of the state, Mr. Moss has presented a formal petition for adoption from Christianna and Lilian Kaklis. Good morning, Ms. Kaklis." He looked from one to the other and chuckled. "I guess that's both of you."

"Good morning," they said together, rising.

"I've reviewed your petition, and it seems to be in order. I'd like to ask...it says here you go by Anna Kaklis...I want to ask you the same question I asked Mr. Haney. What's your interest in this? Are you here because Lilian Kaklis is this little boy's aunt?"

Anna looked briefly at Lily before addressing the judge. "I have to admit it started out that way when we first heard about Andy. I knew Lily wanted him to come live with us, and I supported that because I love her. But then she came up here last week and left Andy with me. I discovered what a special little boy he is. I fell in love with him, and if she weren't asking for custody, I would. We need Andy, and I believe he needs us."

Despite her practiced seriousness in the courtroom, Lily couldn't keep from smiling. She knew from years of handling custody cases that Anna's words were just what any judge wanted to hear. On paper, it was easy to show capable and earnest commitment to adopt a child. But there was no place on the official adoption form to proclaim love.

"Thank you," Cruz said as he shuffled his papers. "Mr. Moss, I'll get to your motion in a moment. I'd like to return to Mrs. Haney."

She stood again.

"You say you want what's best for Andres. What exactly do you think that is?"

"I think he needs his family—all of his family. I said this before, that I know I wasn't a good mother to my girls. But I'm not that horrible person anymore. I've been clean and sober for fourteen years, without so much as a parking ticket." She nodded toward her husband. "Charlie, too. We hold onto each other and it keeps us strong."

Lily recalled her own experience at Redwood Hills, which had been the flashpoint for turning her life around. She had concluded from her social service records that Karen, too, had problems with alcohol, but she would never have pegged her for someone who had seized control of her life.

Anna took her hand and gave it a warm squeeze, as if reading her thoughts.

"I work those steps all the time trying to be a better person." She looked back over her shoulder at Lily. "I never tried to make amends with Lily because I knew she went to a good home, and I thought she was better off not seeing me again. They tell us not to do that when it might do more harm than good."

One of the things Lily had learned early in her recovery was that a person's station in life was irrelevant. What mattered was their common goal of overcoming addiction and helping others do the same. Still, she found it unsettling to listen to Karen's account of working the recovery steps.

"But I tried to make amends with Kristy and she wouldn't let me. The only way I can do that now is through Andres. I want to be a good thing in his life, whether I'm the one raising him or not, and I promise that I'll treat him like the precious thing he is."

Judge Cruz set his jaw firmly and nodded. "Mr. Greene, in light of the new information before the court, has your position on the placement of this child changed?"

"No, Your Honor. As Andres Parker's guardian *ad litem*, I favor the recommendation of the state of California to award permanent custody of this child to Anna and Lily Kaklis."

"Then I guess it's time I talked this over with Andres."

All eyes turned to the back of the courtroom as the big door opened and Andy entered. His hand clutched that of the social worker, who walked to the front to deliver him to John.

Anna chuckled to see Andy's new blue shirt sporting a fresh stain, likely chocolate from one of the vending machines. She gave him a small wave as he walked past on his way to the open floor in front of the bench. She was intrigued by the expression on Karen Parker's face, a mix between what looked like wonder and sadness.

John squatted beside Andy. "Andy, this is Judge Cruz, and he wants to ask you a few questions. You okay with that?"

Andy looked back at Anna and Lily and they both smiled and nodded.

Judge Cruz removed his glasses and peered over the bench. "They call you Andy, is that right?"

By his smile, Andy appeared comfortable in the courtroom,

but his only answer was a nod.

"Come on up here and sit with me."

As John led him around the bench and onto the platform, Anna leaned over and whispered, "Something tells me all those times he played with Dad are about to pay off."

"Do you know why we're here, Andy?"

"So I can live with Lily and Anna?" he replied, as though seeking approval for his answer.

"What would you think of that? Are you happy living with them?"

He nodded.

"What do you like about living there?"

"I have toys and a swimming pool. And Chester sleeps on my bed."

"Who's Chester?"

"He's our dog."

So far, the questioning was going just as Lily had predicted, with the judge trying to get a general idea of their relationship.

"Do you like Lily and Anna?"

"Yes."

"Can you tell me why?"

Judge Cruz was a natural with kids. Anna could almost picture the judge at home with his grandchildren.

"'Cause they're nice to me. They don't get mad at me."

"Why would they get mad at you?"

"'Cause I do bad stuff sometimes," he answered sheepishly.

"Like what?"

"I putted bubble bath in the swimming pool...and I spilled my milkshake in the car...and I peed in the bed."

Anna covered her mouth to hide her smile as Lily poked her playfully in the side.

"You did all those things and they didn't get mad at you? They must like you very much."

He nodded vigorously. "Anna said we love each other."

"Do you love Anna and Lily?"

"Yes."

"I think they love you too. They want you to come live with them and be their little boy. Would you like that?"

"Yes."

"Okay, why don't you go over and sit with them while we finish this up?"

Anna slid over to make room for Andy to sit between them. Then she and Lily clasped hands in his lap.

"All right, I think we're ready to settle this matter once and for all. I know it means someone will be going home unhappy, but maybe we can find a way to mitigate that." He looked directly at Karen. "Mrs. Haney, I had my doubts about you when we started this last week, but this morning you have managed to convince me that you care about this child. You and Mr. Haney are to be commended for the changes you've made in your life. I wish you continued success."

"Thank you."

From where Anna was sitting, she could see Karen's lower lip quiver.

"You told the court that you wanted what was best for this child. Though the state has determined that your home meets the standards necessary for good child care, it is my assessment that Andy is more likely to thrive in the Kaklis home, where he currently resides."

Lily's elated response was evident by the way she suddenly dug her fingernails into Anna's palm.

Judge Cruz turned his eyes toward them. "Parenthood is a sacred trust. As I'm sure you will discover in the years ahead, the duty you have to impart your values on a young mind is both challenging and rewarding. This child may well be the most important legacy you leave upon this earth, and I urge you to consider that with every decision you make."

Anna released Lily's hand and they each took one of Andy's.

"Before we wrap this up, I'd like to express my desire that the adult parties present today find a way to work out their differences in the best interests of this child. I recognize the reservations of Ms. Kaklis, but I also ask that she recognize the tremendous strides Karen Haney has made to overcome her past. I believe Mrs. Haney's interest in Andres is sincere, and I hope she will be allowed reasonable contact." He looked over the motions before him. "That looks like everything. I hereby enter my order that Andres Parker be placed in the temporary adoptive custody of the Kaklises. The state is ordered to monitor his status for a period of ninety days, after which, if it is deemed satisfactory, a permanent order of adoption will be decreed." He slapped his gavel in exclamation. "Good luck to all of you."

As Lily jubilantly hugged Andy to her side, Anna looked over at Karen Haney, whose head was in her hands. Her husband had his arm around her shoulder, and he appeared to be consoling her. The scene struck Anna as profoundly sad, and she felt guilty for the anger she had voiced earlier.

"Come on, Andy. Let's go outside and see if the hotdog cart is there," Lily said. She looked at Anna. "It's going to take about an hour for the clerk to draw up the order, so we might as well hang around."

"You guys go on ahead. I need to check in at the dealership. I'll find you in a few minutes."

They filed out with John and Tom, leaving Anna alone with the Haneys. She sat quietly until they stood together and turned.

As far as Anna was concerned, this moment was Karen's only opening to have a place in Andy's life. She half hoped the woman would write Andy off and walk out the door for good. But if she genuinely cared about him, she would plead for whatever crumb Lily might give her.

"Can we talk?"

Karen gestured to her husband to wait outside.

"The judge thinks you deserve to have contact with Andy. I'm not so sure."

Karen huffed and started to walk away, but abruptly turned back. "I don't have the right to ask for anything from Lily. I know how she feels about me and the things I've done, and I don't blame her. I don't even have the right to be proud of her, because

I had nothing to do with how she turned out."

That wasn't true at all, but Anna didn't need to drive home the point that Lily's whole career was devoted to making sure other kids didn't have to go through the horrors she had known as a child. "I think she'd be the first to tell you that Eleanor Stewart was responsible for everything good about her life. I was lucky enough to know Eleanor, and she was a remarkable woman."

Karen looked away somberly, as if ashamed.

"When was the last time you saw Andy?"

"Kristy brought him to our apartment when he was a year old. She needed money, and I gave her what I could." She opened her purse and pulled out a photo. "I begged her to leave him with me that day. I told her we'd look after him and she could come visit him whenever she wanted."

Anna was actually touched that Karen carried a photo of her daughter and grandson, and that it appeared worn from handling. She was captivated by how much Kristy resembled Lily, but not nearly as much as she was with the infant in her arms. "He's such a beautiful boy."

Karen nodded in agreement as she put the photo away.

"What do you want to happen now?"

It was several moments before Karen answered, and when she did, her voice was meek and contrite. "I wish I could know him, but I don't expect Lily to give me that. I'd be happy if he just knew there was somebody else out there pulling for him...and that if he ever needed me, I'd be there."

Anna weighed her simple request. "Lily's never going to accept you as her family, or as Andy's family. She believes you forfeited that years ago."

"I know, and I wish I could say I've regretted it every day since. But the truth is I only started taking stock of my regrets when I got clean and sober. I feel like I've lived two different lives."

"Lily probably does too. At least both of you saved the best life for last." She started out of the courtroom. "Why don't you hang around in the hallway for a while? We're just killing time until the order's ready."

Karen didn't answer, but by the hopeful look on her face, she would wait.

Lily desperately wished she hadn't eaten that hotdog, as it was now sitting in the back of her throat. She slowly plodded up the stairs, dreading what she needed to do. Andy was following along, stomping on each step as if squashing a bug. "Come on, sweetie. We're going to talk to someone for a few minutes."

Never in a million years did she imagine having a conversation with Karen Parker that wasn't hostile and accusatory. Nor would she have thought Anna would be the one to persuade her to do it.

In her whole career as a family attorney, Lily was hard-pressed to recall a case involving a contest between two family members who were both—at least by the state's definition—determined to be fit parents in which the judge did not encourage them to try to accommodate the other party for the sake of the child. It was standard protocol for custody issues, but Lily hadn't really given it any serious thought at all.

Furthermore, she wasn't moved by the idea that Karen wanted a place in her grandson's life. A fundamental principle of her work in family court was that parents who failed their children squandered the right to have them in their lives, and usually had very little to offer in the way of positive influence. When the judge had granted her and Anna custody, she was ready to whisk Andy away and never look back.

But Anna had prodded her to see the other side, to consider whether there was anything to salvage that might be worthwhile to Andy. Lily doubted it, but she agreed to let Karen see Andy one last time.

"Are we going on the airplane again?" he asked as he jumped over the last step.

"Yes, and that means you'll be sleeping in your own bed tonight."

"With Chester."

191

As Anna had indicated, Karen and her husband were waiting on the bench across from the courtroom. Charles got up and went to the other side of the hall, an apparent sign that Karen wanted to meet with them alone.

Lily stooped and pulled Andy to her. "Sweetie, we're going over there to talk to that woman. She'll probably ask you some questions, and it's okay to answer. Just be nice like you always are." With Andy's hand in hers, she approached the bench where Karen waited. "Andy, this is Karen. She wants to say hi."

Karen's eyes misted as she touched his shoulder. "Hello there, young man. I met you before, but you were only a baby and you don't remember that."

He shook his head.

"I was hoping the judge would let you come home with me, but now that I see how happy you are with Lily and Anna, I think it's best you stay with them. I bet you want to go home and play with your dog."

"His name's Chester."

"What kind of dog is he?"

Lily took a step back and allowed them to talk. It was almost surreal watching Karen interact with him. Her voice was gentle, and her questions were focused on all the things Andy enjoyed about his new home. Lily could almost imagine her as someone else, not at all the woman she had resented for most of her life.

"What made you go into rehab?" she blurted.

Karen's smile vanished instantly, and she nudged Andy. "Go over and say hi to Charlie. He'd like to talk to you too. Tell him all about Chester."

"You said you turned your life around. I want to know what took you so long."

"You were the lucky one, Lily. They got to you soon enough and got you out." She sighed and shook her head wistfully. "I wish I had a cigarette. I quit smoking a month ago when we made up our minds to ask for custody because Kristy told us Andy had asthma and I didn't think he should be around that. Charlie too. I bet we buy a carton and smoke half of them on the way home."

Lily almost chuckled at her misery.

"My mother had me when she was fifteen and the state never looked in on me once. All that stuff you lived with when you were little? That was my life until I was sixteen and ran off to live with some man. It was all I knew."

"Was that man my father?"

She shook her head. "I don't know who your father was. I was seventeen years old when I got pregnant with you, turning tricks so I could eat, living with different people until I wore out my welcome. I loved you so much when you were a baby. I know you probably don't believe that. You were always good...smiling and happy. The problem was that when you drink and take drugs like I did, and when you'll do just about anything so that some man will let you sleep in his bed instead of out on the street, you don't always think about what's good for the baby. I don't expect you to ever forgive me for that, but that's how I was. I just wasn't mature enough to know you were supposed to put the baby first every single time you had to make a decision."

From her vague memories of shabby apartments, men coming and going, and regular contact with the police, it was easy to believe Karen hadn't been ready to care for a child back then. "What happened to Kristy? You were a lot older when she came along."

"I still didn't know what I was doing. I just fed off the people around me, and I still thought more of myself than anybody else. And Kristy was sick and colicky. Nobody wanted her around."

"Why didn't you just let her go when the state took her away? Somebody could have adopted her."

"I was still trying to get my act together. I did all right for a little while, but she wasn't easy like you were. They took her away again when she was eight years old. By then, nobody could handle her, and she ran away for good when she was fourteen. I didn't even see her for four years after that, when she showed up with Andres."

Lily had seen dozens, maybe hundreds, of mothers like Karen, women whose drinking and drug habits dictated not only the company they kept but all of their other choices. Over time she had learned to feel compassion for these women, to realize so many were there because they had come from a similar place and had no Eleanor Stewart to guide them to a better place.

"So what happened fourteen years ago?" Lily's own turning point had been the loss of all the things she loved—her mother, Anna, her job and home, and finally, her self-respect. She wanted to know where the bottom was for someone like Karen Parker, a woman who had never respected herself, who had lost two children and who had been to prison for assault.

"My mother died too," she said softly, her eyes clouding with tears. "When I heard you say that the other day, my heart nearly broke in two."

Lily shuddered to think she and Karen had that, too, in common.

"No, it wasn't the same," Karen quickly added, as if reading her thoughts. "My mother wasn't anything like yours. She threw her life away. I saw her in the hospital the week before she died, and she looked like a zombie, her skin all yellow and her eyes looking like some vampire. I knew I was looking at myself in another ten or fifteen years."

"So you quit for yourself."

"That's the only one you can quit for. I don't care what anybody says." She paused to watch Andy with her husband. "I met Charlie in rehab. We made a pact to help each other and that's what we've done. He's the only man I've ever met who respected me, but that's because when I gave up the drinking and the drugs, there was finally something to respect."

Though the walls of Lily's resentment were weakening, she was nowhere near ready to extend forgiveness. Still, she felt a grudging admiration for Karen's turnabout.

Andy returned from his visit with Charles and tugged impatiently on Lily's hand. "I have to go pee."

"Okay." She was grateful for the segue, an easy window to disengage. "I guess we need to go."

Karen touched her forearm to stop her from leaving. "I

appreciate what you did at the cemetery. I went there on Saturday to give them a check, and they said you came by and paid the balance."

Lily nodded, suddenly aware of her own tears. "I got her a marker too."

"That's what he said." Karen was crying openly now. "I know you'll take care of him. He's a lucky little boy," she whispered.

With Andy in tow, Lily started back toward the stairs when the wall inside her suddenly cracked. She spun back around and pulled a card from her purse. "If you write to me with your address, I'll send you pictures so you'll know how he's doing." She pressed it into Karen's hand and hurriedly walked away.

Chapter 13

"I think he's asleep," Anna mouthed silently to Lily, who watched from the doorway. Anna had rocked Andy for almost an hour to calm him down from the asthma attack that had erupted when he excitedly returned home to his toys and Chester.

Lily tiptoed to the bed and turned down the covers. Andy never stirred as Anna laid him down.

"It's a shame his asthma kicks up like that. It takes all the fun out of watching him get excited," Anna said as they entered the master suite and began to get ready for bed. She was tired from her restless night in San Francisco, but keyed up from the exciting events of the day.

"He'll probably outgrow that part. I did. I'll have to find a pediatrician and see if we can get him on some preventive medication."

"Talk to Kim." Anna puzzled over her advice for a moment. She appreciated that Lily was taking the lead on Andy's health care, but the fair thing to do was divide up the parenting tasks. Except cooking. "Or I can call her. I'll find out where she takes

Jonah and Alice and make an appointment."

"I don't mind. I can do those kinds of things in the afternoon. You don't have that kind of flexibility."

Anna stepped out of her skirt and sat in the bedside chair. "What about when you take the guardian *ad litem* job? You won't have it then either, so we might as well get used to sharing this stuff."

"About that," Lily said, taking a seat opposite her on the end of the bed. "I've been thinking it might not be such a good thing for me to take that job after all. He's just so little to be in preschool all day. By the time we get home, he'll be so tired we won't even get to enjoy each other. Dinner, a bath and a story. I don't want that."

"But…" Anna squeezed her eyes closed to line up the points she wanted to make. The way she saw it, having Andy should add to their lives, not take away from them. "We can have both if we work at it, Lily. This is a job that was made for you. Not only will you love it, but you'll do it better than anyone else. And you'll be helping thousands of kids like Andy."

"Believe me, I've thought about all of that. But it isn't as if I'm not already doing something worthwhile."

"True. But Andy's four years old, which means he starts school next year. He'll be gone all day then. You'll be free to work full-time again, but you'll have missed your chance at this."

"I've thought about all of that. Once he starts kindergarten, he'll get out around two thirty, which means he'll have to go to daycare for at least three hours on top of a whole day in school. Little kids shouldn't have to work grownup hours."

"So what if we hired someone to keep him here at home in the afternoon? Maybe you can work it out to come home early one day, and I can too. And I bet Mom can." She didn't want Lily to have regrets about letting this once-in-a-lifetime opportunity pass her by. "I can even bring him to the dealership a couple of days a week. He'd love that."

By the look on her face, Lily wasn't convinced at all.

"I think you're letting what Karen said in court about both

197

of us working get to you, and you shouldn't, because she's no authority on kids."

Lily heaved a frustrated sigh. "No, but she did say one thing that made a lot of sense, and that was what she realized she did wrong. She put herself first. Parents are supposed to put their kids first, every single time." The last part she said with emphasis.

"So does that mean I should work part-time too?"

She kicked a shoe in Anna's direction. "Now you're being deliberately obtuse."

A fair assessment, but it was still a point Anna wanted to make. "I thought the whole idea was that we were in this together. We're both responsible for Andy, and from his point of view, we ought to be interchangeable."

"Not interchangeable—reliable. He needs to know that if one of us isn't there for him, the other one will be. That doesn't mean we have to share every single task. He'll decide what he wants from each of us."

"Should I give up my bid for VP of the Chamber so that I'll have more time to give him?"

"If that's what you want, yes. But don't do it because you think you have to. If we work together, we can have all the things that truly matter to us."

Anna studied on Lily's counter-arguments and suddenly realized the truth. "So you're saying this job doesn't really matter to you."

"That's exactly what I'm saying," Lily said. She got up and moved to Anna's lap. "I can handle having regrets someday about a job, but not about Andy. Besides, I'm happy where I am, and when it's all said and done, I'd rather be a good mother than a great anything else."

Lily looked over her shoulder to the backseat, where Andy's eyes threatened to close at any moment. "Don't go to sleep, Andy. We're here." She couldn't wait to share their big news with everyone, which they had decided to do in person tonight when they all got together at Empyre's for Anna's birthday celebration.

"I bet Jonah's here already," Anna added, craning her neck to see him in the rearview mirror. She pulled the X3 to a stop and got out, leaving the keys for the valet.

Andy had mastered the latches on his car seat and had freed himself by the time Lily got around to his side.

"You look so handsome," she said, admiring the white shirt and sweater vest he was wearing for the first time. She and Anna had taken bets on how long it would take him to drop something on his new clothes. Anna's guess had been that Lily would drop something on hers first.

They were ushered into the restaurant and greeted by the maître d', a longtime friend of the Kaklis family. "Who is this little gentleman?"

Anna pulled Andy in front of her and rested her hands on his shoulders. "This is Andy. He's part of the family now, so you're going to be seeing a lot of him." She bent down to Andy's ear. "Can you shake hands with Nick?"

When Lily had taken Andy to her office to meet everyone, Tony had taught him to shake hands. Since then, Andy had shaken hands with everyone each time he said hello, including all thirty-two of the children in his preschool.

"Everyone else is already here," Nick said. "I understand someone is having a birthday."

Lily chuckled and shook her head conspiratorially as Anna made a face. "She doesn't want anyone to mention it, so could you call all the waiters out to sing?"

He led them to their usual corner, where the rest of the family was seated at a large round table. Cards were stacked in the center, and Lily added two. She laughed as Andy made the rounds of the whole table shaking hands, finally taking a seat between her and Anna.

"Open your cards so we can eat," Kim said, pushing them toward Anna.

One by one, Anna read their sentiments aloud. The first, from George and Martine, was both sweet and serious. "I can always tell when Mom picks out the cards."

Jonah crawled halfway onto the table to push his card forward. "Open this one." It was homemade, purportedly a picture of Anna and an orange car.

Kim's card featured a wrinkled, toothless woman in a bathing suit. "Never forget that you're always older than I am," she said.

"How can I when you remind me every year?"

Anna reached next for Andy's card, but Lily intercepted. "I think you should save this one for last. Open mine."

She grinned as Anna read the inscription and quickly put it back in the envelope and then inside her purse. "That was from Lily. You'll have to use your imagination."

That left only Andy's card, which Anna set aside while they ordered dinner.

"Thanks for having another birthday so I didn't have to cook," Kim said when the waiter left. "Why don't you have another one next weekend?"

Anna laughed. "Actually, we're celebrating two special occasions tonight."

Lily nudged Andy. "Go over there and sit with Anna."

He climbed into Anna's lap and began to open the card Lily had helped him make.

"We always seem to find ourselves gathered around a big table when it's time to make important announcements," Anna said. "I think I'm going to let Andy make this one."

He suddenly developed a case of shyness and covered his face with his hands.

"Andy, who's that card for?" Lily prodded.

He pointed to Anna as the others waited expectantly for the news.

"And what did we write on it?"

"To Mom."

Anna touched the spot on Lily's dress where she had dropped Tzatziki sauce. "Think that'll come out?"

"You jinxed me."

"I had nothing to do with it. You always spill your food."

Lily wriggled out of the dress and dropped it in the dry cleaning hamper. "Your father was over the moon."

"I know. You would have thought I'd told them all I was having a baby."

"Maybe one of these days…"

"Don't count on it. Last time I checked, you were firing blanks." Anna pulled her dress over her head and tossed it carelessly into the chair. "Oh, and thanks so much for giving me the sexy card in front of my whole family. Were you trying to give me a heart attack?"

"Right, like they don't know we do it all the time." Lily pressed her hips into Anna and unhooked her bra. "I promised you another surprise, didn't I?"

"Some birthday presents make getting older worthwhile." She moaned as Lily squeezed her breasts. "We'd better walk over to the bed while we still can."

When they fell together, Anna won the battle for dominance, pinning Lily beneath her and teasing her nipples until she writhed with want. As her hand slid lower in its intimate quest, she lifted her head to look into Lily's eyes. This was the connection Anna cherished most, the ultimate lover's exchange. Then with a practiced touch, she brought Lily close to climax three times before finally granting her release.

The moments after making love were Anna's favorites, as they reveled in both their physical and emotional closeness. Even as she thought their love could never be greater, she knew it would grow with every passing day. "I love my life with you," she murmured, planting a soft kiss below Lily's ear. It had become her mantra.

They lay together quietly for several minutes before Lily stirred. "Anna?"

Jarred from the precipice of slumber, she grunted.

"Could you see us having a baby of our own someday?"

Her eyes shot open. "You mean one of us getting pregnant?" Lily had always been adamant that she wasn't interested in giving birth, so that only left "one of us."

"Yeah, maybe together...like Vicki and Carolyn did."

Anna propped up on her elbow to look Lily in the eye, just to make certain her chain wasn't being yanked. Their friends from Seattle had used *in vitro* fertilization, and Vicki carried a baby created with Carolyn's egg. "Are you serious?"

"What do you think of it?"

She was too stunned to answer. The prospect of being pregnant didn't excite her, but she couldn't deny that the idea of having a baby in the house did, especially Lily's child. "I think it's something we should talk about."

"Are you open to the idea?"

"I'm...it's one of those...we'd have to..." She pictured herself with Kim's maladies, the swollen ankles, back pain and hemorrhoids. "Oddly, I think I am."

Lily traced a finger along Anna's jaw. "How would you feel about me having your baby?"

"You?" The idea instantly went from an interesting possibility to an overwhelming certainty. "As far as I'm concerned, we'll have a dozen if I don't have to carry any of them."

"Are you serious?" Lily asked.

"Is there an echo in here? When did you suddenly get interested in being pregnant? You've always said you'd be open to adoption, but not to having one of your own."

"I know, but now I have this maternal instinct. I think it kicked in that first day I went to see Andy in the foster home. I've felt like a mother from that moment on. I want us to have more children."

Anna suddenly sat up. "I can't believe we're talking about this like it's actually going to happen. Shouldn't we wait awhile and see how we feel about it?"

"You just turned thirty-six today. How old do you want to be when you're chasing another four-year-old?"

"Not much older." It wasn't chasing a four-year-old that worried her. "I don't want to be the oldest mom at the high school graduation."

Lily kissed her chin. "I bet you'll still be the most beautiful."

Anna fell back onto the bed and sighed. "Now how am I supposed to sleep tonight after that?"

"You'd better sleep now while you still can."

Epilogue

Lily parked her X3 in Anna's space on the back lot. She and Andy had dropped Anna off at work early this morning so they could go to their afternoon appointment in one car. "Can you get out by yourself, or do you want me to help?"

Andy already had the door open. He had abandoned his car seat in favor of the booster seat when he discovered he could get in and out of the car on his own.

"Hold my hand, please." They waited while a car rolled past into the service area.

Andy's sticky hands smeared the glass as he pushed open the door into the showroom.

Lily corralled him before he touched anything else and helped him wash up in the women's restroom. He loved coming to the dealership, and had learned his way around. On days when Lily got tied up in court, Anna picked him up from preschool and let him hang out in her office, the media room, and even once in the garage, where she let him watch her work on an engine.

"Anna Kaklis, please come to the showroom," the loudspeaker

blared.

"Hear that, Andy? Your mom's coming to the showroom, so we don't have to go look for her."

He skipped ahead toward a 760i in Titanium Gray Metallic. Its hood was up, and a well-dressed, handsome gentleman of about fifty was looking it over. Andy stood on tiptoes to peek at the motor.

"Hello," the man said. "Are you thinking about buying this car?"

"It has a B-twelve engine."

"A V-twelve? That's pretty big."

"Uh-huh. And forty-eight balbes." He pointed to a space beneath the manifold.

"I think he means valves," Lily said as she joined them, amazed that Andy knew such details. "Which car is this, Andy?"

"It's the 760i," he said, rolling his eyes indulgently, as if anyone should know that. "And it's got a six-peed step-on-it trission."

"Make that a six-speed Steptronic automatic transmission," Anna said, appearing suddenly from behind. "How are you doing, Dave?"

He smiled and stuck out his hand. "I'm fine, Anna. You're hiring some awfully young salesmen these days."

"Andy, this is Mr. Cahill. Can you say hi?" She grinned as Andy held out his stiff arm for a handshake. "This is my son, Andy. He's been watching the sales DVDs, as you can tell."

Lily beamed to hear the introduction, the first since last week, when the adoption had been finalized. Andres Parker Kaklis, his middle name in honor of his mother.

"Sounds like I should watch them too," Dave said.

"And this is my wife, Lily." She put her arm around Lily's waist. "Lily, I'd like you to meet Dave Cahill, the president of the Chamber of Commerce, and my good friend."

"Nice to meet you, Dave."

"Same here," he said. "Sorry about taking up so much of Anna's time. I couldn't find anyone else gullible enough to be my VP."

"Watch her closely, Dave. She can't wait to take over."

"I believe that. She twisted my arm to come in and trade for a BMW."

"I've got all the paperwork ready," Anna said. "Did you bring that hunk of junk with you?"

Lily scanned the lot near the front door. "Uh-oh, you must drive a Mercedes."

"A Jaguar," he said. "Except Anna called it a four-thousand-pound paperweight."

"Andy, tell him which is the best car on the road."

"BMWs!"

Anna held up both hands. "You got it from the expert."

Lily strolled the lot with Andy while they waited for Anna to finish up with Dave. He rattled off the names of each of the new models, and quite a few of the used models Premier Motors had taken in trade. It wasn't hard at all to imagine him on this very lot twenty years from now enthusiastically showing off the BMW line to the next generation of drivers.

"Anyone up for a test drive?" Anna shouted as she joined them.

"If I didn't know better, I'd say you were stalling," Lily answered.

"And I'd say you know me pretty well. I'm starving."

"I bet." Anna's last bite was a bowl of cereal just before bedtime the night before. "Are you dreading this?"

"Wouldn't you?"

As they turned toward the car, Andy skipped ahead.

"Andy!" Anna's stern voice stopped him in his tracks. "Walk with us."

They dropped him at the Big House, where he would spend the night "camping" in the den with George and Jonah.

"Anna, do you realize this is our first night alone since Andy came to live with us?"

"Ironic, isn't it? A night alone and no sex."

"I vote we call out for Chinese. Then we can lie on the couch together and watch movies until we fall asleep."

"Sounds good."

From her quiet acquiescence, Anna seemed distracted by their looming appointment. Lily reached across the console and took her hand. "You all right?"

"Sure."

When they pulled into the parking garage at the UCLA Medical Center, Lily stopped. "Say the word and we'll turn this baby around."

Anna chuckled. "I'm never going to be more ready than I am right now."

"At least the shots are finished." She had given Anna simple hormone injections for the past ten days in order to stimulate egg production. Today's procedure—egg retrieval under general anesthetic—was much more involved. Dr. Beth Ostrov, the fertility specialist who had worked with Kim and Hal, hoped to extract at least a dozen eggs today, which she would fertilize using donor sperm. They had chosen a man of Hispanic descent because Andy's father had been Latino. "I know you're nervous, but try to think of it this way. If everything happens the way it's supposed to, our baby is going to be conceived this afternoon."

That brought a slow, broad smile to Anna's face. "Have I told you lately that I love my life with you?"

Publications from
Bella Books, Inc.
The best in contemporary lesbian fiction

P.O. Box 10543, Tallahassee, FL 32302
Phone: 800-729-4992
www.bellabooks.com

WITHOUT WARNING: Book one in the Shaken series by KG MacGregor. *Without Warning* is the story of their courageous journey through adversity, and their promise of steadfast love.
ISBN: 978-1-59493-120-8
$13.95

THE CANDIDATE by Tracey Richardson. Presidential candidate Jane Kincaid had always expected the road to the White House would exact a high personal toll. She just never knew how high until forced to choose between her heart and her political destiny.
ISBN: 978-1-59493-133-8
$13.95

TALL IN THE SADDLE by Karin Kallmaker, Barbara Johnson, Therese Szymanski and Julia Watts. The playful quartet that penned the acclaimed *Once Upon A Dyke* and *Stake Through the Heart* are back and now turning to the Wild (and Very Hot) West to bring you another collection of erotically charged, action-packed tales.
ISBN: 978-1-59493-106-2
$15.95

IN THE NAME OF THE FATHER by Gerri Hill. In this highly anticipated sequel to *Hunter's Way*, Dallas Homicide Detectives Tori Hunter and Samantha Kennedy investigate the murder of a Catholic priest who is found naked and strangled to death.
ISBN: 978-1-59493-108-6
$13.95

IT'S ALL SMOKE AND MIRRORS: The First Chronicles of Shawn Donnelly by Therese Szymanski. Join Therese Szymanski as she takes a walk on the sillier side of the gritty crime scene detective novel and introduces readers to her newest alternate personality—Shawn Donnelly.
ISBN: 978-1-59493-117-8
$13.95

THE ROAD HOME by Frankie J. Jones. As Lynn finds herself in one adventure after another, she discovers that true wealth may have very little to do with money after all.
ISBN: 978-1-59493-110-9
$13.95

IN DEEP WATERS: CRUISING THE SEAS by Karin Kallmaker and Radclyffe. Book passage on a deliciously sensual Mediterranean cruise with tour guides Radclyffe and Karin Kallmaker.
ISBN: 978-1-59493-111-6
$15.95

ALL THAT GLITTERS by Peggy J. Herring. Life is good for retired army colonel Marcel Robicheaux. Marcel is unprepared for the turn her life will take. She soon finds herself in the pursuit of a lifetime— searching for her missing mother and lover.
ISBN: 978-1-59493-107-9
$13.95

OUT OF LOVE by KG MacGregor. For Carmen Delallo and Judith O'Shea, falling in love proves to be the easy part.
ISBN: 978-1-59493-105-5
$13.95

BORDERLINE by Terri Breneman. Assistant prosecuting attorney Toni Barston returns in the sequel to *Anticipation*.
ISBN: 978-1-59493-99-7
$13.95

PAST REMEMBERING by Lyn Denison. What would it take to melt Peri's cool exterior? Any involvement on Asha's part would be simply asking for trouble and heartache...wouldn't it?
ISBN: 978-1-59493-103-1
$13.95

ASPEN'S EMBERS by Diane Tremain Braund. Will Aspen choose the woman she loves...or the forest she hopes to preserve...
ISBN: 978-1-59493-102-4
$14.95

THE COTTAGE by Gerri Hill. *The Cottage* is the heartbreaking story of two women who meet by chance . . . or did they? A love so destined it couldn't be denied . . . stolen moments to be cherished forever.
ISBN: 978-1-59493-096-6
$13.95

FANTASY: Untrue Stories of Lesbian Passion edited by Barbara Johnson and Therese Szymanski. Lie back and let Bella's bad girls take you on an erotic journey through the greatest bedtime stories never told.
ISBN: 978-1-59493-101-7
$15.95

SISTERS' FLIGHT by Jeanne G'Fellers. *Sisters' Flight* is the highly anticipated sequel to *No Sister of Mine* and *Sister Lost Sister Found*.
ISBN: 978-1-59493-116-1
$13.95

BRAGGIN' RIGHTS by Kenna White. Taylor Fleming is a thirty-six-year-old Texas rancher who covets her independence. She finds her cowgirl independence tested by neighboring rancher Jen Holland.
ISBN: 978-1-59493-095-9
$13.95

BRILLIANT by Ann Roberts. Respected sociology professor, Diane Cole finds her views on love challenged by her own heart, as she fights the attraction she feels for a woman half her age.
ISBN: 978-1-59493-115-4
$13.95

THE EDUCATION OF ELLIE by Jackie Calhoun. When Ellie sees her childhood friend for the first time in thirty years she is tempted to resume their long lost friendship. But with the years come a lot of baggage and the two women struggle with who they are now while fighting the painful memories of their first parting. Will they be able to move past their history to start again?
ISBN: 978-1-59493-092-8
$13.95

DATE NIGHT CLUB by Saxon Bennett. *Date Night Club* is a dark romantic comedy about the pitfalls of dating in your thirties…
ISBN: 978-1-59493-094-2
$13.95

PLEASE FORGIVE ME by Megan Carter. Laurel Becker is on the verge of losing the two most important things in her life—her current lover, Elaine Alexander, and the Lavender Page bookstore. Will Elaine and Laurel manage to work through their misunderstandings and rebuild their life together?
ISBN: 978-1-59493-091-1
$13.95

WHISKEY AND OAK LEAVES by Jaime Clevenger. Meg meets June, a single woman running a horse ranch in the California Sierra foothills. The two become quick friends and it isn't long before Meg is looking for more than just a friendship. But June has no interest in developing a deeper relationship with Meg. She is, after all, not the least bit interested in women…or is she? Neither of these two women is prepared for what lies ahead…
ISBN: 978-1-59493-093-5
$13.95

SUMTER POINT by KG MacGregor. As Audie surrenders her heart to Beth, she begins to distance herself from the reckless habits of her youth. Just as they're ready to meet in the middle, their future is thrown into doubt by a duty Beth can't ignore. It all comes to a head on the river at Sumter Point.
ISBN: 978-1-59493-089-8
$13.95

THE TARGET by Gerri Hill. Sara Michaels is the daughter of a prominent senator who has been receiving death threats against his family. In an effort to protect Sara, the FBI recruits homicide detective Jaime Hutchinson to secretly provide the protection they are so certain Sara will need. Will Sara finally figure out who is behind the death threats? And will Jaime realize the truth—and be able to save Sara before it's too late?
ISBN: 978-1-59493-082-9
$13.95

REALITY BYTES by Jane Frances. In this sequel to *Reunion*, follow the lives of four friends in a romantic tale that spans the globe and proves that you can cross the whole of cyberspace only to find love a few suburbs away...
ISBN: 978-1-59493-079-9
$13.95

MURDER CAME SECOND by Jessica Thomas. Broadway's bad-boy genius, Paul Carlucci, has chosen *Hamlet* for his latest production. To the delight of some and despair of others, he has selected Provincetown's amphitheatre for his opening gala. But suddenly Alex Peres realizes that the wrong people are falling down. And the moaning is all to realistic. Someone must not be shooting blanks...
ISBN: 978-1-59493-081-2
$13.95

SKIN DEEP by Kenna White. Jordan Griffin has been given a new assignment: Track down and interview one-time nationally renowned broadcast journalist Reece McAllister. Much to her surprise, Jordan comes away with far more than just a story...
ISBN: 978-1-59493-78-2
$13.95

FINDERS KEEPERS by Karin Kallmaker. *Finders Keepers*, the quest for the perfect mate in the 21st Century, joins Karin Kallmaker's *Just Like That* and her other incomparable novels about lesbian love, lust and laughter.
ISBN: 1-59493-072-4
$13.95

OUT OF THE FIRE by Beth Moore. Author Ann Covington feels at the top of the world when told her book is being made into a movie. Then in walks Casey Duncan the actress who is playing the lead in her movie. Will Casey turn Ann's world upside down?
ISBN: 1-59493-088-0
$13.95

STAKE THROUGH THE HEART by Karin Kallmaker, Julia Watts, Barbara Johnson and Therese Szymanski. The playful quartet that penned the acclaimed *Once Upon A Dyke* are dimming the lights for journeys into worlds of breathless seduction.
ISBN: 1-59493-071-6
$15.95

THE HOUSE ON SANDSTONE by KG MacGregor. Carly Griffin returns home to Leland and finds that her old high school friend Justine is awakening more than just old memories.
ISBN: 1-59493-076-7
$13.95

THE FEEL OF FOREVER by Lyn Denison. Felicity Devon soon discovers that she isn't quite sure what she fears the most—that Bailey, the woman who broke her heart and who is back in town will want to pick up where they left off...or that she won't...
ISBN: 978-1-59493-073-7
$13.95

WILD NIGHTS (Mostly True Stories of Women Loving Women) Stories edited by Therese Szymanksi. Therese Szymanski is back, editing a collection of erotic short stories from your favorite authors...
ISBN: 1-59493-069-4
$15.95

COYOTE SKY by Gerri Hill. Sheriff Lee Foxx is trying to cope with the realization that she has fallen in love for the first time. And fallen for author Kate Winters, who is technically unavailable. Will Lee fight to keep Kate in Coyote?
ISBN: 1-59493-065-1
$13.95

VOICES OF THE HEART by Frankie J. Jones. A series of events force Erin to swear off love as she tries to break away from the woman of her dreams. Will Erin ever find the key to her future happiness?
ISBN: 1-59493-068-6
$13.95

SHELTER FROM THE STORM by Peggy J. Herring. *Shelter from the Storm* is a story about family and getting reacquainted with one's past. Sometimes you don't appreciate what you have until you almost lose it.
ISBN: 1-59493-064-3
$13.95

BENEATH THE WILLOW by Kenna White. A torch that even after twenty-five years still burns brightly threatens to consume two childhood friends.
ISBN: 1-59493-051-1
$13.95

THE WEEKEND VISITOR by Jessica Thomas. In this latest Alex Peres mystery, Alex is asked to investigate an assault on a local woman but finds that her client may have more secrets than she lets on.
ISBN: 1-59493-054-6
$13.95

ANTICIPATION by Terri Breneman. Two women struggle to remain professional as they work together to find a serial killer.
ISBN: 1-59493-055-4
$13.95

OBSESSION by Jackie Calhoun. Lindsey Stuart Brown's life is turned upside down when Sarah Gilbert comes into the family nursery in search of perennials.
ISBN: 1-59493-058-9
$13.95

18th & CASTRO by Karin Kallmaker. First-time couplings and couples who know how to mix lust and love make *18th & Castro* the hottest address in the city by the bay.
ISBN: 1-59493-066-X
$13.95

JUST THIS ONCE by KG MacGregor. Ever mindful of the obligations back home that she must honor, Wynne Connelly struggles to resist the fascination and allure that a particular woman she meets on her business trip represents...
ISBN: 1-59493-087-2
$13.95

PAID IN FULL by Ann Roberts. Ari Adams will need to choose between the debts of the past and the promise of a happy future.
ISBN: 1-59493-059-7
$13.95

END OF WATCH by Clare Baxter. LAPD Lieutenant L.A. Franco follows the lone clue down the unlit steps of memory to a final, unthinkable resolution.
ISBN: 1-59493-064-4
$13.95